Ocean's Desire...

*The first novel in the series
from author L.L. Lunde*

Ocean's Desire

L.L. Lunde

OLIVA PUBLISHING

Ocean's Desire
L. L. Lunde

Published by Oliva Publishing
www.OlivaPublishing.com
© 2010

This is a work of fiction. Names, characters, places, and incidents either are the product of the author's imagination or are used fictitiously. Any resemblance to actual persons, living or dead, events, or locales, is entirely coincidental.

ISBN 978-0-9834626-0-6

Printed in the United States of America

*Dedicated in loving memory to
the man who was bigger than life,
the inspiration for Jake Hunter.*

You will never be forgotten.

*Oceans of love,
L.L.Lunde*

ONE

"Father, there is absolutely no way I'll agree to marry a man I've never met before," Lynette exclaimed furiously. Rising from the chair, she began pacing wildly back and forth in front of her father's huge mahogany desk, trying to control her anger.

The entire office spoke of Mac's strong and controlling personality, from the dark wood paneling, the matching burgundy leather wing back chairs, to the bookshelves lining the opposite wall. The floor to ceiling shelves were full of the classics, each one impressively leather bound. This would never be considered a comfortable room or even a welcoming one. It held a dominating mood, which closely reflected Mac's cold and controlling manner, intimidating most visitors. The huge room was exactly what Mac had demanded the designer create for him.

Mac closely watched his daughter as she carefully controlled her temper. Lynnette was a stunningly beautiful young woman, just as her mother had been, Mac reflected, his mind reminiscing of the times he had shared with his wife long ago. His gorgeous love, Mary. She had worn her hair the same way. Her long, loose brown waves flowed down around her shoulders just like Lynnette's did. They had the same lovely brown eyes, the color of root beer, now so full of anger. Lynnette stood taller than her mother had and was much more slender. Too thin almost, he continued, lost in his thoughts. In most ways though, his oldest daughter was a near duplicate of her lovely mother, God rest her soul.

Lynnette should have realized there was trouble brewing the minute her father had called her formally to meet with him at the estate. His dictates were always preceded with a summons to this horribly cold office, she realized in hindsight.

"You will do as I say young lady," Mac responded firmly, bringing his thoughts back to their conversation. "It is my intention to leave my entire estate to you to run as you wish, but only if you obey me in this matter. It is my last dying wish. I insist you do as I tell you, otherwise I leave you nothing and you'll be penniless," Mac stated coldly.

Sitting there regally behind his huge desk, she noticed the strength it cost him to calm down. His illness had added twenty years to his looks in the last six months. Still a large man, he now looked too thin, having lost over forty pounds. His once neatly trimmed grey hair looked thin and scraggly. His wrinkled skin held a grey pallor. He never complained about the pain, knowing that would show a sign of weakness. And Mac wasn't a weak man she recalled, reminded he was a dictator, a tyrant, a ruler of his own little world.

"My time is short, Lynnette. Now that the cancer is progressing quickly, I want you properly married before I die. That is final. My biggest concern is that you'll choose a man who will marry you and then take you for everything, so I will make the right choice for you. You haven't been working on marriage and security. I've been much too lenient with you in this area and I mistakenly left the issue of personal relationships in your hands and for too long you have accomplished absolutely nothing. You have not even been out on a date for months."

"What? How would you know that, father?" she demanded.

Realizing he had obviously been having someone watch her in order to obtain that last bit of information, she stopped pacing to face him, even more furious than before. She hated being controlled. She just wanted to live her life her own way, making her own decisions and her own mistakes. His refusal to answer was answer enough.

Lynnette spoke slowly. "When I date or not is my own business. I am a grown woman and you have no right to dictate my personal life to me any longer." She shook her head in disbelief. "I just can't believe you would do this to me. You've controlled my entire life and now you intend to control it even after you're dea..."

Stopping herself short, she closed her eyes realizing she had gone too far. Her hot temper had once again caused her to speak before thinking. Regretting her callous words, she attempted another approach.

"Father, I'm so sorry for saying that. What I'm trying to say is that I want to choose the man I'll spend the rest of my life with. Someone I'm in love with and who loves me. A man who I can trust. Somebody who enjoys my company and also wants to spend the rest of his life with me. Not some awkward, rich nerd who is probably so hard up for a date he's willing to agree to marry someone before even meeting them."

"No, I am told this young man is very successful, has a sizable portfolio that he built personally and he comes highly recommended by a close friend," Mac interjected.

"He doesn't need your money so that won't be an issue." A single nod of his head indicated the matter was closed.

"If this guy is such a great catch, Dad, then why is he still single and why in the world would he consider marrying someone he's never met?" Lynnette pressed, still hoping to change Mac's mind.

Sitting down once again in the cool leather chair, she smoothed down the short red skirt she wore with the matching jacket. Her golden brown hair was trailing in soft waves down her slender back. Crossing her long legs, she tried to keep from fidgeting.

"As of yet, this young man does not know of this arrangement but I'm told by our mutual friend that he will most certainly agree. Now I will not continue discussing this subject further with you, Lynnette, the matter is closed," he announced sternly. "There is a dinner party scheduled for two weeks from tonight when you will meet for the first time and I will announce your engagement to the small group of family and close friends who will be attending."

"Have you told Keira of this?"

"She knows my intention is to leave you my estate and that you'll look after her when I'm gone, but I haven't informed her of your upcoming marriage arrangement. Nor will I. Your sister does not need to know and this will remain between us, understood?"

Although she was furious with her father, Lynnette found this the most difficult conversation of her life. She knew she was losing her father to cancer, but at the same time he was forcing a man on her as her husband who she had never met. She felt intensely angry and at the same time terribly sad that her father was dying. Sometimes life was so unfair, she thought.

Attempting yet another approach, she challenged him again. "What you're doing to me, father, is wrong. You have no right and I will not be forced to do this. Ever."

Mac replied coldly once again. "I said the matter is closed, Lynnette. The paperwork is already being written up and my mind is made up! I will not tolerate your rebellion and you will marry this gentleman I have chosen or you will get absolutely nothing in my will. Do you understand me?"

Jumping out of her seat she faced him with her hands clenched in fists at her sides. "No, I don't understand and this matter is not closed," she ground out between clenched teeth. "I have not yet agreed to marry this guy. This is the twentieth century, not the 1800s. Arranged marriages are a thing of the past and I have certain rights today as a woman. I intend to choose if and when I marry and I'll choose whom I'll marry. And not a moment before I fall madly in love with him," she added, determined to have the last word.

"Girl, sit down. Now!" he ordered sharply.

Standing, he glared down at her across the huge desk. The look on his face revealed his intense fury at her outburst. Lynnette sat.

"I will tell you this one time only. This silly idea of yours of falling in love is just a fairy tale for little girls. It's not based on reality so forget about it. If you think you can capture a man when you're broke and out on the streets, then go ahead with your stupid plan of looking for your dream man. But remember, you have put in years of training and have been prepared carefully to take over this family business and I swear I will disinherit you completely if you deny me my last wish," Mac shouted down at her.

She had never seen him this angry before, nor had she ever felt such intense hatred toward him .

Seeing it was over, she still tried once again to change his mind. Tears formed in her eyes as she pleaded with him. "Please don't do this to me Father. Don't ruin my life, my only chance at finding true love."

Sitting down slowly and holding the edge of the desk for support, Mac looked away.

"I'll expect you here at the engagement party two weeks from tonight at seven o'clock sharp."

He had controlled everyone in his life for as long as she could remember and she despised him for it. Standing before his desk, she glared at him through narrowed, damp eyes as she literally shook with anger. She spoke carefully to try to control the quiver in her voice.

"I'm running late father and I have to go now. I'll give your request serious consideration in the next two weeks. I'll tell you my decision before then." Turning on her heel, she walked purposely to the door, trying to hold back her tears until she was in private.

Turning back briefly, she noticed her father had already resumed reading the legal documents in front of him as if their conversation had never happened. But it had happened and now her life was in a shambles. She would have to think of a way to get out of this mess, just as she always had in the past.

*　　*　　*

Lynnette stepped anxiously aboard the airplane at LAX as she awkwardly adjusted the strap on the bulky bag hanging over her shoulder. She had always hated flying. Each time she stepped on board an airplane, her imagination raced to all the things that could go wrong with the flight, causing the airplane to crash. Following the troubling phone call she had received from her stepbrother this morning, she was now in a rush to get to Cabo San Lucas to locate her sister, Keira, who was in some very serious trouble down there. It was most likely Lynnette's fault too, she thought, feeling more than a little guilty. Lynnette should have protected her sister better somehow. Now she needed to concentrate on the problem and come up with a plan to get Keira back safely.

Struggling to pull down the short denim skirt that kept riding up one thigh because of the huge bag hanging against her hip, she hoisted the strap higher on her shoulder and continued down the narrow aisle, looking for her seat assignment.

Jake moved slowly forward in line behind her, watching with enjoyment as she fidgeted with her bag. His interest in her would be easily obvious to anyone observing. Jake was tempted to offer to carry her bag but reminded himself he had come on this trip to get away from women for awhile, not to meet yet another one. Jake struggled with himself internally though, for he found this girl quite attractive, tall and nicely curved with long dark hair that looked as if it would be silky to the touch, but he tried to take his mind off her. He just wanted to spend some time alone this week. She wasn't very easy to ignore though. His eyes kept following the enticing movements of her hips as she struggled through the narrow isle with her oversized bag.

Lynnette rarely considered her looks. She didn't think of herself as either exceptionally good or bad looking, just acceptable. The anxious young boys in school had never had any luck getting her to date them. She constantly focused all her energies on improving her mind and increasing her chances to succeed. Over the years, Mac had engrained in her the importance of her intelligence as the most critical element to her hopes of success in this world. No one would ever guess the depth of her own insecurities. She hid them well and had carefully practiced her bold, self-confident façade in order to hide the ever-present uncertainty and apprehension she felt after years of trying to please her father.

Lynnette's best friend and college roommate, Barbara, had always been amazed at all the attention Lynnette received from the guys at school. Every bit of it had gone completely unnoticed by Lynnette as she kept herself constantly busy, from morning to night, focusing all her attention on her studies. Her hard work and diligence had paid off too, she graduated from the university of San Diego with honors.

Now she spent all her time learning to run one of her father's businesses. He had initially built his fortune in commercial real estate holdings, buying sizable empty parcels of land throughout Orange County and then developing strip malls and office parks, overseeing their construction personally. Later, Mac had expanded into education when Lynnette was in high school and showed a serious interest in the business. He was pushing her to take over the company she had helped build which now comprised several privately owned K through 12 schools. She had developed a recent business plan to expand into training centers and teaching supply stores throughout

Southern California. She enjoyed running this part of the business tremendously, more than anything else in her life. She found she was actually quite good at managing it and the people working for her loved her. Mac had begun this part of his portfolio from that first small school in Orange and now he had a hugely successful business which had resulted in a considerable accumulation of wealth due to his diligence, Lynnette's hard work and some other wise investments over the years. Lynnette sighed loudly as she continued waiting for the passengers in front of her to stow their bags, take their seats and clear the isle so she could finally get to her seat. Her impatience was growing steadily with each passing moment.

*   *   *

Macarther Ocean, known as "Mac" to his few close friends, was a very aggressive, ambitious man who drove his daughter hard to be everything he dreamed a son would have been. Mac and his wife, Mary, never had the son he had wanted, so now Lynn, his tomboy and now beautiful twenty-four year old daughter, would have to become everything he needed her to be. He was old, tired and now he was also very ill. The form of cancer spreading throughout his body was untreatable and his time was getting short quickly.

Elliot, who was his long time friend, business advisor and closest confidant, had stopped by Mac's Nellie Gayle Ranch estate that morning to check in on Mac and found him in his study feeling quite ill. Elliot noticed that the cancer was progressing quickly now as he helped Mac upstairs to rest in bed where they continued their visit. Elliot stood near the large French doors gazing down at the impressive view of equestrian riding trails winding through the green belt of tall, mature trees blowing gently in the afternoon breeze.

Mac looked around his spaciously elegant bedroom feeling trapped and frustrated. "Elliot, she's my only heir capable of carrying on my businesses and she had no right to take off to Mexico without my agreement," Mac stated in a raised voice, as he lay propped against the headboard of his huge bed. "She has certain responsibilities. What's in that girl's head anyway? Now she insists she will not marry him. Says she wants to wait to fall in love. Now what ever gave her the idea she has to fall in love to marry? People marry for different reasons everyday."

"Now just calm down there, Mac," Elliot stated, regretting telling Mac of Lynnette's trip south. "You're getting yourself all worked up for nothing. Lynn's a very smart girl and will make the right decision. Just give her some time to adjust to the idea. She hasn't even met the boy yet," Elliot reasoned. Pulling a chair next to the bed, Elliot sat down and continued.

"My nephew is an amazing man, Mac, and although his godmother and her husband raised him and his sisters out in Chicago after their parents died, he and I were always close and in constant communication through the years. As his uncle, he always turned to me first. Lynnette periodically heard of him as they were growing up, but they've never met before, so who knows? She may fall head-over-heels in love with him. Hell, it seems every other girl he meets does. He a good looking man," Elliot added with a knowing grin as he poured Mac a cool glass of water from the crystal pitcher on the nightstand and handed it to him.

As Elliot sat back in his chair, he took a moment to reminisce, recalling a day long ago, when he too turned the heads of many attractive women. Whether he was on an assignment in Europe, Asia, Australia or the South Pacific, it never failed that Elliot would find a beautiful woman to share his time with, but this was of course after he had lost his precious wife to leukemia. In hindsight, he still wasn't clear if he had been trying to get over her death or just distract himself from it in order to survive the pain. Regardless, he had known many pleasures at the hands of various gorgeous women in his time. As a special agent with the Navy and on assignments of a secret nature in most cases, he changed the role he played in each scenario. One time he would be a successful Wall Street businessman on vacation, another a rich Texan traveling on business or a professor from a university on sabbatical doing research for an upcoming novel. He was able to change his identity and demeanor as readily as he could change his accent.

Although Elliot was an older gentleman now, he was still very handsome. He was tall, fit looking and had a full head of silver hair. He moved with an attractive air of masculine confidence. The two friends had seen one another through their weddings, the birth of Mac's two daughters and the unfortunate deaths of both of their wives. Elliot had been as devastated by the death of Mac's wife, Mary, as he had been by the passing of his own wife, years earlier. It was possible he had felt more of a loss at Mary's passing than did Mac.

Elliot never had children of his own so he had taken every opportunity over the years to use his fatherly instincts on Lynnette and Keira. They had been the closest he had ever known to having kids of his own, other than his young nephew whom he had groomed over the years. He loved them each tremendously. The girls loved Elliot and confided in him more than anyone else, often times more than their own father. Elliot understood the girls and he listened to their troubles. He was always there when they needed comfort or advice, unlike their father. Lynnette and Elliot had always been especially close and he had always felt displeased that Mac was so hard on her. He knew she would do almost anything to please her father, but nothing ever seemed to be good enough. Keira had been a sweet little girl as a child, but something had definitely changed as she grew up. They had never shared the deep bond he had with Lynnette. There was just something about Keira that kept him from getting close. Something he could never quite put his finger on.

As Elliot noticed Mac dozing off, he sat back and sighed. He strongly suspected there was more to Lynnette's trip to Mexico than she had told him on the phone when she had called from the Los Angeles airport earlier that morning. He didn't question her any further though. She had sounded rather nervous and upset. He was certainly concerned but hoped she was actually going in order to relax on the beaches of Mexico as she had told him. She certainly deserved a vacation, but he seriously doubted that was her real intent in making the trip. It was out of character for her and she wasn't one to just sit around and relax.

He had several contacts in Baja and was tempted to make a few quick calls to ensure she would be all right, but then decided not to interfere. She would be furious with him for thinking she couldn't take care of herself. She was always trying to prove her independence and he knew it was because of Mac's overbearing ways. He was proud of her for trying at least.

"Oh, Elliot," Mac awoke suddenly, gaining Elliot's attention again, "remember how great it was to be young, chasing after the girls without a care or worry in the world? What I wouldn't give to be back living in those days again."

Elliot nodded remembering the good ole days. "Yeah, but that's what makes it even harder for me to ask my nephew to give up his enviable single status in order to marry Lynn. I love her dearly Mac, you know that. She's an amazing young woman, but I just can't imagine if I were in his shoes that I would be willing to fulfill this request." It was still nagging at Elliot that he had agreed to get involved with this arrangement. It didn't sit well with him, but Mac could be stubborn at times.

Mac looked over at Elliot with obvious concern on his face. "You're certain he'll go along with this aren't you? I don't have the time to come up with another plan and I must see Lynnette properly married before I'm gone. You know that I'll never have peace of mind if I don't see her married first."

Elliot frowned, his brow furrowed in thought. "Mac, you know I completely disagree with you on this matter. Lynnette is an intelligent, capable young woman, entirely able to take care of herself without a husband in her life. Besides, why aren't you as concerned to get Keira's future secured? Are you certain you aren't trying to control Lynnette's life from the grave, my friend?" Elliot threw out knowing he was being painfully direct.

Mac waved his hand in dismissal at Elliot. "I know what is best for my daughters, Elliot, and Lynnette will look after what's best for her younger sister. I need to be absolutely sure though that this young man will keep his word and marry Lynnette."

"I still say you're putting a huge responsibility on Lynnette as an older sister," Elliot frowned. "Don't worry though, my friend," Elliot reassured as he stood. Walking across the large suite to the window, he looked out over the carefully manicured grounds. "My nephew would do anything I asked of him. He has this overwhelming idea he owes me. He always says he wouldn't have made it to college, started his first business or succeeded financially without his old uncle Elliot there to help him out along the way. As you recall, Mac, he and I have always been exceptionally close since his parents died and he never fails to tell me every time he visits me just how much he appreciates the help I've given him over the years. He's a good young man. If he's asked me once, he's asked me a dozen times how he can ever repay me for always being there for him. So now he can... by marrying our Lynnette," he finished with a half-hearted grin at his friend.

The only consolation Elliot took in involving his nephew in this plan was the possibility of the two young people being together. He knew them both very well and felt certain they would be perfect together.

TWO

Lynnette moved slowly behind the person in front of her as she continued inching down the aisle, following close behind as she made her way toward the back of the airplane to take her seat. Her heavy bag was starting to dig into her shoulder as she impatiently moved toward the rear of the airplane to her assigned seat. She swung the cumbersome bag to the opposite shoulder while waiting for the guy ahead of her to stow his luggage and get seated. She was really beginning to feel anxious to get to her sister and frustrated at the lengthy hold up. Why was this guy taking so long?

She attempted to shove past the man who was still struggling to place a large metal case in the overhead compartment when suddenly she was grabbed around the waist from behind and yanked backwards.

Crying out, she quickly spun around exclaiming, "What in the world are you...?" She was interrupted by the loud crash of the heavy metal case as it fell to the floor where she had just been standing seconds before. Startled, she jumped, shocked at the close call, realizing how close she had come to being smacked on the head by that heavy case.

Turning back to thank whoever had pulled her out of harm's way, Lynnette caught her breath. She was looking straight into the huge chest of a very tall, muscular man wearing a rather snug fitting t-shirt. His large body was close up against hers in the narrow aisle. She was surprised at the sheer size of him, noticing his arms and how his t-shirt pulled tighter in all the right places across his chest, accentuating an enormously strong physique beneath.

Never before in her life had she given much more than a brief thought to a man's body. For that matter, she had never before in her life been this close to a man's body. Certainly not a body that looked like this one did anyway.

Stepping back, she tilted her head up to look at his face. Stunned, she found herself looking at the most devastatingly handsome man she had ever seen. He absolutely took her breath away. Gorgeous deep blue eyes stared down into hers; a strong square jaw framed a firm mouth. He had a small inch-long scar along his chin that made him seem a little dangerous somehow. His hair was wavy and dark brown, just long enough to touch his collar, if he had been wearing a collar. She noticed once again the tight fitting t-shirt outlining his masculine frame and thought he must be over six feet tall since she had to bend her head back to look up at him.

Completely forgetting what it was she had turned around to say, she realized her mouth had dropped open at some point. She quickly closed it. Feeling rather disoriented, she took a few slow deep breaths, struggling for more air. What was wrong with her? He was surely standing much too close. Certainly he could hear her heart racing, couldn't he? It was beating much too loudly she thought. Her thoughts were coming too fast. Suddenly it seemed extremely warm on the airplane. Looking back up into his handsome face she knew she could get lost in those eyes. He just stood there staring down at her with an intense look, seemingly as lost in the moment as she was. How could just looking at a man affect her like this?

She realized she was staring into his knowing blue eyes with a dreamy look on her face which made her suddenly feel embarrassment, as if he knew what she was thinking.

Lynnette looked away. Could he possibly be able to tell she was so taken with him? Embarrassed, a pink blush rushed up from her neck to her cheeks.

Jake observed her growing embarrassment with amusement but he didn't want to make her any more uncomfortable than she already was by chuckling, so, stifling a grin, he studied the girl more closely. She is an absolute beauty, he acknowledged. Her lovely face was like an open book, so easy to read. He recognized her reaction to him at once and was very pleased. He was very attracted to her also. She was a delight to look at, he realized with more than a little interest. She was an innocent though, without much experience, if any. When she had first turned to face him, he found her intensely seductive and quite striking. Her brown eyes had an almost exotic, almond shape, which stole his mind of thought. He had enjoyed the feel of his hands on her tiny waist when he had grabbed her to pull her back toward him. Smiling, he hoped to ease her discomfort by trying to make light conversation.

"That was a close call, too close really. I'm glad I saw it coming. You could have been knocked unconscious if that case had hit your lovely head," he said in a deeply masculine voice. "You okay?"

Tearing her eyes away from his to try to make her mind work again, she looked down shyly at her feet. She knew she was acting like a complete idiot but couldn't seem to make a logical sentence form in her head. Taking another deep breath, she coaxed herself to look up and just say thanks. Just simply say thank you, she thought, then find your seat before you make a bigger fool of yourself. Her confidence restored, if only momentarily, she looked up at the handsome stranger and lost her thoughts again, blurting out, "Thanks for grabbing me."

With a sly grin and a glint of amusement in his eyes, he replied easily. "No problem. The pleasure was surely all mine. I'd be happy to grab you again anytime you'd like."

Realizing how he had twisted the meaning of her words and his obvious intent, the rosy blush quickly crept back up to her cheeks again. Closing her eyes in frustration, she was mortified by her own lack of finesse and angry with herself for acting like such a dope. She quickly mumbled, "What I meant to say was, um..., thanks."

Rushing to get away from the embarrassment and his smirk, she quickly turned around, hoisting the strap of her heavy bag higher on her shoulder and nearly fell, racing down the aisle toward the back of the airplane. She had to escape that smug, amused look on his handsome face. How embarrassing. He had been laughing at her stupid, naïve reaction to him.

How was she supposed to react? He made her head spin just to look at him, as he probably did every female he smiled at. She wasn't made of stone. She was just as affected by an extremely attractive man as any other woman would be, although it had never actually happened to her before. It was really quite disconcerting. But with looks like his, she was sure other girls made the same mistake or worse everyday. He's probably totally conceited, she mused, and probably used to stunningly gorgeous women who always know the right thing to say. In comparison to them, she had just acted like some goofy young, inexperienced girl. Well, she was inexperienced when it came to men, but she certainly didn't want it to appear so obvious.

Finally locating her aisle seat, she bent down attempting to shove her bag under the seat in front of her. It doesn't matter what he thinks, she thought, although she still felt the heat of the blush pounding in her face. Pushing the uncomfortable thoughts from her mind, she forced herself to remember he was just a complete stranger who she would never see again after this flight. Just get him out of your mind. Concentrate on what you need to do in the next few days.

As she pushed and shoved on the bag, she was oblivious to the view she was giving Jake from behind. In the short denim skirt she was wearing, it was impossible for him not to notice her long shapely legs and nicely rounded bottom. He felt the immediate reaction the sight of her caused him and with a low groan, he headed toward her.

"Here, let me help you with that bag," he said in a rich, deep voice behind her.

Lynnette jerked upright, startled. "Thanks anyway but I'm managing just fine," she responded more abruptly than she intended.

Turning back around, she knelt back down and struggled to lift the bag into the overhead compartment. She hesitated part way, it weighed more than she realized. Jake quickly reached around her and easily stowed the bag away, closing the compartment for her.

Not daring to look up at his face for fear she would behave like an idiot again, she tossed out a quick, "Thanks," then dropped into her seat. She wasn't about to look directly at him and let him make a fool out of her a second time. She couldn't seem to think straight when she looked directly at him, so she just wouldn't. She didn't especially like the fact he assumed she needed his help. She didn't need any man. She was perfectly capable of taking care of herself.

Bending down, Jake leaned his hands on one of the armrests of her seat. Teasing now, in a low voice so only she could hear him, he said, "No problem. Just let me know if you need anything else at all. If you need me, I'll be right back there," he said indicating the back of the airplane with a slight not of his head.

"I am not in any need of your help and I don't recall asking for your assistance," she bit out tersely. "Thank you anyway," she finished a little more nicely.

She knew she was probably being rude but she couldn't help it. He had struck a nerve with her and she wouldn't tolerate being treated like a helpless female. Her father always did that to her and she had hated it her entire life. It was because of her father that she had learned to be so self-sufficient and she didn't need or require any man's help. Not her father's help, nor this guy's either. Continuing to avert her eyes, she wished he would just go away.

Jake was still leaning down on her armrest, hoping she would look into his eyes once again. She had the most exotic, enticing eyes he had ever seen.

"I'm as capable as any man," she continued when he refused to move. Still avoiding looking directly at him, she continued, "and I don't need a guy looking out for me." Men were really so full of themselves, she thought testily as Jake stood up with a slight chuckle and moved away from her. He found his seat across the aisle, only one row back, and began stowing his carry-on while thinking of her reaction to him.

He wasn't sure whether he was amused or upset. Normally he didn't give a damn what women thought, they were too emotional for him to figure out. But he always felt instinctively protective of them and couldn't help it. He'd grown up in Chicago with three younger sisters to protect, which was probably the reason for his natural urge to protect girls.

Jake had been in more fights over his little sisters throughout the years than he could remember. That's one of the things big brothers did. They'd get into fights to protect their little sisters. Now it seemed to spill over to other girls as well. Protecting girls was instinctive with Jake and he reacted to a woman's needs without thought. Well, that and the simple fact he enjoyed a good brawl now and then.

Taking his seat, as he fastened his seat belt he recalled the time he had come to the rescue of his first love in high school.

Carrie had been a beauty, that was for sure, but she was also a terrible flirt. She would do anything for male attention. That particular evening he had taken her dancing at a local nightclub. She had picked the wrong type to flirt with and when the guy started getting aggressive with her, she immediately cried out for Jake's help. Although he was disgusted with her actions, he knew he had to help her. A man has his honor. It had been an ugly fight and they had both ended up in jail for the night. It resulted in a broken arm for the guy Carrie was flirting with and Jake had received a deep knife cut on his chin, which was still a visible scar. He used his scar to remind himself not to get too close emotionally to any woman. For the most part, he had found they couldn't be trusted. Jake had quickly broken off the relationship with Carrie that same week. She was gorgeous, but too much trouble.

As the airplane taxied toward the runway, Jake found himself glancing over at the girl that had him so intrigued. She had all but pushed him away. He couldn't remember the last time that had happened. Girls were usually a bit too aggressive with him, obviously flirting without any chance for him to do the pursuing, which was definitely a turn off. He wasn't cocky about his looks, just the opposite actually. Looks weren't everything he knew. But his looks always attracted women and he was starting to get bored with the type of girls he had been attracting lately.

Isn't that the reason he was taking this business trip alone instead of bringing a woman along, he reminded himself? Wasn't that the plan, to take a break from women for a while after his last dangerous assignment?

And here you are already showing interest in a girl who doesn't seem to care enough to learn your name? He grinned at the thought. Regardless of his initial intentions, he felt the instant spark of a challenge in the thought of getting to know this beauty. Leave it alone, he warned himself. Time to give it a rest with women, remember?

Jake's mind returned to the fact that he definitely found her good looking. Her long brown hair fell down her back in soft golden waves, her full lips immediately made him think of kissing them and then there was those beautiful brown eyes. He would enjoy staring into them for hours. It would be a pleasure trying to get her to look at him again, he grinned. Yes, he admitted, he certainly was attracted to her, even if he was trying like hell not to be.

He watched her curiously, noticing how nervous she seemed. For a girl who claims to be able to take care of herself, she sure acts awfully jittery and nervous. He couldn't help but wonder what made her so edgy. And what would make her so stubborn about accepting a man's help, he wondered. And was she as naïve as she initially appeared to be? And was she single?

Grasping her armrests firmly, Lynnette chewed nervously on her bottom lip as the airplane started vibrating, gathering speed down the runway. It felt like it was going to shake apart at any moment. She began tapping her fingers on the armrests as she became more and more tense. When the wheels finally left the runway, the horrible shuddering motion smoothed out immediately. She quickly exhaled, not realizing she had been holding her breath.

Lynnette had no idea she was being observed as she laid her head back on the headrest and tried to calm her nerves. Trying to relax, she tried to focus her thoughts on Keira and her immediate problems with Todd, but her mind wandered. Instead she found her thoughts back on the good-looking guy in the tight fitting t-shirt. She could feel her stomach fluttering just thinking about looking up into those gorgeous blue eyes of his, the strong, broad shoulders and those firm yet soft looking, sensual lips. But that can't be right she thought, her stomach now in knots. It must be the result of her fear of flying, she reasoned. Just the thought of a man couldn't make her stomach feel like this, or could it? He had appeared so ruggedly handsome, in a somewhat dangerously primitive sort of way. She wondered what it would feel like to have a man like that pull you possessively into his arms, covering your lips with heated, sensual kisses while his hands…

Frowning in frustration at her lack of concentration, she mentally reprimanded herself on her lack of focus. She didn't know the first thing about a man's embrace or his sensual kisses. She had never experienced either one and she certainly did not have the time to speculate about it now, she knew. Get your thoughts on how to get Keira away from that jerk of a stepbrother, Todd, she reminded herself. Oh how she hated Todd and his horribly evil ways. It made her stomach sick to think of what he had done to her and Keira over the years as they were growing up.

"May I get you something to drink?"

Lynnette looked up startled to see a nice looking flight attendant staring down at her. She had been so lost in thought she hadn't noticed her approach.

"I'm sorry, what did you ask me?"

"Would you like something to drink?" the woman asked again.

"Oh, yes. Um…, water would be fine," Lynnette replied, wiping her brow.

"If you don't mind me saying so, you seem rather nervous. Maybe a glass of champagne to calm your nerves?" the flight attendant wisely suggested.

Lynnette smiled up at the kind and understanding face of the woman and said, "Yes, you're right. I don't like flying much, especially the takeoffs and landings. I think a glass of champagne would be very nice, thanks."

The flight attendant left to get her drink order as Lynnette briefly looked back over her shoulder, spotting him instantly. He was right there, only one row back. He turned and looked directly at her. She tried to pry her eyes away, but they wouldn't obey her.

Looking more closely, she noticed again his finely chiseled square jaw, so perfectly framing his sensual mouth. Her mouth opened slightly as if she were going to speak, but didn't. Looking into his unnervingly blue eyes she could feel the sexual attraction between them. It felt like the air was vibrating across the aisle.

Turning back to face the front of the airplane again, she found herself short of breath, wondering what had just happened between them. She wondered if he was as affected as she was by the feeling. It was overwhelming, yet indescribable.

Pushing her thought of this attraction aside, Lynnette took her drink from the attendant. She began to think back to when she was a little girl; back to the time her life had been truly wonderful. That was when her mother was still alive. They used to do things together as a family, picnics in Heisler Park in Laguna Beach overlooking the ocean and backyard barbeques with close friends. There was always laughter and happiness in the house. Then her mother had died suddenly in the car accident on Pacific Coast Highway when Lynnette was only twelve years old. That's when everything in her life changed for the worse.

She and Keira immediately noticed their father started working all the time and never came home for dinner anymore. The girls resorted to eating in the kitchen with the housekeeper, Angie. Their dad seemed to avoid all contact with the girls as if they reminded him of the wife he had so unfairly lost. He never appeared to consider they, too, had experienced a horrible loss. Life just wasn't the same anymore. And then it got even worse.

Mac had met and married a woman named Claudette Bain a couple of years after her mom's death. Claudette immediately moved into their estate with her son, Todd. She soon took over both the household and the girl's lives.

At first, Lynnette and Keira both thought it might be nice to have an older brother until they learned just how terribly evil Todd could be to them. He had started with little things, like burning Lynnette's homework or throwing away her clothes. Then he began torturing their little rust colored cat, Willy, until it ran away screaming. She had cried and run to her father again, but he dismissively said, "Go talk to your stepmother. She'll handle it." Claudette didn't handle it though. She insisted Todd would never do these terrible things and threatened to ground Lynnette if she didn't stop making accusations against him.

Oblivious to the handsome man still observing her, Lynnette took a long drink of champagne as she remembered with revulsion how Todd and his friends used to corner her in her bedroom while she screamed at them to stop. It was no help though because Todd would always make sure the housekeeper and his mother were out shopping or somewhere else when they came to Lynn's room. Thank God they never truly violated her. They just thoroughly humiliated her time after time.

Todd had tortured her the entire time he had lived with them at the estate and she finally stopped telling anyone, since they never believed her anyway. She finally decided she would have to take care of her own problems herself. There wasn't anyone else she could count on, so she devised a plan.

The next time Todd and his buddies came to Lynnette's bedroom, she was ready. Being one of the top tennis players at school was about to pay off for her. The three of them swaggered in one afternoon with Todd, finding Lynnette standing in the far corner of her room with her hands behind her back. As the first two came towards her to grab her arms, she jumped forward bringing the metal framed tennis racket in front of her, grasping it firmly in both hands. Then she started swinging it with all her might. She swung it aggressively, back and forth, not hearing as it stuck the boys. She didn't care. They weren't going to ever come near her again.

As she continued to advance, swinging the racket wildly in front of her, the boys yelled and cursed at her as they grabbed at their faces with their hands, then finally ran out of her room.

As she reached the doorway, she realized Todd was the only one left inside. She screamed, "Get out of my room and stay out."

Knowing she would smack him too with the racket, Todd spit on the front of her blouse and with a cocky smirk, sauntered out of her room and down the hall. She remembered him calling back over his shoulder at her, "It's not over yet, little sister. I'll be back." And then he laughed.

Again, Lynnette had told her father about what happened, but he allowed Claudette to handle it. Claudette had punished her for lying about what happened with Todd. Lynnette had grown to hate Claudette over time, until her father finally divorced her a few years later. It had been an ugly, drawn-out divorce and Claudette had finally been forced to leave the estate angry and spiteful. Lynnette had thankfully never seen her again.

Shuddering at the memory, Lynnette came out of her reverie surprised to hear the pilot announce they were already on descent into the Los Cabos airport. The nice flight attendant came by to pick up her glass.

Lynnette nervously grabbed her armrests as the airplane banked sharply left, making her stomach flip. Surely any pilot flying in the United States would lose his license flying like this pilot.

She risked a glance out the window, relieved to see the airplane wasn't yet falling out of the sky. Taking a deep breath, she tried to calm herself as she leaned over the empty seat next to her and concentrated on the coastline below.

Even as frightened as she was, she noticed the spectacular view below. There was nothing but dry, brown desert running for miles down the Baja peninsula, meeting abruptly with the beautiful blue waters of the Pacific Ocean. It was a breathtaking contrast of terrain and sea. The coastline was dotted with resorts, golf courses and swimming pools. She could see the main town of Cabo San Lucas set near the very tip of the peninsula known as Lands End, where the Pacific Ocean and the Sea of Cortez meet. Lynnette imagined this would make a very romantic getaway for a honeymoon.

She turned her eyes once again toward the front of the airplane and braced herself for the landing. She decided to focus on coming up with a workable plan. Her little sister's life at this point may very well depend on her. There was no telling what extremes Todd would go to just to get his hands on money. She had racked her brain and still she wasn't sure how to begin looking for where Todd was holding Keira.

What exactly had Todd said on the phone? Nervously drumming her fingers on the armrest, she tried to recall any clues he might have given her by mistake. It amazed her to realize this nightmare had only just begun today, but it seemed like forever. The call from Todd had come just this morning.

"Hello," she answered after four rings, breathless from racing in the front door of her small beach house in Corona Del Mar. She had just finished her daily four-mile morning run along the cliffs and her heart was still beating rapidly as she cooled down.

"Well little sis, you're just the one I need to talk to. It seems you've got a little problem on your hands," the disgustingly familiar male voice stated.

Closing her eyes with a heavy sigh, she wished she hadn't answered or that he would just go away. She knew that wasn't likely to happen any time soon.

"What do you want now, Todd? I'm in a hurry to get to the office this morning and I've got to stop by my father's first."

"Oh, just wait until you hear what's happened. Your whole day is about to get ruined, sweetie." The sarcasm was unmistakable. She hated even hearing the sound of his raspy voice on the other end of the line.

"Todd, you know I hate when you call me sweetie, so cut it out and tell me what you're talking about before I hang up on you." She'd like nothing more than to slam the phone down, but she hesitated out of curiosity.

"Oh no, sweetie," he replied ignoring her request, "you don't want to do that. No, you'll want to hear this, believe me. You remember the last time I asked you real nice-like but you said you wouldn't give me any more of your precious money? Well, I decided to get a little more creative. You see, little sis, I need the money real bad and I need it now or I'm gonna lose out on a partnership in a beautiful new deep sea fishing boat down here in Mexico. You see, I've become a legitimate business partner, sis. Pretty impressive, huh? So, I thought you might just need a little more incentive to get me the money," he said, dragging out the explanation.

"Get to the point, Todd" she demanded impatiently.

"It's Keira, sweetie. I've got Keira down here with me and were having a little vacation."

"Todd, stop screwing around and tell me what the hell you're talking about," she yelled impatiently into the receiver, pacing back and forth in front of the entry table. She now sensed something was terribly wrong.

"Lynn, Lynn, Lynn. You've always been the slow one, haven't you? You're going to be a good girl and bring me the fifty-grand I asked for, then you and Keira can go on back home." His tone turned hard and mean. "Get it now, Lynn?"

"Todd," she ordered firmly, "don't you dare hurt her or I swear I'll…"

"Just get your skinny ass and the cash down here to Cabo by Monday afternoon and she'll be just fine," he demanded sharply. "Oh Lynn, most important, don't make the mistake of telling anyone about this or Keira will pay dearly. You remember all the things I'm capable of, don't you sweetie?"

As she heard the click on the line when he hung up, she realized in a near panic she didn't know where to meet him once she got there. Plus the fact she had never even been to Mexico before and couldn't speak a word of Spanish. Well, she had three days, since this was Friday morning, so she better hurry. She would have to call her office to cancel her appointments and then stop by the bank. There were a million things to do before she could catch a flight, and this was turning out to be a really bad day.

Jake found himself once again looking over at the girl across the aisle only to find her wringing her hands together nervously and fidgeting in her seat. Either she's afraid of flying, like she had told the flight attendant, or this wasn't a vacation she was on. It didn't appear to be a simple case of fear-of-flying. She was way too tense. Something was definitely wrong and he wondered what it was. Possibly she was in some kind of trouble.

THREE

Once out of the airplane and in the fresh air again, Lynnette began to breathe a little easier. The dry warm Cabo air hit her like a blast furnace as she followed the other passengers the short distance across the tarmac to the terminal. The sun had dropped lower in the sky and she noticed on her watch it was already after five o'clock in the evening. The heat of the dry desert air even inside the terminal was nearly unbearable at this time of the evening.

It was only Friday night and here she was already in Cabo. She was way ahead of schedule and so far, things were going fairly smoothly. She had the beginnings of a pretty good plan in her mind and Todd didn't expect her until Monday afternoon. If she could spot him in town before that time and follow him without his noticing her, he may just lead her to Keira. She had no idea what to do from there. She would just have to wing it.

Heading straight for the car rental counter, Lynnette decided it was best to utilize the time waiting for her luggage by renting a car. She set her huge bag down and as the young Mexican at the car rental counter slowly assisted her in his broken English, she finally managed to complete the necessary paperwork.

She waited for him to locate the keys to a compact car as her mind wandered back to the captivatingly handsome stranger on the airplane. She hadn't looked at him again and instead, just walked off the plane, not looking back. In a way, it was a shame she wouldn't see him again. He was quite enjoyable to look at, even if he was a bit of a chauvinist. He was so very devilishly good looking with his dark tan and hard muscles. He sort of reminded her of a pirate. Yes that was it, he looked like a modern day rogue. Thinking of his deep blue eyes and what a gorgeous smile he had, her insides began to flutter with excitement again. I guess it wasn't the fear of flying making my stomach do flips, she realized.

Even as she was handed the car keys and a map of Los Cabos, she continued to wonder what he was doing down here in Mexico all alone. As she walked back to the baggage claim area, a scowl crossed her face as she realized he probably had a horde of beautiful women waiting poolside for him at one of the fancy resorts in town.

Noticing the conveyer belt start its slow circular rotation, she hurried over to locate her suitcase. Anxious now to get to town and begin looking for Todd, she started pacing back and forth while biting her bottom lip, wishing her suitcase would hurry up and appear. It was getting uncomfortably hot and stuffy in the airport with all the other people standing around waiting for their luggage.

Jake knew nervous tension when he saw it and this girl was really wound-up tight as a drum. She hadn't noticed him leaning against the wall across the baggage claim area with his arms crossed casually in front of his chest. His watchful eyes carefully observed her from across the crowded room.

As he picked up his garment bag, she grabbed her suitcase off the conveyer belt, lugging it over to the security guard. As Jake moved closer he could hear the guard asking for her claim ticket. She began feeling around her body frantically and a look of sudden panic came on her face.

"Oh my gosh! No!" she cried out in alarm. "I left my purse on the rental counter." Dropping her bags, she ran off leaving them with the guard, temporarily forgotten. Racing across the tiny airport at breakneck speed, she came to a halting stop when she noticed there was no longer anyone at the car rental counter. There was no sign of her purse anywhere in sight and the small sign on the counter simply read, closed.

After Jake set her bags aside and handsomely tipped the guard to keep an eye on them, he walked over to Lynnette at the car rental counter where she had moved behind the counter to look more closely. Quietly moving up right behind her as she frantically searched beneath the counter for what he supposed would be her lost purse, he could hear her talking to herself.

"You idiot," she mumbled to herself. "I can't believe you lost your purse. Where is that Mexican guy anyway? They can't be closed this early, can they? Oh, how stupid."

As she continued searching, bent over at the waist, head down, looking through the inside of each of the shelves that ran the length of the counter, Jake leaned over and simply asked, "Having trouble?"

Lynnette jumped back startled, perturbed with him for sneaking up on her. She began to get angry. "No, no trouble. Everything here is just fine, thanks," she stated sarcastically.

"You don't look fine," Jake said. "Well, actually you look terrific, but your situation looks rather bleak," he added as his look took in her entire body.

"Would you please stop sneaking up on me? You're making me nervous," she threw back, ignoring the compliment.

"It's not me making you nervous," he responded calmly. "You've been a nervous wreck the entire flight. Now, are you sure this is where you left your purse? Could it possibly still be onboard the airplane? I'll help you find it," he offered.

Upset that he assumed she needed his help, she sharply replied, "Of course I know where I left it. It was right here just ten minutes ago and the guy working this counter must have found it. And, by the way, I don't need your help. I'm doing just fine by myself."

Looking around for the Mexican, she realized he must have left work for the night. She desperately hoped he was honest and had locked her purse up here before leaving. "I'll just have to come back in the morning to pick it up after they open."

Turning back to him, she noticed how extremely handsome he was standing there leaning against the counter looking at her. He was beginning to distract her thoughts again. How could he attract her and upset her at the same time?

Remembering her anger though, she was pleased to have someone besides herself to direct it at, so she continued on in a rush. "It was your fault I lost my purse anyway, so why would I want you to help me find it?"

Lifting a questioning brow at that statement, he asked, "How could this be my fault?"

Not thinking, she blurted out, "You distracted me and I wasn't thinking about what I was doing." Starting back to the baggage claim, upset, she threw back, "Just...oh, never mind. I can take care of myself."

Pausing a moment, he smiled and watched as she stormed off across the airport, her long shapely legs moving enticingly under the short denim skirt. He contemplated what she had just said. She had been so preoccupied thinking about him that she had actually walked off without her purse. Well, she might act like she doesn't like me or need my help, but she does, whether she admits it or not. He was going to enjoy getting her to admit it too! She seemed very attracted to him and he could tell. He was feeling pretty pleased with himself. This was going to be very interesting. He couldn't remember the last time he had enjoyed upsetting a girl this much. With a satisfied grin, he started out after her.

The guard in baggage claim gave her back her carry-on bag, but stated he would have to lock her suitcase up in the airport for the night if she couldn't produce the claim check until tomorrow.

"No, you can't do that. I need something in the bag," she panicked, realizing the money Todd had demanded she bring was inside it. Her last hope of getting Keira back was inside that bag. She couldn't risk losing it. Even if the bag was locked up for the night, what if they went through it and found all that cash? Oh, this day was definitely getting worse by the minute.

"It'll be okay, sweetheart," a soothingly deep voice came from over her shoulder. "Luis here will make sure it's locked up real safe and secure for the night and we can pick it up tomorrow morning, okay?" He was certain there was something very important to her in the bag to warrant her intense reaction though and she didn't seem to be the type of girl who would panic without her toiletries for one night. There was definitely something of value inside and he wondered what it was. He was also wondering what had brought her down here to Mexico.

Hoisting her carry-on bag over his shoulder, he placed his hand protectively on her arm as he guided her away from the guard before she could argue any further. When she started to struggle against him and become disagreeable, he leaned down and spoke quietly in her ear.

"Don't make a scene, sweetheart, it will only make them suspicious of exactly what you've got in that bag." Closing her mouth immediately, she realized he was right. Once out of the guard's hearing range, she asked, "Do you know him? You called him Luis. Is he honest? Do you think he'll search my bag?" Her questions came at him without the slightest pause to allow him a chance to answer. Chuckling, he looked down at her as they walked toward the exit sign.

"No, I don't personally know him. I read his nametag. But yes, I do think he'll lock it up nice and tight for the night and you'll get your nighties and blow dryer back tomorrow." Stopping short to face him, she looked up at him incredulously. He could see she was pissed and assumed it was at him. Preparing for a tirade, he set her bag down and quickly found his assumption was correct.

"You know, you're just amazing. Nearly every time you speak to me, you make me angry. It must just be a natural talent of yours." Hoisting her carry-on up on her shoulder, she struggled muttering, "Nighties and blow dryer, really…"

Falling into step beside her, he easily lifted the bag from her shoulder and continued outside through the double doors, cutting off the rest of her sentence. The warmth of the night air was startling to her. Undistracted, she looked up at his broad back and scowled. "It's even hotter out here," she complained. Even the thin tank top and short skirt didn't help her discomfort. The heat was making her short tempered. She became more uncomfortable as she noticed the heat didn't even seem to bother him.

"You know, since I first ran into you," she stated, "I've been having terrible luck. I'm starting to think it has something to do with you. Why don't you just leave me be and let me take care of my own problems? You might be the cause of all this trouble I'm having today."

Jake set her bag down next to a bench at the curb. "Well then, since you obviously think you don't need my help and you're handling your problems so well by yourself, what will you do now?"

He watched her with interest, his hands on his hips as he leaned against the back of the bench. He found the various emotions crossing her face rather interesting. First there was doubt, then fright, frustration, and then finally anger, directed straight at him again. Her lovely face was certainly an open book for him to read.

Lifting her chin stubbornly, she glared at him standing with her arms akimbo. "I have the keys to a rental car so I'll just drive myself to town."

"Well, I'm sure that seems like a pretty good idea to you, but what happens if you get stopped by the Mexican Policia without any identification or proper papers? This is

Mexico, remember? They would immediately haul your pretty little ass straight to jail."

"Then, I'll just hitchhike to town if I have to," she shot back, stubbornly.

"Okay, so let's say you get yourself to town. Then what? You have no money or credit card, right?"

Beginning to pace in front of him, she angrily replied. "I'm not stupid, I'll wire for money when I get to Cabo." Finally he couldn't stand it any longer and broke into laughter.

"Sweetheart, it's Friday evening and you can't wire for money around here until Monday morning. You're in a very big mess. You're in a foreign country, you probably can't speak the language and you're still too stubborn to admit needing any help. You're even willing to risk your life rather than let me help you. A woman can't hitchhike alone at night in Mexico unless she doesn't mind ending up lying dead out in the desert somewhere, never to be heard from again."

"You're just trying to scare me and it won't work. And I can handle this my...," she stopped mid-sentence when he turned and just walked away. He was still chuckling as he turned back to add, "Wait here. I'll be right back."

She was angry and fuming that he was now ordering her around. She had to think logically. Lynnette sat down on the bench and thought of the truth in what he'd said. She didn't know her way around Los Cabos, she didn't have any identification or credit cards until she got her purse back in the morning and besides, she really had no idea what to do next. Why was it so irritating to accept his help? It was maddening as hell to admit, but maybe she could use his help, just a little. She would die before ever admitting that fact to him though.

Wringing her hands together, she nervously began pacing again. She was worried about Keira and worried about getting her bag back with the money inside. Maybe it hadn't been such a good idea to hide the cash inside her check-in bag, but she didn't know how else to get it down here. She was planning to attempt sneaking Keira away from Todd if she could, but if that plan failed she was prepared to pay him the money he wanted to get Keira out of danger. She would do anything to get her little sister home again safely.

Wishing her problems would just go away, she looked up, startled, as tires suddenly screeched to a halt at the curb in front of her. She was surprised to see him jumping out of a four-wheel drive jeep with huge knobby tires and spotlights mounted on top of the roll bar. She stood there as he came around the jeep and tossed her bag into the back. She began to disagree again, when he caught her off guard, taking her by the waist and lifting her easily onto the front seat.

Overwhelmed by his highhanded action, she stammered, "What..., how dare..., just what do you think you're doing? I'm not going anywhere with you!"

As he climbed in the driver seat, she quickly reached over and grabbed the keys out of the ignition before he could start the engine. Always a fight with her, he thought, although she isn't boring. Fixing her with a scowl, he stared over at her. After awhile, he asked, "Now what? Do you have a better plan? I'm your best shot at getting to town tonight so let me have those keys back before you lose them too. You really aren't having much luck today."

She returned his angry glare.

"You know, you are entirely too overbearing and bossy. Do you really expect me to drive off with you to go..., who knows where? And you thought hitchhiking was a bad idea. How do I know I can trust you? I don't even know you. You're a perfect stranger."

"Perfect stranger, huh?" he suggested with a slow grin. "So you think I'm perfect, do you?" he teased in a slow voice, leaning across the seats toward her. She decided right then he was just as maddening as he was gorgeous. But she wasn't deterred. She was mad as hell, both at him and her frustrating situation.

Seeing the look on her face, he could tell she wasn't in the mood for jokes. As a matter of fact, at the moment she looked like she was either about to kill him or cry.

Leaning back in the drivers seat with a long sigh, Jake slowly raked his fingers through his hair. He was going to have to re-think his approach toward this girl. She was an emotional wreck and he didn't know why. What was troubling her?

Placing both hands on the steering wheel, he looked at her again and could see the underlying fright and vulnerability she was trying so hard to hide from him. She really was holding up fairly well considering her situation. She did have herself in a real mess. She couldn't help it if she was all emotional about it, he decided. She was a female. And quite an enticing female at that, he admitted to himself. But she did have a point. She didn't yet know him and whether or not she could trust him. He was a complete stranger to her.

She watched him as he looked at her with those intensely blue eyes. She wondered just what it was about his eyes that made her think he could actually read her mind. She hoped he didn't know the turn her thoughts took as she sat there observing his huge arms as he ran his fingers through his dark, wavy hair. What a perfect male body. He was still just sitting there staring at her with those spectacular deep blue eyes of his and she could feel herself losing concentration again. It wasn't long before she could sense in him a warmth, a genuine concern for her and a sort of gentleness. Still looking at him, she felt relatively sure she would not have to worry about her safely with him, he wouldn't harm her, but she didn't want to let him off the hook too easily. She had no intention of making anything easy for this guy; he was just too quick to take charge, in her opinion. She would just keep quiet to see what he would say next. She was well aware that her options were few at the moment.

Looking very serious, he quietly agreed, "Look, you're absolutely right. You don't know me, but I am your best choice for help right now. Possibly your only choice. I know you're scared and wary, you should be."

"I'm not scared. I'm just hot and miserable. It's too hot here. I'm not scared," she stubbornly interrupted, but he put up his hand to stop her, and then continued.

"Look, you don't have any money, you have no papers or I.D. This is a foreign county and our rules in the states don't apply down here. You really are in a dilemma and I can't just leave you out here at the airport all alone."

Noticing her softening a little he pressed on. "Just let me help you out. I'll give you a lift now and in the morning we'll come back to the airport, find your purse, get your suitcase and you'll be on your way, okay?"

Contemplating his little speech and noticing the honest look on his face and concern in his voice, Lynnette turned away for a second and allowed herself a small grin. He really was quite charming in an overly masculine, highhanded way.

"By the way, my name is Jake. Jake Hunter. So formally we're no longer strangers," he smiled wide and she looked away, warning herself to beware of that big smile, knowing it could be dangerous. It was unsettling how absolutely gorgeous he was when he smiled at her like that. Glancing over at him, she conceded a bit.

"Okay, Jake, you're right. You've made some very good points. My name is Lynnette Ocean and since I don't have a choice, I'll trust you and take you up on your offer for a ride."

Handing him back the keys, he started the engine and pulled out of the airport and on to the main road leading to town. Lynnette had to grab the handrail on the dashboard to keep from falling out the side where a door would have normally been.

"Where are you from Lynnette Ocean?"

"I'm from Orange County up in California. How about you?"

"I live in Long Beach and have for ten years now. I love it there." Jake was pleased to learn she lived near him.

"So, Lynnette, where did you make your room reservation?" he asked loudly over the roar of the engine, and the wind loudly whipping around in the jeep, as he got up to speed. Looking over, he could see her long hair blowing wildly around her face.

"Reservations?"

"Yes, where are you staying in town?"

"I don't have a room reservation yet," she yelled back to be heard, trying to hold down her skirt in the buffeting wind. Jake looked over at her dumbfounded, realizing she wasn't joking.

"You've got to be kidding me. You show up on vacation in one of the hottest tourist spots on the west coast during the Bisbee Fishing Tournament without making a room reservation?" he asked in disbelief. "This town is completely booked weeks in advance of the tournament." Cocking his head to one side he stated, "Now I can see how you get yourself into so much trouble. You don't think!"

Perturbed with him again, she crossed her arms and fixed him with a scowl. As usual, she was unable to stop herself from replying before thinking, which was definitely one of her downfalls. "For your information, I'm not here on vacation and I didn't even know I was coming until this morning. There wasn't enough time to make a room reservation, so I just thought I would get a room when I got here. I didn't even know about any stupid fishing tournament."

Catching herself before she revealed too much information, she stopped herself from saying another word, knowing it was very dangerous to tell him anything about Todd or the situation with Keira. She sat there quietly fuming. No reservation and no rooms available. Again, she had goofed up and now had no place to sleep. Even if she could find a cheap room, she was going to have to swallow her pride and ask Jake for a small loan to pay for it until tomorrow.

Jake thought over her comments. As far as he was concerned, she shouldn't even be in Mexico on her own. She had gotten herself into more trouble just in the past hour than he could have ever imagined anyone could. It was unbelievable. She was almost a danger to herself. What in the world would bring someone like her to Mexico on less than a day's notice if it weren't something urgent? And why had she been in such a hurry to get here? He didn't know anyone who came to Cabo besides people on vacation or possibly people with business dealings, as was his case. There were also those hiding from the law down here in Mexico, but he knew that wasn't her situation. He was going to start getting answers out of her, and soon.

She sat staring out the windshield, struggling with the wind in her hair, trying to keep it from tangling around her head. Jake couldn't resist stealing glances in her direction as she reached up to gather all that beautiful, long wavy hair together in her hands. As she raised her arms over her head, her tank top pulled tightly over nicely rounded breasts. She was enticing him without even knowing it, giving him reason to pause a moment. Although she's a bit stubborn and troublesome, she sure was a beauty, he thought with pleasure and anticipation.

Dragging his eyes back to the curving desert road, he realized he liked the thought of having her at his mercy. He would enjoy playing the role of her protector, whether she liked it or not. She certainly needed it. Surprisingly, he found himself delighted with her argumentative disposition. The women in his past were always so proper and polite, always on their best behavior for him. They were constantly reminding him of his financial position and his single status, trying to work their way into a committed relationship with him in hopes it would lead to marriage. Their attempts were as transparent as they were futile. He had never been interested in tying himself down to any of the scheming women he had met in the past.

Jake had become a very successful businessman and he now had accumulated the kind of wealth most women would love to get their hands on. None of those other women would ever openly disagree with him. They would whine when they didn't get their way, but they were always predictable. In contrast, he rather liked this girl's spunk. She certainly is a fiery little thing, he thought, knowing he'd enjoy nothing more than to spend some time taming her.

Knowing it was a bit deceiving, he decided to keep his financial standing a secret from her, at least for now anyway. He personally challenged himself to win her over with his charm. Once he was sure she was truly interested in him then he'd see where it went from there.

Smiling, he realized he was in for a much better trip than he first imagined. "Lynnette, I know the perfect place for you to stay tonight. I'll take you there now and show it to you. By the way, what are you doing down here if you're not here for a vacation?" he asked directly.

"I'm meeting someone," she answered too quickly. "He doesn't expect me for a couple more days though," she hedged, turning away. She hoped he wouldn't ask any more questions. She didn't have a good back-up story worked out in her mind just yet. She certainly couldn't tell him the truth. It was much too dangerous for Keira's safety.

Meeting a guy? Jake frowned, realizing he should have known. But what kind of boyfriend would let an innocent beauty like this show up in Mexico without meeting her at the airport? He hadn't heard her mention she arrived early. He hadn't heard anything after she said she was meeting her boyfriend. He was still frowning, not realizing he'd drawn the wrong conclusion. He wondered why he was suddenly so bothered by the thought of another guy with her. It was certainly none of his business anyway. He had no claim on her himself. Not yet.

As they drove along in silence, Lynnette took note of the spectacular coastline as they headed down the coast towards Cabo San Lucas. The two-lane road was built high into the side of the cliffs and wound its way along the beautifully rugged coastline. Looking out at the dark blue sea she saw a few scattered sailboats along the horizon and some fishing boats heading back to the harbor for the night. Looking out the other side toward the west, she witnessed the most breathtaking panoramic view of the desert; unlike any she had seen in her life. It was absolutely beautiful. Again she daydreamed of being here on a romantic holiday with a handsome man, imagining they would be in love and happy together, only to catch her wandering thoughts. Frowning, she dragged her thoughts back to the present situation.

Jake expertly maneuvered the powerful jeep off the main road turning on to a dirt road heading down toward the water. As he wound his way through a huge grove of coconut palms and wild bougainvilleas, each blooming in bright shades of red, purple and orange, she caught her breath as the road suddenly opened up to a spectacular view of a white sand beach in a small private cove.

"Oh, this is beautiful," she said in awe as her gaze took in the gorgeous blue-green of the sea and scattered banana trees growing among date palms. Leaning forward in her seat, she could see a few Spanish style homes, nicely hidden among the lush tropical landscape.

"Absolutely gorgeous," she said utterly enthralled by the view.

Glancing over at Jake who was noticeably quiet, she found him looking at her strangely. The intensity of his gaze darkened and he stared at her as if studying each feature. The look in his eyes grew warm and held hers. Her heart quickened just looking at him. She noticed his strong, square jaw with the scar on his chin. His dark hair was tousled from the ride and he looked so ruggedly handsome that a slight sigh escaped without her notice.

Not taking his eyes off her, he said, "You really are pretty when you're not yelling at me."

Feeling uncomfortable with his undivided attention, Lynnette felt her mouth go dry when she tried to speak. Admittedly, he was the most gorgeous man she had ever met. He was certainly too good-looking for his own good. Nervously, she licked her lips finding she couldn't speak. Her breathing was labored as she tried to get some air. What was happening to her?

Oh, how it made him want to kiss her when she ran her tongue over her lips like that, he thought. His eyes smoldered as his gaze returned to her eyes.

She wondered why he was staring at her. Not realizing just what her actions were doing to his resolve, she nervously moistened her lips once again so she could speak. "What?" she asked.

"It intrigues me when you lick your lips like that," he nodded briefly.

Biting her lower lip, she pulled away and looked out the windshield trying to think straight, to regain control over the situation.

"Yeah, that does too," he interrupted her attempts at control with a deep, sexy voice. "Biting your lower lip just like that." He put his arm over the back of her seat, moving in closer, his eyes never leaving her mouth.

Realizing he was about to kiss her, the reality of the situation hit her. Here she was sitting in a jeep with a stranger in a foreign country on a stranded stretch of beach, completely alone and vulnerable, she realized she could be in serious trouble. It wasn't that she disliked the idea of him kissing her though. Nearing panic, she attempted to regain control of herself.

"No, just stop," she said breathlessly. "You said you were taking me to town to get a room. Unless I'm seriously mistaken, there isn't any town here and I don't see even one hotel on this beach.

Pulling back with a slight grin, secure in the knowledge she had wanted him to kiss her, he threw the jeep in gear and drove across the white sand to one of the beach houses.

"What I believe I said, Lynnette, was that I knew the perfect place for you to spend the night. Here we are," he announced, stopping the jeep in front of a big white-washed hacienda style house with a red Spanish tile roof and heavy wooden door at the front entrance.

"Wait a minute, what is this place?" she asked suspicious of his intentions. "I'm not staying here with you. That wasn't part of the deal," she stated getting upset again.

Ignoring her, he continued. "This beach is called Santa Maria and this place," he said proudly looking around him, "is where a good friend lets me stay whenever I'm in town," he lied casually. "It's quite comfortable and Rosa always keeps it immaculate. She's amazing."

"Rosa? Who's Rosa?" she asked, eyes narrowed.

Getting out of the jeep to walk around the front, he tossed out, "Come on in and I'll introduce you."

Feeling a little better knowing there was another woman there she tried to calm herself. Then it dawned on her it might be his girlfriend.

"That must be nice to have a friend loan you his place whenever you want," she said as she attempted to step out of the jeep. She hesitated contemplating the rather huge step down as being nearly impossible in her skirt.

Jake saw her dilemma, reached up, placed both hands on her trim waist before she could argue, then set her easily down on the bottom step leading up to the house. Stepping back from his lingering touch, she exclaimed, "I'm perfectly capable of getting out of a vehicle without your assistance."

With a charming smile he responded. "It's much more fun doing it my way, but as you wish, sweetheart." Reaching into the back of the jeep, he grabbed both their bags and headed up the steps towards the big wooden front door.

In spite of herself, she enjoyed his endearments. Hearing him refer to her as sweetheart made her heart flutter, although he probably used that name for all women so he wouldn't confuse their names, she warned herself. She couldn't help but notice the way the muscles in his back rippled as he lifted their bags out of the jeep. As he turned back, he threw her another one of his devastating smiles, making her head spin. She was really going to have to watch out for that smile. It was really quite overwhelming, making her totally defenseless. She would have to concentrate hard to stay out of trouble with this guy.

As he walked inside the front door with her bags, she realized her mistake in hesitating at the jeep. "Hey, wait a minute. Where are you taking my bag? I just told you I'm not staying here with you."

She ran up the front steps after him. He had ignored her, disappearing inside the house.

FOUR

"Jake," she called out to the empty house. There was no answer. "Hello, Jake? Where are you?"

The foyer was so much cooler than outside; it was wonderfully refreshing to be out of the extreme heat.

Jake apparently had disappeared from sight, but their luggage was sitting just inside the foyer. She was tempted to grab her bag and bolt out the door but was distracted by the spectacular view of the beach from the elegantly furnished living room in front of her.

It was absolutely beautiful. Red Spanish pavers led to three large arched windows through which she could see a spacious patio deck overlooking the white sand beach. Taking the two steps down into the living room, she admired the white leather couches and chairs, which contrasted beautifully with the dark wooden end tables. Throw rugs were strategically placed over the tile floor and expensive looking artwork and throw pillows added splashes of greens, reds and blues that accentuated the gorgeous view of the ocean through the windows. This was definitely an elegant room designed for an elegant man, whoever he was. It was both masculine and welcoming. She would love to meet this friend of Jake's, the one who had ordered this lovely room designed.

Just then, she heard voices coming and saw Jake enter the foyer through a wide archway next to the front door, closely followed by a very short, stout Mexican woman who was rapidly speaking to him in Spanish. Lynnette couldn't understand a word she was saying but the little woman appeared very pleased to see Jake as she continued on with her animated dialogue. She probably already knew him since he had obviously borrowed this house from his friend on previous occasions.

Tossing Lynnette a wink across the room, Jake turned to the tiny woman and announced, "Lynnette, I'd like you to meet Rosa. Rosa, este es mi amiga, Lynnette," he rattled off in perfectly eloquent Spanish.

Rosa gave her a welcoming smile and once again, they began a dialogue in her native language as Lynnette advanced across the room and up the step towards them. Lynnette smiled back and looked questioningly up at Jake, not understanding a word the woman was saying. He quietly studied her face for a few moments before speaking.

"I was right, wasn't I? You don't know any Spanish at all, do you?"

Scowling at him, she angrily crossed her arms in front, obviously piqued at his correct assumption.

Jake understood Rosa's chatter perfectly. She was excited, thinking he had finally brought his special lady on vacation to his home with him. She was happy to finally meet her and told Jake she was very pretty. Jake knew Rosa was just an old romantic at heart, so why tell her the truth now. Let her enjoy the deception for a while. He decided to let it go for the time being since it was easier than trying to explain the complicated truth.

Lynnette watched as Jake calmly patted Rosa's hand, saying something apparently sweet to her that caused her to smile up at him warmly. Then she bustled back through the archway to the back part of the house.

Gently taking Lynnette's arm, Jake offered, "Come along with me. I'll give you a tour of the place, then Rosa can show you to the guest room."

Lynnette was about to object again about staying when he noticed the look on her face. He quickly hushed her by placing a finger over her lips.

"Don't worry. My plan isn't to ravage you while you're sleeping," he grinned. " You can have the guest room all to yourself."

Smiling, he placed his hand lightly on the small of her back as he guided her down the Spanish tiled hallway. She felt like the skin where his fingers touched her was on fire. She was overwhelmingly aware of him standing so close as he showed her every room of the charming place.

They worked their way through the house and she found each room was even more impressive than the last. The interior designer had continued the theme of the elegant look of the living room, but introduced new colors as you moved throughout the house. Downstairs, there was a full gym at the end of a long hallway, a huge guest bedroom and bathroom, complete with a sunken tub overlooking the beach, a dining room and a wonderfully designed kitchen in which Rosa looked completely at home. The master bedroom and bath were upstairs along with an office. The house was even larger than it looked from the outside.

"Well, how do you like it?" he asked proudly, leading Lynnette back into the living room.

"It's absolutely gorgeous," she answered, "and no, by the way, I'm not staying here with you tonight. I couldn't. It just wouldn't be right. We just met, but thanks for the offer."

She figured she couldn't trust being alone with him all night; he was far too clever. She knew she couldn't trust herself being alone with him. He was too handsome and tempting.

Jake didn't acknowledge her statement as he moved across the room toward a desk in the corner. He picked up some mail and began leafing through it. Puzzled, she thought it strange he would go through someone else's mail.

"Jake, I said I can't..."

"Yeah, I heard you the first time, Lynnette. Don't worry, I'm not even staying here tonight," he stated, distracted by a particular piece of mail he was reading. "You can have the entire place to yourself. You'll be perfectly comfortable here until morning," he finished not even looking up at her.

Thinking it was rather rude to open up his friend's mail, she frowned at him. "You're not staying?" she asked hesitantly, not wanting to seem too curious, yet feeling bothered at the thought of him leaving. "Where are you going?" She had tried sounding nonchalant, but failed. He hadn't appeared to notice.

Still distracted by the mail he was intent on reading, he absently answered. "I'm going down to the docks to see if Ariel's arrived yet. I haven't seen her in months and I'm anxious to she her again."

A woman! He's going to meet a woman! He won't be back until morning, meaning they were...

She felt both irritated and depressed at the same time. Disturbed, she glanced over to see that he was still going through the large stack of mail.

"Well isn't that nice," she stiffly responded. Walking toward the patio door, she coldly said, "You two have a wonderful time. I'll be ready to leave early in the morning if you would be so kind to drop me off at the airport. I'm going out for a walk now."

Looking up suddenly, Jake saw the back of her as she headed down the patio stairs toward the beach. That's odd, he thought as he folded up the mail and filed it in the drawer. I wonder what's gotten her pretty tail feathers ruffled up all of a sudden? Deciding it was another one of those odd things about women he'd never understand, he headed up the stairs, taking them two at a time. He changed into something cooler since it was still quite hot for this late in the day. Checking his watch, he realized there was just enough time to get down to the docks before it turned completely dark outside. He could feel his excitement building inside, very anxious now to finally see Ariel.

Lynnette spent over an hour walking along the water's edge, thinking. Poor Keira. Lynnette hoped Todd wasn't being cruel and that she was okay. Saying a quick prayer, Lynnette's thoughts switched to her father. She couldn't believe he really expected her to marry someone she had never met before. Knowing her father, this fellow probably was some uptight accountant type who spent his free time counting his money. She would have to call Elliot when she got back. He would surely know what to do about this marriage farce her father had cooked up.

She had felt very uncomfortable earlier when she had lied to Elliot about her trip since he had always been so honest and loving to her. He was always there when she needed someone to confide in and share her troubles with, even more than her own father. She had never once lied to

Elliot about anything before and it didn't set well with her now. This was an exception though. There was no other way to handle it. Todd had been very clear about her not telling anyone about the situation and she wasn't about to risk Keira's life. This was her problem and she would handle it like she had always handled her problems in the past, alone.

Lynnette stopped and sat down in the soft sand, looking out over the blue water wondering if it was warm enough to take a swim. It looked more than inviting. Luckily she had thought to slip a swimsuit and some jeans into her carry-on bag. Maybe she would go back to the house and change. Filling her hand with white powdery sand, she let it run slowly out through her fingers as her thoughts returned to her messed up life. She knew somewhere deep inside she had always wished she had been born Elliot's daughter instead of Mac's. Elliot was so sweet and compassionate. Elliot had let her know he was aware that Mac pushed her too hard and he had interceded whenever he could, but there wasn't really much he could do about it. Mac was a very headstrong man with his own ideas. He was hardheaded and stubborn.

Deciding to change into her bathing suit before it got too late, Lynnette returned from her brief walk to discover Jake had already left the house. He sure was in a hurry to get out of here, she scowled. He's probably in such a rush to see his girlfriend he couldn't stand being here a moment longer, she thought with irritation. What did it matter to her anyway? She didn't like him in that way. He was bossy, overprotective, rugged and sexy... Catching herself, she decided it was time to get her mind back to the real reason for her trip here.

Still feeling too hot to eat before her swim, she decided to find Rosa to get a cold drink. She would take a moment later to sit down to study the local map she had picked up at the car rental counter. It was probably a good idea to get as familiar with the area as possible before looking for Todd. Once she did locate Todd and he, hopefully, led her to Keira, she would have to know the quickest and safest route back to the airport if they were going to make it out of here in one piece.

She found Rosa in the kitchen scrubbing a wooden cutting board. Using her hands to motion since she couldn't speak any Spanish, Rosa was able to understand Lynnette's wish for a drink. Rosa quickly and efficiently prepared a tray with a glass of ice and a pitcher of lemonade. Just perfect. Rosa took the tray out on the patio as Lynnette fetched the map from her carry-on bag, which had mysteriously made its way into the guest room. Rosa definitely was efficient.

Passing by the bookshelf in the front room on her way outside to the deck, Lynnette stopped to look over the selection of books over the desk. Spotting a book on deep-sea fishing, she pulled it down and took it and the map outside hoping to learn something about Todd's new fishing enterprise. It might just help her locate him. He had promptly failed at everything else he ever tried, but fishing, now maybe that was something even Todd could succeed at.

*   *   *

Jake stopped short as he walked toward the docks. You could spot her immediately among all the others; she was so outstanding, so spectacular. Feeling now the anticipation and complete pride of ownership throughout his body, he hurried toward the fantastic ninety-five foot sailing yacht known simply as Ariel. He wondered what Lynnette would think of Ariel if she were standing here next to him.

Climbing aboard, he immediately noticed the newly redone teak deck. It was apparent they had done an exceptional, high quality job. He always demanded the best and usually got it.

"Miguel, you down there?" Jake called out as he climbed down the steps leading below deck.

"Hey Jake, good to see you, jefe. ¿Cómo está usted, mi amigo?" Miguel, a strong and stocky Mexican reached out his hand in a hearty handshake. "The yacht, she is great, yes?" Miguel asked in his thick accent. "Handles the water better than she looks," he added with enthusiasm.

Miguel had been working on Jake's fleet of yachts now for over six years, ever since Jake had first met him on one of his first trips down to these very same waters. Miguel had been eager to learn, anxious to sail and was a natural at navigation. Now he was not only one of Jake's top skippers, but also a close and trusted friend.

Heading back up on deck, Jake commented to Miguel on the various improvements he had ordered done since the time he had purchased the vessel in San Francisco eight months earlier. The interior joinery had been replaced along with the teak deck and the hull had been taken down bare inside and out for rework and paint. It had cost him a bundle but he had never even considered the amount. He had fallen in love with this particular yacht immediately and now he would add this ketch to his fleet of skippered sailing vessels that his elite clientele hired out for charter. Any one of his fleet of fine sailing and motor yachts offered the perfect getaway for the wealthy and successful, itching for a vacation with a hint of adventure and a whole lot of relaxation. Not to mention the excellent cuisine they would experience at the hands of his gifted staff.

"Where is Maria?" Jake asked, now reminded of her great cooking. Maria was Miguel's wife and without a doubt, the best cook on Jake's payroll. She cooked better than many chefs he had enjoyed in the past.

"She spends most her time down in the galley. She loves this ship, Jake. Even better than the last one we worked on for you. It is hard for me to get her to go home now," Miguel said laughing.

Jake smiled down at Miguel, giving him a hearty pat on the back as his thoughts went back to Lynnette again. They seemed to wander there no matter what he was doing. She really seemed to be getting to him. What had gotten into him?

Hurrying through a quick checkout on the rest of the improvements he had ordered done, Jake headed immediately back to the jeep with a new purpose in his step. He'd decided to go back to the house again to see Lynnette. His mind looking for a reason for this sudden decision settled on the thought she had probably never been to Mexico before and maybe she would enjoy a tour of Cabo this evening. It was still early. They could have a late supper together. He couldn't seem to force himself to stay away from her, although he knew he probably should.

Miguel and Maria stood side by side at the deck railing, watching Jake walk away up the dock. Discussing what in the world could possibly drag Jake's attention away from this new yacht he loved so much, Miguel's face looked puzzled while Maria's had the knowing satisfaction of a woman wise beyond her years.

"I guess you may be right," he said in Spanish. "It must be a woman," Miguel agreed. Maria laughed at the pained look on her husband's face and gave him a big hug, saying, "Our Jake, he is falling in love maybe."

Taking his wife's hand in his, he calmly disagreed. "No. Not our Jake, my wife. You are just an old romantic woman. He is not the falling in love type of guy."

FIVE

Jake entered the dark house to find the lights were all turned low and there was no one inside. Rosa would have already left to go home, but where was Lynnette? She wouldn't be asleep yet, it was much too early. He wandered down the hall to the guest room to make sure. She wasn't there. When Lynnette didn't answer his repeated calls, he began to get concerned. He stepped out on the patio deck to take a quick check around the property before getting seriously worried. That's when he heard her laughter. It sounded like music to his ears. By the sound of it, the laughter was coming from the water and she was obviously having a great time. As he took a seat on the patio chair, he could hear splashing mixed with the sounds of giddiness. He couldn't see her just yet because his eyes had not adjusted to the darkness. He could feel his growing anticipation of seeing her standing there before him in some skimpy bikini, dripping wet. Running his hand down his face, he tried to clear the alluring image of her from his mind.

Lynnette had never before taken a swim in the ocean at night. She laughed, imagining her father's stern voice ordering her not to do it, that it wasn't safe. He wouldn't let her do anything because she might hurt herself. But she didn't care now. It felt great playing out here in the water. For the first time since the plane landed, she wasn't feeling miserably hot. She actually felt wickedly wonderful. That's what made it even better in her mind, the fact she was thoroughly enjoying something that Mac had always forbidden her to do. In the past, she would have never considered going against him. For the first time in her life she felt totally independent and free from her father's never ending dominance and powerful personality.

Running out of the water on to the soft sand, she found the air temperature had dropped only slightly although it was already dark. She was still quite comfortable wearing only her bikini. Feeling happier than she had in years and able to forget her problems, if only for a short while, she ran back to the house and up the steps to the deck. Crying out as she tripped over something in the dark, she began to fall. Realizing too late that it was Jake's outstretch legs that had caused her to fall, she felt his strong arms reach out and catch her, pulling her firmly onto his lap.

"What in the world do you think you're doing?" she exclaimed. "You nearly scared me half to death." Squirming in his lap, she attempted to get up but he easily held her firmly in his strong arms. Looking up at him in the darkness, she could barely make out his features in the indirect lighting coming through the windows. There was no mistaking the look in his eyes as he stared down at her though. She also noticed the unsteady rhythm of his rapid breathing, matching her own unsteady gasps. Her skin was on fire where his body touched hers. She could feel a warm glow beginning to burn deep and low inside her body. Her thighs quivered slightly where she rested on his firm legs.

Suddenly realizing his obviously natural male reaction to her ongoing wiggling around on his lap while wearing next to nothing, she immediately became perfectly still and glowered at him.

"What are you doing back already? Didn't your girl, Ariel show up?" she asked sarcastically, trying to struggle to her feet again.

Laughing lightly at her useless attempts to stand he admitted she was completely charming while irritated. Distracted by her damp skin, he answered, not realizing she mistakenly thought his yacht was another woman.

"No, she was there all right. I was anxious to come back to tell you about her."

Suddenly excited to share his enthusiasm about his new yacht with her he rushed on. "Oh, Lynnette, she was so beautiful, even better than I remembered. There she was tied up at the docks and as I climbed aboard her, she was just spectacular..."

"Stop right there, Jake," she demanded working free of his grasp finally and gaining her footing as she backed away. Her mouth hung open in disbelief, standing there outraged that he would come back here and tell her the sordid details of his sexual encounter with another woman. Fury in her eyes, she stood there in shock at his unthinking crudeness.

She found her voice again, declaring, "How dare you pretend interest in me, then run off on some escapade with some sleazy girlfriend and have the audacity to come back here to tell me the sordid details of your latest conquest. If you think for one moment I want to hear about you tying up some woman at the docks and doing..., who knows what with her, well then..."

"Lynnette, what in hell are you talking about?" he demanded while standing, confusion written on his face. They stood toe to toe, shouting at one another.

She continued, yelling louder as if he hadn't spoken, "doing some..., some weird sexual..., whatever to her, you're mistaken mister. You are undoubtedly the most disgusting, egotistical, self-centered, male chauvinist I have ever laid my..."

Pulling her to him, he brought his mouth firmly down over hers, partially to shut her up, but mostly because he couldn't resist the temptation any longer. Seeing her standing there in her bikini, chest heaving in anger as she ranted on about some nonsense, he just couldn't handle it anymore.

It worked too. She was definitely quiet now. At first she let out a startled cry when he pulled her into his arms, but the moment his mouth slanted down over hers, tasting her sweet lips, she melted into his body. He knew she was just as helplessly lost in the kiss as he was as he ran his hands up and down her bare skin. She felt wonderful to him.

Jake began to tease her mouth with his tongue, biting lightly on her bottom lip with his teeth as he lightly moved his hands up and down her back, pulling her closer against his body. She responded timidly at first and then breathlessly she ran her hands up his muscled arms and circled them around his neck. Losing control, she aggressively gave in to the kiss. Her helpless whimpers and the deep moans coming from him were the only sounds to be heard besides the waves rhythmically crashing on the beach behind them. Their bodies moved together, their lips devouring one another's with a passion neither had felt before.

Lynnette tried to focus her mind, attempting to regain some semblance of self-control over the physical need washing over her body like a powerful ocean wave.

Placing both hands against his broad chest, she pushed away weakly, tying to steady herself. Her eyes were still closed as she breathed in deeply. Her mind whirled in circles and she couldn't think straight. Licking her swollen lips, she could still taste Jake's wonderful kiss and slowly opening her eyes she looked up at him.

Jake gazed down into her eyes, a dark gleam in their blue depths. She could see the muscles in the side of his strong square jaw clench as he struggled internally with himself. They continued just staring into each other's eyes, a silent communication between them. His was a question of continuing their physical explorations further and hers an answer of silent hesitation.

This girl was magnificent, he thought, so full of untapped, heated passion, yet she had been so timid and shy in the beginning. When she did cut loose though, she kissed him like he had never been kissed before in his life. It brought out some of the most arousing sensations he had ever experienced and all that just from a single kiss. He was eager to get back to it, but he would have to be patient. He sensed her inexperience and that she still had some fear and hesitation to overcome. He would control his desire, bide his time and carefully romance her. He knew he must push aside for the moment the fact that she still intended to leave first thing in the morning.

Pulling away from his arms uncomfortably, she quickly grabbed the towel she had left hanging over the chair and began walking back into the house when he stopped her.

"Wait just a minute, woman. You can't kiss me like that and then just walk away," he ordered in a deeply sexy voice. "I want to talk to you for a minute. Come back here and sit with me. Please," he added more gently.

Hesitantly, she wrapped the towel snuggly around her body as she slowly came back to the patio table and took a seat. She was still trying to collect her thoughts. Never in her life had she been kissed like that and it had left her deeply confused. She still felt a tingling deep inside which made her somewhat uncomfortable. She wasn't at all sure she could sit near him without wanting him to kiss her like that again. It had felt amazingly wonderful, but also a little frightening.

Jake took a deep breath and patiently asked, "Now what in the world were you ranting on about earlier? Something about a girlfriend?"

"I don't rant, Jake," she stated, "and you most certainly do know what I'm talking about."

"I honestly have no idea what you were talking about, Lynnette" he insisted.

Clearing the arousal from her mind, she attempted to focus on the conversation at hand. Answering slowly as if speaking to the dumb witted, she explained.

"Your girlfriend, Jake. You said you were going to meet some gorgeous woman on the docks. Now I can't remember her name. It was Andrea or Adrienne, or something like that."

Uncomfortable under his direct gaze, she stood and walked over to the deck railing with her back to him, pulling the towel up protectively around her body again. He was sitting there looking so irresistibly handsome and she still found it much easier to speak coherently if she wasn't looking directly at him.

Continuing to gaze out into the dark, she said, "I found it very distasteful of you to go on about another girl while you continually tease me with your flirting, not that your silly flirting has affected me at all," she suggested.

"Liar."

"No I'm not. Anyway, I just thought it was rude of you and I didn't like it."

When he spoke again, his voice was low, soft and strangely deep. "Lynnette, you're absolutely gorgeous when you're jealous."

"I'm not jealous. That's just ridiculous." She could hear his voice moving closer behind her and felt shivers of anticipation.

"And you're lying about my flirting not affecting you. It is. I can tell." Unconsciously she swallowed as he moved even closer yet placing his warm palms on her bare shoulders. He pulled her back gently against his firm body, wrapping his arms slowly around her waist.

"Ariel is not my girlfriend, sweetheart," he whispered softly in her ear. "She isn't even a woman. She is female though. I'll explain it to you later on."

Placing sweet kisses lightly on her shoulder and up the back of her neck, she could feel his warm breath on her skin. Lynnette felt a spark of fire ignite deep down inside her and dropping her head back against his solid chest, she began to lose herself again in the heat of his touch.

Then her stomach growled so loudly it was impossible for him not to have heard. He began laughing as she blushed, mortified at the timing of her hunger pains. A grin slowly spread across her face quickly turning into hysterical giggles.

Moving away from her, he grabbed her hand and offered, "Come on, you sound starved. Let's go out to dinner. I'll show you around Cabo and I also have a surprise for you waiting outside." He led her by the hand back into the house and said with a grin, "Run change into a pair of pants. It's all part of my surprise. I'll meet you out on the front porch in ten minutes."

A short while later, she stepped from the cool interior of the house onto the front steps, feeling the warm desert air hit her. It was amazingly warm still. Her wet hair was combed back; she was wearing a pair of jeans and sporty top with slip on sneakers. Anxious to find out what Jake's surprise was she found she wasn't prepared when she saw him sitting astride a large shiny, black and chrome motorcycle.

Oh my, she thought, as the fear quickly set in. He expects me to get on the back of that thing with him? I won't do it. I just can't do it. It was another thing, in a long list of things, her father had always forbidden her to do, insisting it was much too dangerous. But she had gone swimming in the ocean alone in the dark this evening, hadn't she? It had been a wonderful experience, something she would have never done before feeling so independent of her father. Maybe I'll just get on that bike and love it, she argued with herself, as she stood there completely frozen on the top steps of the house, looking petrified.

Jake saw the frightened look on her face and knew immediately this was going to be her first ride on a motorcycle. Well, there's a first time for everything, he thought. Grinning handsomely up at her, he motioned enticingly with his index finger for her to come down the steps and get on. As he started up the Harley-Davidson, she walked toward him slowly as if in a trance. She could feel the ground shaking from the vibration of the motor, the loud rumble of the engine nearly deafening as she strained to hear him yell something to her.

"Never ridden on a bike before, huh?

"Sure I have," she lied, yelling over the roar of the engine. "It's just been awhile."

Her lie didn't convince him for a moment.

"Throw your leg over the back of the bike," he grinned, obviously excited about some aspect of riding doubled up that she wasn't aware of yet. He anticipated the fact she would have to hold him around the waist and sit very close behind him in order to even remain on the back once they took off. Bending down each side of the bike while expertly balancing the heavy machine, he lowered the passenger foot pegs helping her to solidly place her feet on them.

"Lynnette, you're going to have to hang on to me so you don't fall off the back, okay?" he hollered back over his shoulder. "There's no sissy bar behind you so keep your arms around me and lock your fingers together. Don't let go, even at a stop sign. Without a backrest on this bike, I could lose you halfway between here and town."

She didn't obey, but rather placed her hands hesitantly on his sides. She was being careful not to touch him anywhere she shouldn't. It might be silly after the passionate kiss they had just shared on the patio, but suddenly she wasn't at all comfortable touching him now. She tried not to notice the rippling muscles in his back or the way his waist tapered down narrowly from wide shoulders.

Jake revved up the engine, dropped it into gear and took off. Lynnette panicked at the sudden thrust of power and immediately threw her arms around his waist, scooting up tightly against his back, hanging on for dear life. Glancing back over his shoulder, he pulled out on the main road that lead to town with a satisfied grin on his face.

SIX

Pulling up in front of his favorite restaurant in the small town of Cabo less than thirty minutes later, Jake was more than pleased to find Lynnette had enjoyed the motorcycle ride. She was obviously scared at first, but after just a few minutes of feeling the warm night air blowing through her hair, she began to relax. Yelling back over his shoulder to find out if she was having fun, she had answered with such pure enthusiasm that he stole a glance back to find her actually beaming with delight. She loved it! She certainly seemed to be quite an amazing girl.

Parking the bike near the harbor, across the narrow street from the restaurant, Jake called out to a young Mexican boy around twelve years old who appeared to be just hanging out. Removing his wallet from his jeans, Jake asked in Spanish if the boy would be there for the next hour or so. The boy tried hard to answer in his broken English that he would be there so Jake handed him a ten-dollar bill. The kid's face glowed with delight.

"You'll get another one of these if my bike is still here when I get back from right across there," he indicated the restaurant with a nod of his head. "We're going to be watching you from right up there," Jake said pointing up to the patio overlooking the marina.

After tousling the boy's hair and patting him companionably on the shoulder, Jake placed his arm around Lynnette and guided her across the road to the stone steps leading up to the restaurant.

Glancing back at the look of wonder on the young boy's face, she looked up at Jake. "That's a lot of money to these locals, isn't it?" Jake nodded as they continued up the steps.

Thinking a bit longer, she stopped to face him, asking, "You paid him, but you don't really expect him to protect your bike do you? He's too little."

"I expect his family can really use the money and I won't miss it. It also teaches him not to expect a handout, he's earning it." He started up the steps again with his arm around her and Lynnette found she enjoyed the protective feel of his arm . Strange, that's out of character for me, she thought. She liked the attention they stirred when entering the double doors. The entrance was raised, causing them to descend the steps down to the front desk. She smiled, noticing the reactions of several women who had spotted Jake, reinforcing the happiness she felt being with him. That and the fact he continued to maintain his large hand on the small of her back, possessively, and was only paying attention to her.

The view from the Italian restaurant looking out across the bay of Cabo San Lucas was awesome at night. The multitude of lights from across the harbor reflecting on the water looked purely magical. The Mexican waiter seated them near the patio railing at a lovely set table, complete with a white tablecloth and burning candle, setting a quaintly romantic mood. Sitting, Lynnette looked around to see if anyone noticed she was seriously under-dressed for this type of restaurant.

"Don't worry, gorgeous," he smiled in amusement at her obvious discomfort. "You look absolutely beautiful tonight."

The wind on the ride had blown her hair dry and it looked wild and sexy. Her face was flushed from the wind and the excitement of the ride. He couldn't imagine her looking better.

Blushing at his compliment, she could feel the heat rise into her cheeks. Smiling at him shyly, she looked down at her menu and attempted to slow the wild beating of her heart. This guy was too much. Now he was reading her mind and saying the words she'd always longed to hear from a man, but had only dreamed she would. Plus the fact he was so good-looking sitting there in the candlelight with his hair windblown from the ride. She itched to run her fingers through its dark, wavy length. She must surely be losing her mind. They had only just met that day and she was already so overwhelmed by him it was sinful. You better watch out, she warned herself again. If someone seems too good to be true, it usually means they are. She wondered what could possibly be wrong with him, what flaw would she find. He seemed so perfect, other than the fact he was a bit too domineering and take-charge for her liking. He also seemed rather stubborn when he made his mind up about something. Then reality struck her hard and cold. She remembered her argument with her father earlier that same morning.

What was she thinking? This situation with Jake could never go anywhere. She was supposedly promised to another man in marriage. True, she hadn't yet agreed to the arrangement, but she knew she would never be willing to walk away from everything she had worked her entire life for and lose her inheritance because she had just met this seemingly fantastic man. Jake was pretty close to the man of her dreams as far as she was concerned. She could probably change his high-handedness over time. She also hoped she would someday be able to think coherent thoughts while looking at him.

Jake was observing her over the top of his menu noticing how her mood seemed to change suddenly. Something she was thinking about was upsetting her and he assumed it was linked to the reason she was down here in Cabo in the first place.

Interrupted by the waiter's arrival, she agreed to Jake's suggestion of a bottle of dry red wine before they ordered dinner. He spoke to the waiter in perfectly fluent Spanish. Once again they were alone.

"Tell me why you're really doing down here?" he asked directly, looking at her with true concern.

"Why did I come here? You brought me here for dinner, silly. Remember?" Purposely side-stepping his question, she tried to change the subject. "Where did you learn to speak Spanish so well?"

Realizing she wasn't yet ready to confide in him, he answered her question. "I learned the basics from language tapes while on various lengthy sailing trips as a teenager. Then when I started coming down here to Mexico, I had a chance to use Spanish more often and it became easy. It's fairly easy to learn and really is a beautiful language."

He didn't mention the fact he was fluent in three other languages in addition to Spanish. It had served him well in the past in various countries while on special assignments for the government. He never spoke about those secret assignments with anyone. No one other than his uncle, that is. It was his uncle who provided him the details regarding the assignments he was given whenever they came up, which weren't often. When they did come up though, Jake immediately dropped everything and went undercover until the mission was accomplished. He worked as field agent for a special ops group just as his uncle had years before. His uncle had recruited him after concluding his service as a U. S. Navy Seal.

At a loss for another subject, Lynnette waited until the waiter finished serving the wine and took a nice healthy sip to soothe her nerves. She knew she shouldn't be sitting here enjoying a fancy dinner while her sister was in such serious trouble. Until she got her purse and money back, there wasn't much else she could do.

"I noticed the map and book on fishing boats on the coffee table while you were out swimming," he inquired. "Are you interested in fishing while you're down here?" Looking directly at her, he was very aware she had no more interest in fishing than he did. He correctly suspected it also had something to do with her reason for coming here.

Fidgeting in her chair, she delayed her answer by taking another long drink from her wine glass. "Well, I've never been fishing so I don't know yet if I'll like it. I was just curious, that's all," she hedged.

She had promised herself not to tell Jake anything about the situation with Todd and Keira. It was just too dangerous. If he got it in his mind to get involved, he just might accidentally get Keira hurt or killed by interfering. Todd had been very adamant about her not telling anyone, so she wouldn't mention it. She would just take care of the situation by herself.

Jake refilled her wine glass, realizing getting her tipsy might be the easiest way to get the truth out of her. She certainly was stubborn. He still suspected she was in trouble and he wanted to know the reason.

Feeling the beginning effects of the wine, Lynnette began to loosen up somewhat. Leaning forward in her chair, Jake caught a delightful view of her luscious cleavage. Her low-cut top allowed him a wonderful view that she wasn't aware she was sharing with him. Looking over his shoulder, he ensured she wasn't also sharing it with anyone else.

"Maybe you could tell me more about this area, Jake. The view from up here is just gorgeous, but it's not at all what I expected. I always thought Cabo was a tiny fishing village.

"Yes, the view from here is fantastic," he replied slowly as he regained some semblance of control. Prying his eyes away from the ample vision before him, he looked over the railing at the bay and sighed.

"It was ten years ago when I first came here by sailboat. They had just finished the only road down here shortly before that. That was really the beginning of all this growth you see now." Sipping his wine, he sat back in his chair and continued.

"On the one hand, the growth has been good for the people of Mexico. It's brought work and plenty of tourist dollars, but on the other hand, the growth happened so quickly they brought a lot of workers over from the mainland causing the locals living in town to move further inland to the back side of that hill over there," he pointed out with a nod of his head. "Much of what they've done has ruined most of what I originally loved about this place."

The waiter came by their table and poured them both more wine when he noticed her glass was empty. Jake continued.

"Cabo is no longer the escape it once was for criminals from the states, which is the up-side." The mention of criminals brought Todd to Lynnette's mind.

"It used to be a place you could run to where there were no phones, televisions or noisy jet skis. You really got away from it all. Now everything has changed, not necessarily for the better. Anything you can get in the states is available right here in Cabo now. I still enjoy it, but I definitely have mixed feelings about the growth down here. It would be a damn shame if they did here what they did to Acapulco," he finished. The emotion in his voice indicated the passion he felt on the subject.

Lynnette leaned forward as if confiding a secret, once again offering Jake's eyes the pleasure offered by her low-cut top. Whispering with a slight slur, she confided, "Ever since we were landing today, I've been thinking what a lovely, romantic spot this would be for a honeymoon. Especially the fact it's so close to home so the couple wouldn't have to wait so long for…" Realizing the turn of her thoughts, she stopped herself and quickly changed subjects.

They ate the rest of their meal over small talk, interspersed with comfortable moments of silence. She caught him more than once looking at her with a strangely thoughtful expression that she was unable to understand. When they were finished with dinner, Jake requested something additional in Spanish. He refused to translate when she asked.

"It's a little after dinner surprise for you."

Even tipsier now, she was now slurring seductively. "Well, aren't you just full of surprises, Jake Hunter? I can't wait to see what you've got planned for us after dinner." Once again she leaned forward to smile at him, unknowingly offering him that tempting view he was now growing to love.

Eyes burning with desire, he placed both arms on the table and leaned forward. "I want to stay with you at the house tonight, Lynnette" he announced suddenly. She obviously had no idea the affect she was having on him. He was using every ounce of his willpower not to toss the dinner table aside and throw her down on the patio tile right there and then. He wanted her so fiercely he literally ached with desire.

Realizing just then that she had been teasing him, although unintentionally, she now understood the intense level of his craving. It somewhat scared her, which sobered her up a bit. Sitting back in her chair she looked out at the view of the water and tried to clear her fuzzy mind. She had entirely too much wine tonight and was now too tipsy to handle the result of her reckless actions. This is exactly why she didn't often drink alcohol. She preferred to be in control of her actions in all situations and she certainly was not in control of this one.

Two waiters arrived just then at their table with a cart full of a half dozen bottles of various liquors and a flaming canister. What they did next was nothing short of fascinating to Lynnette. Diners from the other tables were turning around in their chairs to gape at the show the waiters proceeded to put on at their tableside.

The lights on the patio were dimmed low but she could see one waiter mix a variety of liquors in a snifter, then he lit it on fire. The dancing flame was spectacular and Lynnette was amazed as they poured the burning liquid back and forth from one metal container to another, pulling their arms further and further apart during each pour. All the while, the liquid was aflame throughout the pour. She was amazed the waiter didn't burn himself in the process. The second waiter then dipped two coffee cup rims in sugar and then they poured the burning liquid into the cups, adding hot coffee before presenting it proudly as a Mexican coffee. Lynnette clapped with delight as they cleaned up and moved the cart away. Jake smiled openly at her enthusiasm. She was such a delight to be with, he thought.

During the entire show, Jake's chin rested between his thumb and forefinger as he closely watched her. He was fascinated by the honest, wholesome expression of pleasure she exuded. He could read the fears and pleasures on her face so clearly it was fascinating how expressive she was. She was nothing like other women he had dated in the past. There was no pretense, no game playing, and no acting of any type. She was just..., herself. And she was lovely. He wondered if he could actually get serious about this woman. He would have to play it very careful to avoid getting hurt again.

The coffee helped Lynnette sober up a bit, as most of the alcohol had burned out of the liquor. She sincerely thanked Jake for a wonderful meal and he realized it had been a long time since a date had actually thanked him for buying her dinner. Not required, but certainly nice to hear. Lynnette was certainly from a different mold than the rest.

Walking back to the motorcycle he reminded her of his earlier question. "Lynnette, you never answered me. May I stay the night with you tonight?"

Looking up at him, the lights reflecting off the water so romantically, she could see the look of desire clearly on his face. He was so attractive it was nearly impossible to resist him. She knew she would have to look away to break the strong pull of temptation.

Looking out across the harbor she answered faintly. "No, Jake. I don't think I can…, it's too quick. We just met today and it's moving way too fast for me. I really don't…"

"That's alright. No need to explain. I understand and will respect your decision, but I had to ask." He leaned down to brush a light kiss across her lips. "But don't expect me to stop trying. I'm a patient man, but you're also a very beautiful woman, so I'd be a damn fool not to try again," he said laughing as he climbed onto the Harley. Looking at her with that sexy smile of his, he added, "And just so we're perfectly clear, my dear, I'm no fool."

Jake tossed another ten-dollar bill to the young boy, and then they rode down to the harbor. After locking the bike, Jake took her hand in his as they walked down the docks toward the Ariel. "Watch your step, honey. The wood on this dock is uneven in places." Stopping in front of the bow of his huge yacht, he asked her, "What do you think of the Ariel?"

Lynnette had a questioning look on her face but didn't say anything. She was still tipsy but tried to think back to what he had said on the deck at his friend's house. Recalling his exact words, she repeated them quietly, "…

there she was, tied up at the docks and as I boarded her, she was spectacular?"

Suddenly looking up at him she exclaimed, "This is your girlfriend? A boat?" A slow grin spread across her face as she added, "There never was a woman you were meeting down her, was there?"

"No, sweetheart, there was no woman. By the way, this isn't a boat, it's a yacht," he corrected with a grin.

"Okay. Whatever. It's amazing. Who's is it?"

Then remembering he intended to keep his wealth a secret from her for the meantime, he amended his answer. "I work onboard this one, among others. I just happen to like this one particularly well. By the way, do you get seasick?"

"I don't think so, but then again, I've never been out to sea on a boat before," she giggled. "Nor do I plan to do so tonight," she added warily, not knowing if he planned to take it out with her now. He seemed to be prepared to do anything at anytime. But she had plans for early in the morning. She needed to start looking for Keira as quickly as possible.

Lynnette looked at the Ariel more closely, walking along the dock to the stern, Jake close behind her watching. "It really is a beautiful boat," she stated, forgetting his earlier correction already.

"It's a yacht, honey. Not a boat."

Distracted, she didn't respond.

"I really think you should get me back to your friend's house now though," she said. "I need to get to the airport first thing in the morning to pick up my bags and the rental car."

Scowling, he had hoped she would not leave him as soon as she picked up her things, but that seemed to be her plan.

They rode the motorcycle back to his house. He knew he needed to find a way to keep in touch with her after tomorrow morning. He also wanted to find out her true reason for being here.

Walking her into the living room, Jake slid open the large glass doors exposing the room to the refreshing sea breeze blowing gently in the night. He invited her to sit on the couch. Lynnette could hear the comforting sound of the surf and thought it sounded better than any stereo system she had ever heard in her life. This place was really great. She could stay here forever.

Jake sat on the couch next to her, handing her another glass of wine. She knew she shouldn't drink any more, but thought she would just sip a bit on this last glass. Jake began telling her humorous stories of his experiences while open ocean sailing as she laughed. He recalled the time he had fallen overboard while trying to relieve himself off the stern of a boat. He had been young and new at sailing back then so the crew had laughed and teased him for the remainder of the trip after fishing him out of the water. She listened attentively as he told her of a time the boat under full sail had been surrounded by a large school of more than fifty dolphins. They had jumped and swam along with the sailors for over thirty minutes before breaking off and it had been spectacular.

Jake thought Lynnette looked the prettiest when she was laughing and uninhibited. She was so intent on his stories, she didn't take note of the fact she drank another full glass of wine. Somehow, Jake expertly maneuvered the conversation back to her situation without her expecting his next comment. "I suspect you're in some kind of trouble, Lynnette, and I intend to help you out with it, whatever it is."

"What are you talking about?" she stammered getting up from the couch and making her way unsteadily out to the deck. She definitely needed more air. Her mind wasn't working as quickly as his and she needed to think clearly now. Darn it, she shouldn't have drank any more of the wine. He was definitely clever, this one.

Jake followed her to the railing where she stood. "Lynnette, don't walk away from me. Maybe I've only known you for a short time, but I can read you like a book and know you're hiding something from me. If you're afraid of someone or something, please just tell me what it is and I'll help you. You just need to trust me."

"I have no idea what you're talking about and I am not in any trouble. Everything is just fine," she stated emphatically. "I came down here to get away from things for awhile." She moved away from him again and down the patio steps onto the cool white sand.

"Well then, if you just came down to enjoy yourself for awhile, why don't you stay with me here instead of moving to a hotel? I have plenty of room and the view is spectacular," he invited, following her out toward the water's edge.

She was definitely tempted. He was so..., intriguing and attractive but she knew she couldn't stay here. She needed her freedom to search for Todd and try to locate Keira before it was too late. She hoped to find her tomorrow or the next day at the latest and be on the first flight back to Los Angeles. But she wasn't going to tell Jake that. No, she had to separate herself from him before they became any more involved.

Continuing to walk slowly along the water's edge as small waves lapped at the cool sand beneath her feet, she responded to him over her shoulder. "Thanks, Jake, but I just can't stay. I have some things I nee..., I want to do while I'm down here. Some sightseeing and maybe fishing, I'm not really sure yet," she lied. "I admit to being tempted, but I really can't."

Jake stopped walking accepting the fact she would be leaving in the morning no matter what he said to her tonight. He made his decision then and there to change his approach.

"Well then, I guess I'll see you in the morning," he stated suddenly. "I'll just drop you off at the airport first thing tomorrow. Good night then."

He turned and walked away so abruptly it caught her off-guard. She turned to watch him leave in amazement, feeling perplexed. He was just going to leave her out here in the dark along a secluded beach alone? Frowning at his back, she turned to follow his path back across the sand toward the lights of the house in the distance. She was sorry they couldn't continue developing a relationship any further. It just wouldn't work out. It was better to stop now before it possibly caused them both pain. At least she was trying to convince herself it was better this way.

Suddenly out of nowhere, a mangy looking dog appeared and it was growling angrily at her. It was acting like it was going to bite her if she moved one more step. She screamed, scared half-to-death. Her scream was loud and instinctive. She loved dogs but this aggressive creature looked wildly savage, frightening, like it was about to attack her. She panicked. Turning, she raced down the beach as fast as she could. Hearing a loud whistle, she stopped and turned back to see the dog running back the other way. Exhausted and terrified, she dropped to her knees in the cool, damp sand and began to cry hysterically.

She knew it wasn't just her fear of the dog making her cry. It was everything. It was the overwhelming stress of the entire day. Her father planned to force her to marry someone she had never met, her constant worry over Keira, Todd trying to extort money from her again, losing her purse and the suitcase full of money. It was all just too much. She completely lost control, sobbing loudly into her palms. She wanted to crawl in a hole and just make it all go away. Her life was a total mess.

Jake ran up quickly, seriously worried about her. Kneeling down, he gently pulled her sobbing body into his arms, holding her tightly against his chest. He had no idea just how badly Max had scared her. She was still crying uncontrollably.

"It's okay now, honey," he consoled in a deep soothing voice as he smoothed back her hair away from her face. "That's just Max, the neighborhood mutt. He looks and sounds scary, but he's really just a big ole lovable dog with a loud bark. He lives here in the cove and is a little overly protective of his territory." He rocked her body gently and her sobbing became more of a light crying in a short time.

"He's really a big baby when it comes down to it. Nothing at all to be scared of," he continued, stroking her hair back gently as he held her.

"Come on now honey, stop crying. He's gone now. I wouldn't ever let anything hurt you." Running his hands up and down her back and trying to comfort her, he wasn't aware of the long term promises coming from his own mouth. He was just enjoying the feeling of her in his arms.

Jake sat down in the sand pulling her on to his lap. She continued crying, but easier now. Burying her head in his chest, he held her as they listened to the waves gently rolling in. After a short while, she cried herself out. Stirring uneasily in his arms, she now felt embarrassed for losing control. Sitting upright, she looked up at him sheepishly.

"I'm sorry. I don't normally cry like this," she sniffled. "I'm usually quite strong. I don't know what got into me.

"You were just scared, " he said gently, pulling her back into his embrace again. "That's nothing to be embarrassed about. Max can act pretty fierce when he wants to," he added, settling his chin comfortably on her head.

Lynnette then became acutely aware of Jake's large body holding her. He felt so muscular and strong. She could smell his natural masculine scent which was uniquely his own. She was feeling light-headed.

"You feeling any better now?" he asked, tipping her chin up with his finger.

She could see those intriguing, mesmerizing eyes focused solely on her and couldn't seem to breathe. He looked so wonderful to her.

He thought she looked absolutely awful. Even in the dim light Jake could see her red, swollen eyes and her makeup smeared down her cheeks still wet with tears. He gently wiped her tears away with his thumbs. Slowly, he lowered his face and gently touched his mouth to hers. He lightly teased her lips with his own. She reached out, placing her hand firmly against his chest in a half-hearted attempt to push him away. She continued pushing with more force, knowing in her own mind this was a really bad idea. His kiss was beginning to get the best of her though and she involuntarily opened her lips allowing him just what he desired. He pulled her up closer against his body as his tongue entered her mouth, exploring, teasing, making her crazy with wanting him.

She began kissing him back, hesitantly experimenting with her tongue the way he had. When she heard a moan from deep inside him, she knew he was hungry for her too. It gave her an amazing feeling, one she had never felt before. The kiss became deeper and more aggressive.

Wrapping her slender arms around him, she could feel the strong muscles moving in his back as she ran her hands down the length of his torso. She explored further, moving her fingers down along the length of his arms, feeling his biceps bulging as he held her close and felt herself becoming more aroused by the moment. Lynnette was vaguely aware she was quickly losing control as she ran her fingers wildly through his hair.

Jake's mouth covered hers. With an unquenchable desire, he couldn't seem to get enough. His mouth moved skillfully across her cheek, then behind her ear. He pulled back her hair to get better access. His lips ran down the length of her slender neck as he leaned her back on his lap.

His tongue moved yet even lower as he slowly slid her strap off one smooth shoulder.

She felt her skin quiver in response and she moaned in delight. He now had full access to what she so badly wanted him to taste. She was melting in his arms. What an amazing feeling. She never dreamt a man could make her feel like she did now. She was floating in ecstasy.

Pulling her off his lap, he gently laid her on the sand, sliding his body down over hers. Looking up into his face in the moonlight, she could see his barely controlled, pent-up desire for her. Holding his weight up on his elbows, he lay there across her body and then slowly kissed her lips ever so gently. She could feel the cool sand against her back, the cool night air on her bare skin and the warmth of his body over hers.

Angling his head to kiss her more deeply, he tasted her mouth again with a driving urgency. She could feel his arousal as he rubbed his firm body against her. With his knee he tried to spread her legs apart. That brought her back to her senses immediately.

What in the world was she doing lying in the sand making out in Mexico with a guy she had only met just that very day? About to have sex out here on the beach in the open? Was she a nut? What about protection? What about love? Did she need her head examined? Placing her hands against his chest, she began pushing him away. "No, Jake. I can't do this here. Not now, not like this."

Pausing painfully, Jake looked down into her troubled eyes, knowing she was right. This wasn't the place or the time.

"Yeah, you're right," he ground out between his teeth.

Rolling on his back, he exhaled loudly. This was sheer misery. He wanted her so badly right now he literally ached with the pain of it. He covered his head with his arm and tried to think of something else, anything else, to give his body time to adjust to this sudden change of plans.

Realizing he appeared to be upset, Lynnette leaned over and placed her hand hesitantly on his chest, trying to apologize. He snapped back at her, slowly asking her not to touch him just yet. He needed time. She didn't understand. Was he mad at her? No, that couldn't be since he just agreed she was right. She had no idea what he was going through, but it surely looked uncomfortable. If only she had more experience at these kinds of things, then she would know what to do.

SEVEN

Saturday morning, Lynnette woke up slowly feeling groggy and tired from staying up too late the night before. She was disoriented and a little hung over from drinking too much wine. She did not immediately recognize her surroundings, as the room suddenly became a flood of bright light. She sat up, squinting, holding her aching head in both hands as it really began to throb. Then she spotted Jake standing by the windows where he had just opened another shade. She quickly pulled the covers up to hide her breasts, knowing she normally slept in the nude, but not remembering if she had pulled on a nightgown or something the night before. Lifting the covers back to take a peek, she realized she hadn't. Embarrassed, she flopped back on the pillows, covered her face with the blankets and moaned loudly.

"Come on, wake up sleeping beauty. We don't have all day and it's time to get up. Rosa made us breakfast and it's out on the patio deck getting cold." He walked over to the side of the bed and started poking at the lump under the covers. She flipped on her side away from him, her head still hidden underneath the blankets.

"Come on out from under there girl. It's a beautiful day outside," he ordered cheerfully, slapping her soundly on the behind through the blankets.

Lynnette moaned from under the covers. Uncovering her head and shoulders, she grumbled, "What makes you wake up in such a great mood? Doesn't your head hurt or do you just enjoy the pain?"

Chuckling at her, he set a bottle of aspirin he had figured she'd need on the nightstand next to a tall glass of water and left the room, informing her he would be waiting for her out on the patio.

As soon as he left, she frantically tried to remember how the night before had ended. Was he in such a good mood because they had...?

No, surely that hadn't happened. She would be able to tell. But what had happened after they came back to the house from the beach? For the life of her, she couldn't remember. She had certainly drank too much last night. She had never over indulged in alcohol before and would have to be much more careful in the future.

Throwing back the covers, she hurried to get dressed and ready for the day that lay ahead.

It was time to get down to business. She had to find Todd if she could. Then she needed to get Keira safely home, hopefully tonight or tomorrow. Showering and dressing quickly, she took two aspirin, packed her few things and carried her bag to the front entry hall.

Stepping out onto the patio into the bright sunshine, she quickly slipped on her sunglasses to protect her sensitive eyes. Looking around in the daylight, she realized just how beautiful the view from this house really was. It was spectacular in the daytime.

"If I were your friend and owned this place, I'd come down here and never leave. This place is really fantastic." She sat down across from Jake and grabbing her cup of coffee, began to drink hoping it would help ease her hangover. Across the white sand she watched the light surf surge along the long length of curved beach from one point to the next. It was an outrageous view from the deck as the sun rose slowly over the Sea of Cortez.

"Rosa made us omelets and muffins. Here you go. Eat up." Jake tried serving her but she placed her hand over her plate and slowly shook her aching head. She knew she couldn't eat a bite. Her stomach was churning and she figured she would be lucky to eat by dinnertime the way she felt.

"Well then, if you're ready, let's go."

She couldn't believe his attitude this morning. He was already halfway to the front door, not even pausing to look back to see if she was following. He sure seemed awfully anxious to get rid of her all of a sudden. What in the world happened? Was it about last night? Then she realized it was probably because she had told him she wouldn't have sex with him. Yeah, that must be it. A guy like Jake probably didn't often get rejected and now he was in a big hurry to dump her. Likely, he wanted to try his charms on another woman. What a conceited ass. Becoming more irritated by the moment, she stood and stomped off toward the front door.

Trying his best to ignore her instead of kiss her, he picked up her bag and stepped out the front door and down the front steps to the Jeep, tossing it in the back.

Wanting to thank Rosa for her kindness, but realizing she was being silly since she would never be back here again anyway, she closed the front door behind her and climbed in the Jeep.

The drive was horribly uncomfortable. Jake ignored her completely and she sat there in the passenger seat fuming the entire ride. She was so angry with him, she didn't even notice he wasn't heading toward the airport until ten minutes into the drive.

"Wait a minute. This isn't the way to the airport. It's behind us, isn't it? Where are we going?" she demanded.

"I have a quick errand to run. It won't take but a minute," he responded without looking at her.

"Fine," she mumbled, looking out across the bleak brown landscape.

He was so distant and remote this morning. He was acting so differently from last night. She couldn't believe the difference in his demeanor today. Men are so oddly strange. They are infuriating, she decided.

Jake pulled the Jeep to a stop outside an old church and jumped out. Reaching into the back, he grabbed two big boxes she hadn't noticed earlier and carried them inside.

"Coming?" he tossed back over his shoulder as he disappeared inside.

Climbing out, she frowned realizing this was the first time he hadn't helped her get down out of the Jeep. Although she had insisted she could get out by herself, she frowned at his rudeness and then followed him inside.

It was dark and cool in the huge old stone church. Once her eyes adapted, she noticed a dozen or more children gathered around the two boxes Jake had set down in the middle of the room. They excitedly began to open them as Jake spoke with a priest in the far corner.

Mesmerized by the odd scene, Lynnette watched as the kids excitedly tore into the boxes as if it were Christmas morning. One box was filled with new clothing for the youngsters and the other was jammed full of toys. She looked up in time to see Jake hand the priest a check. She noticed the look of delight on his face as he shook Jake's hand again. Jake approached the group gathered around the goodies and bent down to receive the offered hugs, patting the backs of the older boys who were over the age of hugging a man. Jake's face glowed with happiness at the pleasure these simple items brought these poor kids. To them, these were treasures.

Then Jake noticed one small boy off alone, standing against the far wall seemingly hesitant to join the others. Reaching into the box, Jake lifted out a baseball and mitt and then walked over to the timid boy. Leaning down, he spoke some Spanish to the youngster as Lynnette and the priest looked on.

Suddenly the boy's face brightened and Jake handed him the glove. He quickly helped fit in onto his small hand and stood up to his full height. He tossed the boy the baseball, which the kid caught carefully and then looked up into Jake's face with pure pleasure. Jake tousled the boy's hair, then turned and walked toward the door. He walked past her, not even bothering to look over at her.

Once they were settled back in the Jeep and heading for the airport, she finally asked him the one question that was bothering her the most.

"Jake, what did you say to that little boy who was standing by himself to make him so happy?"

He looked over at her, then back at the road again. He had a thoughtful look on his face.

"I told him I thought it looked like he had a good arm and with practice, he could possibly be a good baseball player someday. Then I told him that the glove and ball had been mine when I was his age and that I grew up to play ball in college."

"That was clever of you. He seemed to really respond to that story."

Looking over at her he said, "I wasn't being clever. That was my glove and baseball when I was his age."

Lynnette just sat there. She didn't know what to say. She thought about how sweet and caring he had been with those kids. Although she was still mad at him, she couldn't help but be impressed with his act of kindness. At least the guy had a heart when it came to orphans she thought glumly. She wished she too were on the receiving end of his kindness.

The entire ride to the airport, Lynnette sat staring out the windshield not believing how Jake could act this cold today, after being so interested in her last night. He wasn't even speaking to her and only answered her questions with short, clipped replies. He actually seemed anxious to get rid of her.

She should never have let down her guard with him, she reprimanded herself. Guys can't be trusted. They were only after one thing and since she hadn't let him have that, he was now giving her the brush off. Hadn't she been taught by examples in the past not to trust men? They would only use you or hurt you. Why in the world had she let down her defenses with Jake? At least she hadn't had sex with him last night or she would be feeling much worse toward him today.

Getting madder by the moment, she noticed Jake was already pulling into the airport. He hadn't spoken one word to her the entire drive besides his clipped replies. He had pretended to like her last night when he thought he might get lucky, but now she was getting really furious. He was being a complete ass.

Pulling up to the curb, Jake jumped out and set her bag down on the edge of the curb so quickly she was still trying to climb out of the Jeep as he stood there waiting. When she turned to face him, he stepped away from her as if wanting to avoid her attempting to hug him good-bye.

Lynnette couldn't take it any longer. She finally lost her temper, ignoring the fact they were standing in public.

"Jake, why are you acting like this towards me? After last night, I can't believe you're being like this!" she yelled at him, stomping her foot in frustration. She wished she didn't care and could just be cool and walk rudely away from him.

"Oh, I bet I know why," she added sarcastically. "It must be because I wouldn't have sex with you last night, right? So now you're in a rush to move on to the next woman, aren't you?" She stood there fuming, waiting for an answer. There was fire in her eyes.

Jake just stood there looking down at her calmly, not answering. People outside the terminal were beginning to stop to listen. Maybe this deceptive idea of his wasn't such a good idea after all. She was a lot more of a hot head than he had anticipated and was making quite a scene at the moment.

"You must think you're so irresistible," she continued loudly. "Well, you're not. I'm even madder at myself for thinking maybe I could trust a man for once. I should have known better. You're all the same and I was stupid for thinking you were different."

Jake was beginning to think he would have to change his plan and try calming her down. She was really causing a scene and people were now stopping to stare.

"And I'm really glad I didn't have sex with you," she continued hollering at him. "Just go on now. I don't ever want to see you again."

Regardless of the few women now clapping at Lynnette's tirade, Jake could see the hurt in her eyes as she turned to storm inside the airport. Jake felt truly sorry for her pain. He wanted nothing more than to take her in his arms and hold her, telling her how wrong she was about his intentions, but he reminded himself he was doing all this pretending to protect her.

Smiling sheepishly at the people still standing around, he frowned as he climbed back in the Jeep and drove quickly out of the airport. At least she had been completely fooled by his act. His intention was to make her mad, but he hadn't realized she had such a nasty temper. He just wanted to get away from her in order to follow her without her knowledge. To do that, she had to think he had no further interest in her. It was the only way he figured he would ever learn what she was doing down here in Cabo San Lucas and what kind of trouble she was in. He couldn't walk away and leave it to her. He actually cared for her. She thought they were through.

He was definitely not through with her yet though. In fact, he was afraid he was starting to really fall for her. She intrigued him, entertained him, infuriated him and aroused him, unlike any woman had before her. He hadn't wanted to feel this way about her or any woman right now. His life had been going along just fine the way it was. But, he also couldn't deny how he felt.

Jake pulled off the road, just outside the main entrance to the airport and hid the Jeep behind a small block shed. He got out and walked to the corner of the building where he would wait for her.

Lynnette marched through the airport fighting back the tears, trying to remind herself they had just met and it didn't really matter anyway. Unconvinced, she found the Mexican guy at the car rental counter and retrieved her lost purse, thanking him as she proceeded to the baggage claim. She traded her claim check for her suitcase full of money. Checking to ensure everything was still inside, she assured herself nobody had looked inside and then carried her bags to the little red Volkswagen she had rented. She deposited her belongings inside.

Trying to stay focused on her purpose, she knew she would have to be organized if she were to be successful so she pulled out her map of the area and set it neatly on the seat next to her. Backing out of the parking space, she headed for town to hopefully find an available room for rent so she could begin searching for Todd.

The day was now very hot and dry. It was already late in the morning. By noon, Jake figured it would be nearly a hundred degrees outside. The dust from the car tires driving by rose high in the air and blew out across the open desert. He was beginning to feel very dry and thirsty. Then he saw her.

Jake pulled out and followed far enough behind so she wouldn't notice him. She drove to town and stopped at the Casa Blanca, a quaint, whitewashed, two-story motel in the heart of town. He watched from down the road as Lynnette got out and walked into the office. Once she was inside, he pulled around the corner and parked. Jake continued to watch until he saw her enter a room on the second floor. Noting her exact room number, he then headed down the street on foot to his favorite bar for an ice-cold beer.

EIGHT

Lynnette changed into a cool, sleeveless summer dress and unpacked her few clothes. Searching the room for a safe place to hide the locked suitcase of money, she finally decided to tuck it beneath the bed. That done, she grabbed her purse and sunglasses and headed out the door hoping to spot Todd in town. Frowning, she stopped in her tracks realizing she needed to spot Todd before he recognized her. Running back to her room, she grabbed her straw hat. Surely, with the hat and her sunglasses on he wouldn't recognize her. Not as easily anyway.

She had walked through three clubs so far, with no luck. Lynnette felt she would soon pass out from the unbearable heat. In the first two bars, she had been offered three drinks and two dates. Absently brushing off the latest most aggressive offer, she reprimanded the guy for his drunkenness in the middle of the day and stalked out leaving him and his friends staring after her.

The narrow dirt roads were lined on both sides with small, colorful shops offering Mexican style clothes, shoes, silver and various knickknacks for the interested tourist. Many of the shops were now empty and only a few people sat quietly at the scattered tables outside the restaurants.

There were very few people out on the dusty streets shopping in the heat of midday. Everyone with half a brain would be down at the beach or in a pool staying cool, which is where she wished she was at the moment. There was no sign of Todd anywhere. She felt hot, tired and frustrated. She still had a slight headache from earlier, but she had to keep looking if she was to find Keira. At least she had something to do to keep her mind off Jake, not that it was working. Her mind continually wandered back to various thoughts of him as she continued her search.

She had such mixed emotions about Jake. She was angry with him for acting the way he had towards her this morning just because she wouldn't have sex with him on the first night they met, but she was also miserable she would never see him again. A part of her had hoped they might somehow continue their relationship and get to know one another better. She had thought he was really different than other men and couldn't believe she had been so far off in her judgment. Then there was the sweet side of him helping the kids out at the church. He had been so kind and loving toward the children. Then she remembered her father's dictate again, reminding herself not seeing Jake again was probably for the best. She was supposed to marry someone else so what was the point. Once again she pushed thoughts of Jake from her mind and entered yet another restaurant/ bar in search of Todd.

Jake was standing across the room, leaning against the long wooden bar talking with an old buddy when he spotted her in the doorway. She didn't see him yet but he recognized her immediately. It looked as if she was trying to hide from someone, wearing some silly hat and shades as a disguise. Taking a long drink of the cold beer he held lightly in one hand, he vaguely heard his friend's conversation as he continued to watch her closely.

She stood out like a neon light in her short dress with those long, shapely legs and attractively curved body. She couldn't disguise herself from him if she wore a potato sack over her head. The mental image of her would be forever ingrained in his mind. But why would she be sneaking around anyway, hiding behind a plant, stealing peeks around the room looking ridiculous? She must be looking for that idiot of a boyfriend she was supposed to meet up with tomorrow. Why be so sneaky though? Did she suspect he was cheating on her and thought she could catch him in the act?

Jake still wasn't listening carefully to his buddy's story until the fellow startled him by punching him in the arm.

"What in the hell are you starting at, man?"

Jake nodded his head toward Lynnette in answer.

"Oh yeah," he observed with enthusiastic approval. "Now I see why I couldn't hold your attention. Understandable. She's a real looker, isn't she?" he observed, chugging down more beer.

Just then, Jake's eyes narrowed as he spotted two rather stocky Mexicans getting up from their table. They had been sitting with a small group of guys across the bar. They were heading straight for Lynnette. She hadn't yet noticed them either. She would make a horrible spy, he realized.

Anyone observing Jake at that very moment would have assumed he was relaxed and having a casual conversation at the bar, when in reality, he was completely alert to the scene unfolding before him, ready to jump in at any second. Taking another slow sip of beer, he nodded absently at a comment from his friend. It had something to do with the Japanese fishing out the local waters.

"They actually block the entire entrance to the Sea of Cortez with their nets, then..." his buddy droned on, only slightly exaggerating the facts.

The two Mexicans each took Lynnette firmly by an arm, leading her toward the back corner of the bar. Jake frowned, his face set but he subconsciously clenched his right hand into a fist. He slowly set down the beer with his left.

Lynnette realized Todd had spotted her as soon as the two guys grabbed her. She fought off the temptation to run out the door, knowing running would be stupid. She did come to meet Todd, but found him revolting. Stiffly, she walked with them toward Todd. Stopping in front of his table, she shook off the guys who still held her arms and removed her hat and sunglasses, setting them down on an empty table nearby.

"Hi, Lynnette," Todd snarled. "So good of you to come. These here fellas are my new friends." She could feel their lecherous eyes on her and felt a shiver crawl up her spine.

She noticed Todd hadn't changed much since she last saw him. It wasn't that he was unattractive exactly, just horribly intimidating to her. She swallowed, trying her best not to show him her fear. Whenever he noticed he was getting to her, he had always continued on longer, only making it worse. Todd hadn't shaved in awhile and it appeared he had added weight to his six-foot frame. His beady brown eyes grazed over her body as he observed her, causing her to shiver in disgust again.

"Well, I'll be damned sis. You've gotten even sexier since last time I saw you. Since the last time we were together…" he trailed off suggestively with a gleam of lust in his dark eyes.

Her fear instantly dissolved in to anger as she realized he was insinuating to his friends they had been intimate together. She was incensed.

"Todd, you disgust me and I hate you more than you could ever imagine. Now, where is Keira?" she demanded.

Ignoring her, Todd continued. "I see you couldn't wait to see me so you showed up early. How nice. I've been anxious to see you too, sis," Todd said sarcastically. "Sit down and have a drink with us," he ordered, motioning to the empty chair across from him.

"No," she replied sharply. Her stomach turned at even the thought of a drink. "Is Keira alright? Where is she, Todd? I want to see her now," she demanded.

"Oh no, sweetie. That's not the way it goes," Todd ground out between clenched teeth. His lips pulled back in a forced smile. She wasn't acting scared enough for his pleasure or enough to impress his new friends. "First you give me my money and then I'll give you Keira. Where is the money, Lynnette?" Maybe he should intimidate her a little, just to show off and impress his new partners. He would enjoy reminding her who was boss.

Lynnette wasn't intimidated though. She squared her shoulders bravely and pressed him further.

"I want to see her now, Todd, so I know she's alright. Otherwise, you don't get any money," she challenged him.

The two glared at each other. He felt a mixture of emotions. Arousal from looking at her standing there facing him and raw anger that she had access to all that easy money instead of him.

On the other hand, she felt only intense hatred for him.

"I want the money, Lynn," Todd growled.

"I don't have the money on me and I'm not going to get it until I see Keira," Lynnette insisted aggressively.

Todd jumped up, shoving the table aside in one swift motion sending empty beer bottles and glasses scattering across the floor. Lynnette jumped as some of the glasses hit near her feet and shattered. Todd was furious that she would try to embarrass him in front of his business partners. He decided he would just have to show her he really meant business.

She saw the infuriated look on his face and recalled the many times he had tortured her as a young girl. He had an uncontrollable temper and she might have just pushed him too far. She was scared, she admitted to herself. He looked mad as hell and ready to kill.

As the bartender started to come around the bar, he stopped short as Jake raised his hand in warning. Nodding in understanding, the bartender returned to the bar for the time being.

Lynnette sensed she was in trouble. Backing away, she bumped into something solid blocking her exit. Todd, she noticed, had an oddly curious look on his face as he looked over her head. Turning around, she found it was Jake standing directly behind her and he was looking furious. He was glaring angrily past her at Todd.

She was thrilled to see him. That was her initial reaction anyway. Then she remembered why she was mad at him.

"Jake, what are you doing here?" she asked, sounding confused. Just a few hours ago he acted like he never wanted to see her again and now he was here coming to her rescue again. What was going on?

"Lynnette," Todd growled from behind her. "I told you to keep your mouth shut about this. You really fucked up big time sweetie."

Jake was thinking this idiot was her boyfriend. Not once taking his eyes off Todd, Jake menacingly stated, "I'll tell you just once not to speak to her like that."

Jake's stance was aggressive and the lines of his face were drawn like granite. Lynnette still stood facing Jake, her jaw hanging open. The sexy scar on his chin looked white to her.

"Stay out of it, mister. You're badly outnumbered here," Todd stated confidently. "She isn't worth the trouble anyway." Todd looked over at his two buddies smugly, ensuring his back-up support. Just the look in Jake's eyes alone had the other guys at Todd's table backing away.

Lynnette began to panic, thinking her stepbrother would harm Keira because of Jake's interference. Lynnette swung back around to face Todd once again.

"Todd, I swear I haven't told him a thing. Don't you dare do anything to hurt Keira, please," she begged.

"Then get him out of here, Lynn. Now," Todd barked at her.

Turning back toward Jake, she pressed her hands against his solid body and began pushing him away. She whispered softly so only he could hear.

"Please, Jake. Just go away. I can handle this, really I can. I don't need your help and you'll just make things worse if you try."

"Who is Keira, Lynnette?" Jake asked loudly. Standing his ground, his eyes were still pinned on Todd. Jake was wondering what this guy was threatening to do to this other girl and why. Glancing briefly in each direction, Jake noted the exact position of each of Todd's buddies at the moment, as well as those watching on with interest from a distance.

"Never mind, it's not your problem. Please, just go now. You'll only make it worse." She tried pushing Jake away again. She pressed against him again with both hands as hard as she could. He wouldn't budge.

Jake calmly said, "Lynnette, I'm not going anywhere so stop pushing on my chest." He gently took her hands and placed them at her sides while continuing to watch Todd. He needed to keep a distance between himself and Lynnette in case a fight suddenly broke out. He didn't want her getting hurt accidentally. He grinned as he realized that in a way, he was actually looking forward to a good fight. It had been a long time since he had been in a brawl and he would enjoy connecting his fist with the mouth of this big talking jerk named Todd.

"What did you ever see in this guy anyway, Lynnette?" Jake asked to insult Todd into action. "You're much too good for a guy like this and besides, he stinks."

Lynnette looked up at Jake, confused. "What? He isn't my boyfriend, Jake. He's my stepbrother."

That caught his attention. Surprised, he briefly looked down at her, one eyebrow raised in question.

"Your brother?"

"Well actually, no. He's my stepbrother, or was when his mother was previously married to my father." She continued to stare up into Jake's handsome face. "They divorced and now we're not even related."

"Your brother?" he repeated again, as if to himself. "Good," Jake grinned down at her in pleasure at the news. He turned his concentration back to Todd.

By this time, Todd was getting more agitated by the moment. "Lynn, get him the hell out of here now. I'm warning you," he yelled.

"Shut up," both Lynnette and Jake turned and yelled back at Todd at the same time.

Jake continued watching Todd, but addressed Lynnette again. "Where is your boyfriend then?"

"Boyfriend? What are you talking about? I don't have a boyfriend," she answered, confused by his question.

"Hey, this is getting completely off track," Todd interrupted again. He was still furious with Jake's insults. "You two lovebirds discuss your relationships later. Come on, Lynn. Let's go take care of our business now." Reaching out, Todd grabbed her lower arm to pull her out of the bar.

Jake had Todd's wrist in his grip so fast and hard, Todd hadn't even seen it coming. He cried out in pain at the strength of Jake's grip.

"She isn't going anywhere with you. Let her go. Now." Jake's slow voice was strangely calm.

Todd released her arm immediately, jerking back in pain, feeling embarrassed and really angry once Jake released him. He stood there glaring up at Jake, rubbing his wrist. He turned to Lynnette. "You get one more chance.

Meet me back here tonight at dark. Come alone or you'll regret it," Todd ordered. "Believe me."

Todd turned and stormed across the bar toward the door followed by the two stocky Mexicans. The rest of the group watching slowly filed out of the room, giving Jake wide berth as they passed him.

Lynnette tried to run after Todd, but Jake stopped her.

"Wait, Todd, please," she pleaded. "I'll go with you now, just don't do anything to Keira, please," she begged as Jake restrained her. "Promise you won't hurt her," she cried out as Todd continued out the door, ignoring her.

"Let go of me," she struggled, trying to free herself from Jake's gentle grip. "I have to follow him."

Turning her around forcefully to face him, Jake held her firmly by both arms.

"You will not follow him now and you will not meet him here tonight by yourself, Lynnette." He stared down at her, his face stone cold. "You won't do a thing without me, understood?"

What's this, she thought? He can't order me around. She felt he had just issued her a command; one she had no intention of obeying. In anger, she knocked his hands away.

"What? I don't remember asking for your opinion or for your help. Just stay out of this, Jake. It has nothing to do with you and it's none of your business anyway," she ordered crisply.

Now Todd was gone and she'd never be able to catch up and follow him to find Keira. Turning to pick up her hat and glasses, she began to leave. Jake tried to reason with her again.

"Lynnette, those guys are trouble and you should not meet with them tonight alone. Trust me. Let me come with..."

"No," she yelled, glaring at him. "Just leave me alone. You've screwed up everything enough already, don't you think?"

She paused, looking away so he wouldn't see the lie in her eyes. Tensely, she added, "I told you Jake, I don't want to see you again and I meant it. Just stay away from me!"

Turning, she marched across the dark room and out into the bright afternoon heat, tears streaming steadily down both cheeks.

NINE

Anger boiled inside Jake. Damn it, she was a stubborn woman. Shaking his head in disbelief, he wondered if she realized the danger she could be in. Women were a blasted curse on men, as far as he was concerned. Fine, she wanted him to leave her alone? Great. He would forget he ever met her. She had been a problem for him ever since they met anyway. Sure thing, he would leave her alone to deal with her issues herself.

Deciding to take his mind off Lynnette and her problems, he headed down to the Ariel to check on the crew. It was late Saturday afternoon and he could use a distraction. Hell, if she wanted to run off on some dangerous excursion alone without his help, then let her. He was just trying to help her out. She'd shown no appreciation at all. Damn it! He didn't need her, she needed him. She was acting like an idiotic. Damn it, women were more trouble than they were worth.

Arriving at the marina, Jake immediately spotted Miguel waving to him from the deck.

"Hey, Jake," Miguel called out, "you have a phone call down here.

Moving quickly down the gangway and along the dock, Jake stepped easily aboard the huge ketch as Miguel explained in broken English. His accent was stronger when he was rushed. "David from the main office in Long Beach is been trying to get hold of you all day."

Jake frowned, taking the phone. "Thanks. I'll take it in the pilot house." He was still in a foul mood. Speaking into the phone, he requested brusquely, "Hold on a minute."

Climbing down the steps heading below deck, he walked through the galley where he asked Maria to make him a rum and Coke. "Heavy on the rum, Maria, but go light on the Coke. I'll be up in the pilothouse. Thanks," he added.

Jake spoke into the phone as he sat down at the navigation station. "Yeah, Jake here."

"Hey, you're a hard guy to find," the excited male voice said on the other end of the line. "Good news here, boss. We've just got our first booking for Ariel already. The Allisters from Boston called this morning. Said they'd be here in just over two weeks to charter Ariel for a twelve day trip up the coast of California to San Francisco," he rushed on. "They're already familiar with the yacht from an acquaintance of theirs who was a former owner. Found out it was for charter through a broker and they've already booked and paid half down as a cash advance to hold the reservation. They insisted. Great news, huh?"

"Yeah, that's very good news," Jake replied without any excitement in his voice. He took his drink from Maria as she moved a coaster over to his chart table. He realized they would have to leave almost immediately in order to finish the certification paperwork, stock the galley and be ready by the charter date. Jake inquired into other business matters briefly, then offered direction on a few other specific issues before hanging up.

As he sat back and sipped his drink, he began wondering if he should try to find Lynnette before he left port. He would barely have time to say good-bye. That is, if she would ever talk to him again. She was pretty upset with him for interfering when she left the bar. Shaking his head in frustration, he realized he shouldn't even be thinking about her. She'd told him to leave her alone, hadn't she? Yet he was finding it nearly impossible to put the thought of her out of his mind. There was just something different about her, something so intriguing to him. He envisioned images of her with her hair flying wildly behind them as she rode with him on the motorcycle; he saw images of her lying beneath him on the cool sand under the stars or images of her scantily clad body in a bikini as she squirmed uncomfortably in his lap.

Enough, he decided. Time to get back to business. Frowning, Jake rose from his chair and informed Miguel and Rosa to notify the rest of the crew they would be leaving the next morning at one o'clock a.m. sharp. This would be his first trip aboard her and he was as yet unfamiliar with the yacht, so he grabbed his checklist from the cockpit and headed below deck to begin a check of the engine room first.

Although it was a sailboat, if the winds were dead the twin engines would ensure cruising at up to ten knots and the stabilizers would add to the comfort and safety of future charters. The yacht was equipped with all the necessary state-of-the-art navigational and electronic equipment available. The yacht had several 'optional' electronic upgrades he was only able to obtain through his contacts in the military. Jake had onboard some technology the public wasn't even aware existed yet.

Heading back up on deck, Jake checked over the rigging and the sails. He realized with the new automation installed, they could handle this beauty with as few as a three-man crew. They would have a five-man crew onboard for this first trip, but that was acceptable to him. He could absorb the extra cost without noticing, plus it would also give him a chance to train more men at one time.

Leaning down to rest his elbows on the railing, Jake looked out over the harbor. The huge orange sun glowed low on the horizon. The heat of today was much milder than yesterday and more comfortable. It made him think of Lynnette's ongoing grumbling about the extreme heat. It was the oddest thing for him to still be thinking of her. In the past, sailing had always been uppermost on Jake's list of interests. There was nothing that could distract him from sailing or his time on the yachts. Girlfriends in the past had been known to become more jealous of the time he spent on the water than the time he spent with other women. Being on the ocean was his first love.

Now though, as he explored the newest and finest addition to his fleet, the thoughts that continued to creep into his mind weren't thoughts of its new interior upgrades or the remodeled galley or the improvements to the engines. They were of Lynnette. Was she okay? What was the big secret she was hiding from him? He had a nearly irresistible urge to go find her, to spend just a little more time with her until he had to leave. Try as he might, he couldn't imagine leaving without seeing her again. The truth be told, he didn't want to stop seeing her at all. He decided to take off for a bit to try to locate her.

Jake didn't find her in her room at the motel Casa Blanca, nor did he see her anywhere else either as he slowly drove his Jeep through the dusty, quiet town. He recalled she was supposed to meet Todd at the bar at sunset, and it was about time, but he didn't see her there either when he stopped. It was now getting dark and he had no idea where she was. He was certainly worried, but it was ridiculous trying to find her. She didn't want to see him anyway and he had several things to do in order to leave just after midnight.

Frustrated, he drove back to his house at Santa Maria beach. He had a number of calls to make and some mail to handle before leaving. His frustration was increasing as he worked at his desk and he was continually losing concentration. He decided that what he needed was a hard work out in his gym and then one of Rosa's tasty meals. Maybe he would ask if she had time to stay a bit later tonight for instructions since he was leaving again so soon. Then he would get packed for the trip north. There was no reason he couldn't locate Lynnette in Orange County once they docked in Long Beach. He decided this would not be the last she saw of him.

A little while earlier, Lynnette had begun changing into her black slacks and long-sleeved black knit top as soon as she returned to her room just before sunset. She knew it would be more difficult to be spotted in the darkness if she were dressed all in black. She jumped upon hearing a loud knock on the door shortly after returning and then peeked through the curtain to see Jake standing just outside the door. Her emotions were in such turmoil as she moved hesitantly toward the door. She placed her palms flat against the surface as if to touch him. It would feel so wonderful to let him kiss her again and to feel his arms around her body once more. A part of her wanted so desperately to throw open the door and rush into his arms, but the other part wanted to hit him for risking her sister's life by being so stubbornly persistent and interfering.

Waiting until she heard his heavy footsteps as he walked away, she swiped angrily at the tears slowly streaming down her cheeks. She quickly finished getting ready, hoping to arrive at the bar early to find a place to hide across the street before Todd arrived at sunset. If only he would lead her back to Keira so she could make sure she was alright. At this point, she wasn't even convinced Keira was in Mexico. Todd was not only good at extorting money, he was a great liar too.

Stacking the money in her dark backpack, she pulled it on over her shoulders and left the room just as the sky was growing dark. Hurrying down the street, she turned the corner only to find herself face-to-face with Todd's two stocky Mexican partners. She froze. The instant they recognized her, she took off running. They tore off on foot after her.

She panicked. Turning back the way she had come, she ran as fast as she could down the dirt road. It was dark now and much harder to see where she was going. Being careful not to step into a hole in the road and sprain her ankle, she tried to stop a couple of the cars driving by. No luck. They were Mexicans who spoke only Spanish and she couldn't make them understand she needed help. Looking behind her, she could see the two were gaining on her and would catch her for sure if she dared to stop again.

Feeling terrified, she continued running up one street after another, turning left, then right. Each block was darker than the one before. Her lungs felt they would soon burst and she knew she couldn't keep up this pace much longer.

The shop windows were all dark as she ran past. Nothing seemed to be open. Stopping just around a corner, she leaned against the building trying to catch her breath.

She sucked air into her lungs, trying not to make too much noise. The pack on her back was getting really heavy. Knowing she was getting further away from the tourist area and heading toward the back side of town where the locals live, she knew she had to double back and get back to the main part of town.

Taking off again when she heard their footsteps getting near, she made the next left and ran with everything she had down to the waterfront where she might possibly find some help. The two heavy set men were panting, but still running down the hill after her, although they were falling back now. They obviously didn't run four miles every morning, she thought with some relief. They could be dangerous though, she thought and were not far behind her, so she turned another corner and started back toward the main part of town, darting into side streets attempting to lose them.

Maybe Jake had been right. She realized now that Todd's plan all along was probably to have these two guys grab her and force her to tell him the location of the money. Maybe they weren't planning to hurt her at all. Well, she sure had made it easy for them, hadn't she? She had the money right on her back inside the pack. Just great!

Finding a road that led all the way back down to the harbor wasn't difficult. She could see the main lights of town up ahead. Continuing to run as fast as her legs would carry her, her lungs were burning. She needed the money in order to get Keira back. She desperately hoped she could reach a group of tourists before the two goons reached her. Gasping for more air, she continued running.

Finally, she made it back to the main part of town. Where were all the tourists? She was in a near panic. There was nobody around. A glance at her watch confirmed more time had passed than she realized. It was getting late now and she was exhausted. There wasn't even anyone out on the docks. Risking a chance to quickly look back, she couldn't see the two men yet, but could still hear them approaching. Looking around wildly, she spotted the docks and thinking quickly, decided to hide on one of the boats.

Racing down the length of one dock, she risked losing her footing to glance back over her shoulder again. Yes, they had spotted her and were following her through the dozens of boats. Ducking down low so they wouldn't see which way she was going, she turned and crept along but soon ran out of dock. She was trapped.

Quickly climbing aboard the huge boat in front of her, she cleverly hid herself under the tarp that covered the little boat hanging off the back of it. Hoping it would stop swinging before they got near enough to notice, she held completely still, waiting. She waited and waited. It seemed like hours. It felt like forever. She didn't even dare to take a peek for fear of revealing herself. This night had gone so terribly wrong. She was no closer to finding Keira and they were probably searching the boats or waiting at the gate to the docks for her to attempt leaving. She didn't dare risk it. There was only one way to get off the boat docks and that meant she would have to wait until morning when there were other people around. Carefully removing the pack from her back, she used it as a pillow and after a very long while, she fell fast asleep, thinking of Jake.

TEN

Jake arrived aboard the Ariel shortly after midnight, early Sunday morning. The night air was finally cool and the moon hung overhead as a peacefully glowing crescent. The town was finally dark and sleeping. There wasn't any activity on any of the other boats in the marina and all was quiet on the water. The crew of four, one mechanic and three to work the rigging, were all up on deck, working quietly and efficiently together in the near darkness. Jake could hear Maria down below deck in the well-lit galley, banging pots and pans around, humming to herself happily as she worked. Jake didn't recognize one of the four crewmen. He figured he must be a new employee.

Jake strode over to Miguel, slapping him on the back. "Well, Miguel, what do you say? Are we ready to get underway?"

Miguel's excitement was evident in his accent. "Give me thirty more minutes, then we'll untie and shove off."

Jake had every confidence in Miguel's capabilities and his word was true. He knew they would be shoving off in thirty minutes. Walking together across the deck toward the pilothouse, Jake asked Miguel about the new crewman.

"Yes. I found him here in town looking to sign on as crew. His credentials seemed like they should be and he seemed to know his stuff. I would call his references but could not get anyone on the phone. He has much more open ocean experience than most, so I thought we could give him a try," Miguel explained. He knew Jake paid his crew very well but was also very discriminating of whom he brought onboard. He then demanded the best out of each of them once hired.

"Good. Just keep an eye on him for awhile and let me know how he's doing?"

Jake sat down at the navigation station to begin charting their course north.

Clearing his throat uncomfortably, Miguel shoved his hands deep inside his pockets. "Jake, I do not like to butt in where I should not, but Maria and I, well…, we see that you are kind of bothered lately and we wonder if maybe it be from a lady. She wanted me to check to see if everything is okay."

Miguel obviously wasn't at all comfortable asking Jake about his personal life, but the question brought a small grin to Jake's face. It relieved Miguel's anxiety tremendously. Jake could only imagine how Maria had pestered Miguel to death to get him to find out what was going on, otherwise Miguel would have never asked. Miguel had always been a very good and reliable friend over the years and Jake didn't really mind him asking questions. He knew it was because they sincerely cared about him.

"You tell Maria her concerns are not necessary. Everything is just fine," Jake answered, his guess proven correct by the relieved look on Miguel's face. Jake gave him a sly look as he grasped Miguel's shoulder firmly and teased. "And you really shouldn't let your wife nag you like that. You have a question, ask me. I consider you a friend, Miguel, so if I don't want to answer, trust me, you'll know it right away."

With a heavy sigh, Jake walked across the pilothouse. "You're right though. It is because of a woman. I'll tell you something, Miguel. This one's different. She's..., well she's someone unique, very special. Although it hasn't worked out between us, I have to admit she comes real close to being the one woman I think I could really get serious about. At least I'd like the chance to find out. There's just something different about her. It's strange though, because on the one hand she's infuriating as hell, but on the other hand, I know I would never grow tired of looking at her or just being with her. She's gorgeous. It may be over for us though."

Jake sat back down at the chart table and stared off into space. Miguel sat across the room and waited. After awhile, Jake spoke again.

"No, it's definitely not yet over between us," he finally stated distantly as if talking to himself. Miguel finally rose from his seat, walked over to slap Jake on the back in understanding of how a woman can confuse a man so and then he quietly left the room, leaving Jake alone with his thoughts. After a bit, Jake stood. It was time to shove off.

Jake quickly finished plotting their course. He took a few minutes to familiarize himself with the navigational and electrical equipment that had recently been installed. He was beginning to feel the excitement of the trip too now and although he regretted not seeing Lynnette again before leaving town, he was anxious to feel the helm of this yacht in his hands once again. He wanted to experience the exhilaration of controlling the strength of the sea and wind through the feel of the wheel. He would try to keep himself busy the entire trip, therefore keeping his mind off Lynnette. Maybe it wasn't meant to be for them, he thought with a tug of disappointment, but damn it if he wasn't already missing her.

Entering the galley, Jake gladly accepted the big steaming mug of strongly brewed coffee Maria offered him and took a sip. Maria was a plump and pretty Mexican woman Miguel had met on the mainland of Mexico three years ago. Miguel had fallen in love with her quickly and Jake could understand why. She was sweet as could be and was one hell of a fabulous cook.

Jake snuck up behind her while she was busy working at the sink. Careful not to spill his coffee, he leaned down and wrapped one arm around her thick middle and teasingly whispered in her ear. "I've really missed your great cooking, sweet lady."

Maria squirmed out of his arm, giggling like a schoolgirl. "You stop that now, you silly man. You are just a big flirt."

"You got that right. Now, are you certain you have all the supplies you'll need onboard so you can whip up those marvelous meals you're so famous for?"

Blushing at the compliment, she answered, "Yes, we got everything we need." Continuing, she added, "Senior Jake, with all your joking, I can still see in your eyes your heart has been hurt. The ocean will help you heal, no?" Maria's English was not terrific, but her sense of observation was absolutely flawless.

"I see you've already spoken to Miguel. I never will be able to hide anything from you, Maria. You sometimes seem to know more about me than I know about myself," he responded with a quick kiss on her cheek. He left to go back up on deck with his mug still steaming. Thoughts of

Lynnette nagged at the back of his mind as he wondered what had happened to her with Todd and his two idiot friends. There was no help for it now. She'd made it this long in life and before yesterday, he hadn't been there to protect her. She would be just fine, he reasoned.

Jake walked the entire deck, checking with the crew for any last minute adjustments. Miguel introduced him to Eric, the new crewman. Eric shook his hand firmly, possibly a bit too firmly. Jake could almost sense a rebellious insolence in the guy and felt an instant dislike for him. It was probably unwarranted, but there nonetheless. On the other hand, Eric would probably come in very handy pulling sheets and climbing rigging if he was as strong as his handshake implied.

Giving the order to cast off, Jake started up the engines. Initially, they sounded loud in the quiet of the early morning hour, but they ran smoothly. Once the crew had tossed all dock lines aboard, Jake put it in gear and pulled slowly away from the dock. Cruising steadily out of the marina in the darkness, they left the harbor and within a few minutes were headed out to sea. He set a heading to round the tip of Lands End. As they passed it in the minimal light from the crescent moon, they could barely make out the famous arch near Lover's Beach. They left the Sea of Cortez heading west and entered the Pacific Ocean. There they could feel the rolling of the steady Pacific swells beneath the solid deck of the yacht. The motion of the sea beneath Jake's feet made him feel right at home. How he loved the feel of the wind in his face, the smell of the salt air in the night and the view of the starts shining brightly overhead against a black velvet sky. The sound of the water lapping against the hull sounded like heaven to him. He truly loved the peaceful serenity of being back at sea and wondered if Lynnette would enjoy sailing with him. Pushing thoughts of her from his mind he focused completely on the sheer pleasure of being at sea again.

Once they were rounding the tip of the peninsula, Jake gave instructions to the crew. "Let's get that main up to steady us in these swells." Jake's excitement was evident in his voice.

If the light breeze Jake felt now continued to increase, he reckoned that by daybreak, they should be able to fly full sails. The winds usually increased right before the sun rose or set. For now, the skies were clear, the stars bright and the evening just perfect for cruising.

Standing at the wheel of his magnificent vessel, Jake felt better than he had in a long time. This is where he belonged and he loved to be, at sea behind the wheel. Getting his captain's license years ago had been a wise move. Few men really loved what they did for a living. He happened to be one of them. Whether he was on a secret assignment for the Navy in another country or working on his continuously profitable charter yacht business, he had to admit he loved his work.

Miguel worked on deck with the others, carefully watching over the crew as they familiarized themselves with the sheets, halyards and rigging. Every sailboat was a little different, but the fundamentals were all the same when it came to sailing. Although it was dark, Jake observed them at work in the dim moonlight. He made a mental note of which guys he would pull aside later to train more extensively in certain areas as he had done with Miguel several years ago. He had several other charter yachts at various exotic ports around the world and was always looking for another exceptional sailor to take the lead role as skipper aboard those yachts.

Maria thoughtfully brought Jake a second cup of hot coffee. He enjoyed the chilly breeze and the feel of the Pacific swells as he drank from the mug. Allowing himself to relax, the next few hours passed quickly as he noticed the sky off the stern lighting up the horizon with the coming sunrise. It was one of the most beautiful Sunday sunrises. As Jake suspected, the winds increased just as he noticed the sky getting lighter on the horizon. It wasn't long before Jake set his coffee down and told the crew to also raise the headsail and mizzen sail.

"Let's get them all up," he hollered to the men on deck, referring to the sails. "No reason to wait any longer than necessary to get a feel for how she'll handle in the wind."

It was only when all the canvas was raised and trimmed properly that Jake really felt the full pull of the wind in the sails thrusting the Ariel forward through the swells. Jake's favorite moment was when he cut the engines. The silence was overwhelmingly awesome. He could hear the steady pull of the wind and the rhythmic power of the swells against the bow. He could hear the strain on the lines, the snap of the head sheets and the creaks of the joints. Jake felt exhilarated and rejuvenated. This was what he loved best about sailing, the silent serenity of the sea joined in harmony with the sounds of the sailboat. He enjoyed the sure knowledge of being in total control of the powerful vessel in the elements. Knowing you were setting your own course and not veering from it and heading toward a specific destination. Unlike real life itself, he thought slightly unsettled by the irony of it.

The winds were steady and the sails were trimmed properly. Jake was feeling great as he enjoyed the next hour with the early morning sun on his back. The crew was busy around the deck and he could smell the aroma of the breakfast Maria was busily preparing as it traveled up the gangway from the galley below. It was making his stomach growl in hunger. Yes, he thought to himself, this was going to be a very good trip. He felt better about leaving already. Maria had been correct when she said the ocean healed the heart.

Just then one of the crew ran up with a concerned look on his face. "Captain," which was the title they always addressed Jake by when onboard at Miguel's insistence. It was a matter of respect and his crews all respected and trusted his ability.

"You better come have a look at this," the crewman urged.

Turning the wheel over to one of the others, Jake strode to the stern of the yacht where the rest of the crew was gathered. One of them lifted up a corner of the tarp covering the dinghy so they could see inside. There was Lynnette sweetly curled up in the bottom of Jake's shore boat, still sound asleep.

ELEVEN

Not even the motion of the sea was rousing Lynnette from her peaceful slumber. Jake realized she must be exhausted as he closely watched her beautiful face while she slept.

"It seems we have stow-away, sir," one crewman finally remarked, breaking the silence of the group.

None of the men could read Jake's mood, although the expression on his face seemed rather curious. He continued to watch Lynnette sleep a moment longer, then came to his decision.

"Cover her up and let her wake on her own." Moving away, he pointed to one man and added, "You, keep an eye on her and tell me the minute she wakes up. I'll be working down in the engine room with the mechanic." He instructed Miguel to start both engines for a checkout, and then headed below deck.

Jake informed Maria he would be skipping breakfast as he passed through the galley. He had lost his appetite. He felt the need to work with his hands while he thought through the situation. He needed to figure it out. Feeling the intense heat in the engine room from the moment he walked in, Jake removed his shirt and worked in his jeans.

As he and the mechanic worked together silently, Jake wondered what Lynnette was doing onboard the Ariel. Maybe she'd had a sudden change of heart and finally realized she did want his help after all. Yeah, that must be it, he concluded with a slight grin. She'd climbed aboard his yacht, hadn't she? He had shown it to her just last night after dinner. She knew which one he'd be on and had come right to it. More than likely she had gotten into more trouble with Todd and his gang of buddies last night, which he had warned her of, then she'd run to the docks to find him and he hadn't been there. He frowned. He was pleased she had possibly come to her senses though. He hoped she would finally be willing to tell him what this business was about with Todd and the girl named Keira.

It was loud and hot down in the engine room and sweat began to drip off Jake's body as he continued to work, now deep in thought. Pulling out a bandana from his back pocket, he wiped his forehead.

Maria poked her head inside the engine room to inform Jake their newest "passenger" was finally beginning to wake up. Brushing quickly past her, he wiped his greasy hands on the cotton cloth as he headed up the stairs, taking them two at a time. Maria noticed she had never seen Jake looking so intense before. He was usually focused on whatever task he was working on, but now he looked anxious and eager, almost excited. Instead of heading back to the galley to finish breakfast, Maria headed after Jake to make sure she didn't miss a thing.

Lynnette began to slowly wake up from a deep sleep, as if she were rising up through a long tunnel. She was groggy and completely disoriented by her surroundings. Was that motion she was feeling? Where was she? Then it came back to her in a rush. She had run down to the docks and hidden in a dingy on one of the boats last night. She must have fallen asleep while waiting for the two Mexican guys to leave. She felt so terribly groggy.

Realizing she must have slept the entire night away, she knew she had to get off the docks and back to her room right away. Grabbing her bag from under her head, she began to climb out of the dingy, surprised by a large blond man who helped her off the dinghy and into the yacht. Guys were standing around and there was a strong breeze blowing her hair wildly around her head, blocking her vision. Steadying herself against the motion of the deck beneath her feet, she gathered her hair in both hands, looking around. Oh my gosh, they were out to sea! She felt panic at the knowledge they were no longer tied off at the docks. Frantic, she ran to the starboard railing praying the dock would still be there next to the boat. Looking out toward the coast, there was no sign of Cabo or of any civilization anywhere. Stumbling across the deck to the starboard rail she only saw ocean for as far as the eye could see. Little did she know that Cabo was just a short distance away, just around the rugged point behind them.

"Oh no," she moaned. "What have I done?" Turning back to the tall blond guy, she pleaded with him. "You've got to turn the boat around so I can get back to Cabo. I'm not supposed to be on this boat. It's a mistake. I have to get off."

Eric was eyeing her with definite interest and knew she was in a panic. He decided he would have to get to know her a little better. She was a hot-looking babe and he was already bored. Time to have a little fun. Not bothering to mention he was just a hired hand and not in the position to turn Ariel around, he pulled himself up to his full height.

"Well, hello there," he said slowly, moving closer to her. "I'm Eric. Who exactly might you be?" Eric's bold gaze raked down Lynnette's snug fitting outfit.

Feeling very uncomfortable under his close scrutiny, she instinctively moved a step back. Something about him made her feel wary.

She heard one of the other men state, "Here comes the captain. He decides if we turn back or not."

Looking up toward the bow of the boat, her breath caught the instant she saw Jake walking across the deck towards her. His eyes were intense and un-readable, focused directly on her as he approached. The motion of the deck made it necessary to reach for the railing behind her for balance to prevent her from falling. Was it due to the motion or from seeing Jake again? What in the world was he doing here anyway?

Jake wore only jeans and his chest and arms were glistening with sweat. How could a man be so sexy wearing only jeans? The smooth skin of his upper body was tanned and muscular. His long hair just touched his shoulders and was curly and disheveled. Lynnette was robbed of all reason. In her imagination, she pictured him lowering his face to steal a passionate kiss, his arms enfolding her firmly in his embrace. Frozen, she continued to observe him, fascinated, as he steadily strode sure-footedly across the rolling deck. He didn't even appear to notice the movement of the deck beneath his long, sturdy legs.

Jake stopped directly in front of her. Reaching down he took her chin lightly in his fingers and guided her mouth toward his. Pausing a brief moment to study her soft lips, he looked into her eyes before bringing his mouth down over hers in a possessive kiss.

She was only aware of his heated breath mingling with hers, the warm lips covering her own and strong arms that held her from falling weak-kneed to the deck. Her head was swimming and she was feeling light headed and dizzy. Whether from the kiss or the motion of the water, she wasn't certain. Just as abruptly as he had approached, he pulled away and let her go. She grabbed the railing for support.

Dazed and speechless, she suddenly remembered with embarrassment the eyes of the many curious men standing around them. They had all just witnessed that amazing kiss. She watched him as he dismissed the crew, offering instructions to each one as he did so.

"Miguel, you take the wheel and check on the course heading. One of you two," he said, pointing toward the two wide-eyed young men, "go and help the mechanic with the work on the port engine." To the last one standing there, he paused as if out of tasks, "find something to polish or varnish somewhere." Grinning, he looked directly at Lynnette as he slowly said, "I'll take care of our stow-away personally."

As everyone left to get on with their work, Lynnette felt a confusion of dread and anticipation at Jake's words.

Miguel never missed much and was the only one standing there who had noticed the angry scowl on Eric's face as they all witnessed Jake kissing her.

When the last of the group moved slowly away, she asked Jake, "What are you doing here?"

She saw amusement on his face. There were crinkles at the corners of his splendid blue eyes and he was failing at suppressing a grin. Stepping forward he gently placed a hand on either side of her face. Tilting her head up, he firmly placed another kiss on her lips.

He knew the second he'd seen her sleeping in his dinghy, he would never have been able to get her out of his system. There was just something about her that drove him like a moth to light. She was both passionate and fiery. She pleased him.

"It's good to see you, Lynnette," his voice deep and husky. "I'm glad you finally came to your senses and came back for my help. You really shouldn't try to handle this situation with Todd on your own."

Pleased she was here with him, he didn't notice the confusion on her face. Trying to recover from his kiss, which had left her heart beating fast and her mind senseless, she tried to concentrate and follow his conversation.

"Jake, I have no idea what you're talking about."

"You came aboard the Ariel to find me last night, right?" he asked. He was content in knowing she wanted his help. "You finally realized you were in way over your pretty head and needed my help after all."

"Well, then you figured all wrong," she retorted in anger, not caring at all for his condescending attitude. She didn't need his help. She didn't need any man's help.

"The truth is I didn't come looking for you at all. I was just simply looking for the quickest hiding place I could find in the dark last night and that was it," she said pointing to the dinghy. "I told you before that I don't want or need your help. I can…"

"…handle it by yourself," he finished for her with a bit of sarcasm. "Yeah, I know. Look Lynnette, you got into trouble last night, right? Otherwise you wouldn't have been looking for a place to hide." Grasping her by the shoulders he aggressively asked her, "Don't you realize yet that you can't handle everything in life alone? Sometime, you're going to have to start trusting someone. Someone who cares about your safety and what happens to you."

"Turn this boat around and please take me back to Cabo," she ordered him, knocking his hands away. She crossed her arms tightly in front of her, directing her angry gaze up at him.

"Why?" he tossed back.

"Because I asked you to, that's why. I can't tell you what's going on, Jake, you know that. I just have to get back. Turn it around now."

"No," he answered forcefully.

Stomping her foot in anger, she shrieked, "Oh, you make me so mad." She turned her back stomped off to the starboard railing and stood there, furious with him. She could see the coastline clearly, could even hear the waves crashing on the beach.

"Give me one good reason why I should and maybe I'll consider it." He was beginning to lose his patience with her. "As soon as you're ready to explain what the hell is going on with Todd, then I'll decide if we go back or not. Got it?"

Turning, Jake headed for the cockpit when he heard her yelling back at him.

"Fine, then. You won't take me back? I'll just swim to shore and walk back." She was frustrated and angry, not thinking clearly at all.

Pulling her backpack onto her shoulders, Lynnette quickly climbed over the wooden railing, reminding herself she had been a competitive swimmer back in high school. It didn't look too far to the beach. She could hear Jake yelling for her to stop, but pushed off with both feet and jumped into the ocean. Shocked as she hit the surface, the cold water quickly seeped inside her clothing. She began to crawl through the water, swimming hand over hand towards the shore.

Jake had seen what she was about to do but still couldn't believe his eyes. He was stunned. Most men wouldn't have the nerve to jump into this water, this far from shore. Was the woman completely nuts? Didn't she know there were sharks out this deep? It was crazy to think she could make it all the way to land from here.

In a flash, Jake removed both shoes and pulled his wallet out of his back pocket, throwing it down as he raced across the deck. He barked orders to the crew. "Man overboard. Miguel, bring her around. You," he said pointing to Eric who was the closest one standing nearby, "drop the dinghy and come pick us up." Grabbing the life-ring hanging on the rail, he quickly threw the strap over his shoulder and made a perfect dive over the side and into the frigid water.

Lynnette hadn't thought about just how heavy the backpack would become once it filled with water. The stacks of money inside were weighing her down too much and she was already getting fatigued. It also hadn't seemed so far to shore from up on the deck but from down here she had her doubts if she could make it. Struggling to keep her head above water, she began to feel real panic. This was a really dumb idea, she thought belatedly, but he had infuriated her with his overbearing, controlling ways. She hated being told what to do and wouldn't be dictated to

ever. She would never do what he ordered her to do.
Never.

Jake couldn't see her due to the choppy white-capped
water. Kicking to thrust his body higher up out of the chop
and using the floatation device, he finally spotted her. She
was just ahead, but obviously struggling to keep her head
above water. He could see the panic on her face. Putting
his head down, he crawled toward her, his strong arms
pulling him quickly through the rough water.

Out of breath, he soon grabbed her around the waist
instructing her to grab hold of the life preserver. "Here, let
me pull that pack off your back. It's dragging you down."

"No," she exclaimed, breathing hard and spitting out
water she choked on. "I'm not letting it go."

"Lynnette, use your head. It's weighing you down like
an anchor. Take it off the let it go," he ordered.

"I'm not letting it go, so just forget it," she sputtered,
going under briefly.

"Woman," Jake's tone was furious, "when I get you
back on that boat, I'm going to throttle you. What in hell
were you thinking jumping into the water this far from
shore?" He continued to kick, never letting her go. "Don't
you realize the dangers of being out in water this deep?" he
yelled.

Just then they heard Eric approaching in the dinghy.
Jake left Lynnette hanging on to the edge of the boat as he
lifted himself up easily over the side. Reaching down, he
grabbed her under the arms and hoisted her into the boat,
dropping her into the bottom like a flailing fish. He looked
at her briefly, his anger obvious in his narrowed eyes.

Trying to sit up, she looked away and pulled the pack off her bag setting it away from him. She hoped he didn't inspect the contents.

They rode back to the yacht in silence as she stared at Jake's wide back. She could see he was barely controlling his temper and dreaded having to face him up on deck. His jaw tightened each time he clenched his teeth in anger.

Jake was feeling so angry at the moment he could hardly hold back. Maybe he should just beat her senseless for being so damn stupid. Jake couldn't image anyone in his entire life that made him so angry so easily. Didn't she have any clue of the danger she continually put herself in? It was amazing she had lived to be an adult with no more common sense than she possessed.

They tied off to the stern of the yacht and climbed up the ladder to the deck. As Miguel turned the boat back to a northwest heading, the crew prepared to raise the dinghy into its harness so they could once again get underway. Up on deck, Jake glared at Lynnette as he grabbed the backpack out of her hand. She tried to yank it back, but his grip on her arm was too tight.

"What in the hell have you got in here that weighs a ton and is worth more to you than your own life?" he demanded angrily.

Squatting down on the deck, Jake unzipped the bag and looked inside the opening. He was dumbfounded. It was a bag full of cash. Looking up at her through narrowed, angry eyes, he slowly shook his head and carefully zipped the bag shut again. Rising to his full height with the bag firmly in one hand, he grabbed Lynnette's arm with the other and dragged her across the deck to the stairwell leading below deck.

TWELVE

She had to run to keep up with his long stride since he was walking so fast. Her clothing was thoroughly soaked and heavy, plus she was getting nervous. He was holding her wrist so tight she couldn't get loose of his grip, but she continued to try anyway. The look on his face had the entire crew stepping back with intimidation. He looked mad as hell and she knew she better think fast. She remembered his promise to throttle her once they were back on deck and fervently hoped he had forgotten he'd said it.

Jake dragged her down the stairwell to the deck below, pausing briefly to make sure she didn't lose her footing. He pulled her quickly through the galley, ignoring the incredulous look on Maria's face as she stared wide-eyed at them. Jake continued pulling her along behind him down the wooden corridor to his own private quarters.

Throwing open the door, he tossed her inside, threw her bag on the floor, then slammed the door shut behind them. He slowly turned the key in the lock and removed it, placing it in the top drawer of the desk in the corner of the room. Lynnette stood frozen in place as Jake turned to face her, his eyes glaring. She could see he was seething, struggling to control his anger. She watched as he moved purposely to the closet to remove one of his shirts, which he shoved at her.

"I'll give you exactly two minutes to dry off and change into this," he motioned toward the private head off the stateroom. "I'll take our wet clothes out to Maria to dry.

Then you will explain to me exactly what the hell is going on."

Lynnette was beginning to shiver, whether from the wet clothes or from Jake's intense fury, she couldn't tell. Without a word, she moved away from the puddle forming beneath her feet and went into the bathroom to change out of the dripping wet clothes. Stalling for time in the bathroom, she tried to figure out just exactly what she was going to tell Jake. Pulling off her drenched clothing, she toweled herself dry and slipped into Jake's huge, white cotton shirt.

She couldn't very well tell him the truth. Todd was a cruel and intensely mean individual and she would be placing Keira at risk. No, she definitely must keep their personal business to herself. But what should she tell Jake? Should she fabricate an elaborate story to pacify him, she wondered as she rolled up the long sleeves of the shirt to just below the elbows. No, she wasn't that quick with a good lie. She would just have to convince him to turn the boat around, somehow.

Gathering up her wet clothes, Lynnette opened the door and stepped into the cabin just as Jake was straightening up to his full height. His back was to her and he was pulling up a pair of dry jeans over his muscular legs and bare buttocks. Her eyes widened in surprise as she stepped back into the bathroom and quickly shut the door behind her.

"Get out here, Lynnette. Now," Jake's voice boomed through the door.

Hesitantly, she opened the door as Jake stepped forward still buttoning up his jeans. Grabbing the wet clothing from her arms, he marched to the door.

"I'll be right back," he stated firmly. "You wait here." She jumped as he slammed the door shut behind him.

Lynnette began pacing back and forth, wringing her hands together nervously. As she chewed on her lower lip, she tried to figure out how she could convince Jake to turn back. Somehow she must get back to Cabo without Jake learning the real truth. He would definitely cause more trouble with Todd if he knew what was going on, especially with that nasty temper of his.

Looking around, she was distracted by the magnificently impressive interior of the yacht. She browsed around the large room, noticing the highly polished teak walls, the elegant brown leather sofa and the oversized bed with the matching custom bedspread and pillow case coverings. She noticed the stateroom was wonderfully decorated with a very elegant, masculine feel to it.

Off the main room was the large in-suite bathroom where she had just changed. At the far end of the room, she saw what looked to be a chart table underneath several shelves of leather hardbound books.

Wandering over to the window, she thought about what she would tell Jake. She jumped as he suddenly burst through the doorway. Once again, he locked the door behind him.

"We're not leaving this room until you tell me exactly what I want to know."

"You can't keep me locked in here like a prisoner," she tried reasoning with him. The blue eyes boring into her were a much darker shade of blue as they pierced her.

"I can and I will. Damn it, Lynnette, you have got to be the most stubborn woman I've ever met. You infuriate me.

Now tell me what this business is with Todd once and for all," he demanded.

"No. I won't, and I won't be intimidated into telling you anything either," she retorted holding her ground. Oh, how she hated being told what to do, especially by a man.

Grinding his teeth in frustration, he began to advance toward her as he slowly said in a deep voice, "You're acting like a spoiled child, you little brat. I ought to put you over my knee and slap fire from your ass. It would serve you right. My patience with you is about used up, so I'm warning you, don't push me any further."

She was outraged. "You wouldn't dare," she spat back, infuriated he would even consider such a thing. She would never allow any man to do anything so humiliating and demeaning to her.

"Oh, wouldn't I?" he moved steadily toward her.

Moving in one quick motion, Jake grabbed her arm and sat down on the edge of the bed. She struggled and tried pulling away from his grasp, but he was firmly holding both her wrists together behind her back in his one large hand. He pulled her facedown over his lap as she began kicking and screaming at him furiously. He easily held her in place but looking down suddenly realized his shirt had ridden up and was exposing her in their struggle. It was almost his undoing. He quickly reached down and pulled the shirt down to cover her firm and beautifully rounded ass.

Uncomfortably clearing his throat, he spoke. "Lynnette, I'm doing this to teach you a lesson. My patience goes only so far and I will have my way in the end. You will tell me the truth about this matter one way or the other."

He was aware she could hear him even thought he had to yell to be heard since she continued screaming at him to let her go. He calmly continued.

"I've asked you a number of times to tell me what is going on with Todd, but you continued to refuse me an answer. You say it's none of my business," he said loudly, "but it became my business when I started to care about you and it will be my business until it's been resolved. Now this punishment should remind you not to act like a brat in the future. I'm bigger and stronger than you and no matter how stubborn you can be, when I ask a question, I want the truth."

Lynnette could feel his thighs digging into her hipbones and ribs as she fought to free herself. This was the most demoralizing, degrading thing any man had ever done to her and she hated the helpless feeling of being so overpowered. Fighting with all her strength, she couldn't get loose of his grip and her shoulders began to ache from struggling. He was ranting on about something she tried not to hear, when suddenly, she felt the first sting of a slap as his hand struck her bottom. She screamed at him even louder. It was not a hard slap. It didn't even hurt since it was through the fabric of his long shirt she was wearing, but it infuriated her nonetheless. He continued his assault, again and again, until she finally stopped struggling and lay still across his lap, silently fuming inside. She utterly despised him at that moment.

Finally, as she lay still across his lap, he stopped, mistakenly thinking he had broken her nasty temper. He knew he hadn't really hurt her. It was then he finally noticed the attractive curves of the woman instead of the behind of a stubborn brat. He struggled to put aside the arousing thoughts that the sight of her was conjuring up in his mind. Releasing her hands, he pulled her up to sit next to him on the bed. He suspected her bottom was now a bit red, but her face was beet red now also. She must be embarrassed, he incorrectly assumed.

"I'm sure that didn't hurt much. I was careful and went easy on you. I needed to make my point though. Now, I want you to answer my question, Lynnette."

When she looked over at him, he knew right away he had been mistaken about breaking her temper and stubbornness. He had incorrectly assumed her red face was due to embarrassment. If looks could kill, he would be a dead man on the spot. Sparks were flying from her shiny brown eyes and she looked enraged. To him, she looked fantastic.

"I hate you for doing that to me," she yelled at him. "I'm getting out of here and away from you, you ass, you..., you brut, you...," she screamed, running out of insults.

She made a run for it, but he stood up in a flash and grabbed her quickly, swinging her around to face him, which was his mistake. She brought her leg up, attempting to knee him hard in the groin. Luckily for him, his legs were so long she only connected with his upper thigh. Her true intention wasn't lost on him though.

Breaking free, Lynnette raced toward the table across the room to elude his grasp as he quickly moved back and forth across the other side, trying to determine which way she would run. Faking one direction, she then made a dash the other way and headed for the door. He watched as she tugged on it with both hands, remembering too late that it was locked. Slowly, she turned around knowing she was trapped. He stood there looking at her with her hair wildly messed up and concluding she looked the most amazing when she was furious.

Lynnette felt like a cornered animal as she pressed her back up against the door. Jake advanced slowly toward her, a menacing gleam in his gorgeous blue eyes. If only he weren't so darn handsome, she though, then her body wouldn't react toward him the way it was now. As he stood his full height directly in front of her, she could feel her breath quicken and an unfamiliar fluttering deep down inside.

"You jumped overboard and put yourself and my crew at risk," he stated calmly. "You deserved what I just did to you, Lynnette."

She didn't move or speak until he reached out to take her by the shoulders. She began pounding his chest with her fists, both arms wildly flailing at his body. She struggled to get away, knowing it was hopeless as he just held her firmly in his strong grasp.

Deflecting her blows to his chest while he recalled what she'd tried earlier, he moved his lower body closer to prevent her from trying to knee him again. He pressed his hips tightly against hers, her back to the door. Grasping her arms firmly by the wrists to stop their assault on his body, he easily pinned them against the door above her head. She continued thrashing back and forth in an ongoing attempt to get free.

Jake's eyebrows rose as his gaze moved down to her generous breasts moving freely beneath his thin white shirt as she continued her attempts to get free from him. Sucking in his breath, he observed their movement briefly, noticing the darker hint of peaks standing out through the flimsy cotton. She noticed the direction of his gaze and immediately ceased her struggles.

Jake closed his eyes and dropped his chin to his chest as he leaned his elbows on the door, still holding her wrists in his grip trying to control his intense desire to take her right there. In his anger, he had not stopped to consider she would have removed all of her wet undergarments so Maria could dry those as well. Everything she had on would have been thoroughly soaked. Clenching his teeth, he struggled internally with himself for physical control.

Lynnette heard a low sounding groan come from somewhere deep inside of Jake. When she looked up into his eyes, she saw the intense passion in their blue depths. The tingling within her began again.

Instinctively, she moved her legs tightly together as she felt Jake's full arousal pressed tightly up against her belly. Breathing became difficult. Her breasts rose with each deep breath and they felt tender, aching for his touch.

"God, woman, you're driving me crazy with wanting you," he groaned through clenched teeth. "Damn it, I don't know whether to throttle you or make love to you," he finished in a low, passionate voice.

She realized she wanted him too. He was the man of her dreams and she wanted at that moment to be with him, to give herself to him more than anything else in the world.

As he continued to stare down into her beautiful eyes so full of uncertainty, he also saw there the passionate heat of her own desire. Gently, he leaned into her body, lowering his head down toward her, concentrating on her lips, which she nervously licked, causing Jake to suck in his breath again. Ever so softly, Jake kissed her moist lips, teasing them with a light brush of his own.

He wanted to make her feel the same intensely painful desire he was now experiencing. He wanted her to come to him willingly. He wanted her to want him just as badly as he wanted her.

She couldn't stand much more of his teasing. She wanted to touch him, but couldn't. Her hands were still pinned high against the door. She wanted him to devour her mouth with kisses like he had before on the beach, yet he didn't. He just kept teasing her, brushing light caresses across her lips until she thought she would go mad with desire. She knew she shouldn't allow this to happen but she couldn't resist him any more.

Forgetting her anger, she leaned forward, taking his mouth aggressively, sucking his lower lip within the soft folds of her mouth. Jake moaned his pleasure and she felt encouraged. She dangerously taunted his lips with a light flick of her tongue.

Jake suddenly let go of her wrists and grabbed her abruptly in his arms, pulling her tighter against his hard body. His grip was so sudden that she lost her breath, as his mouth came down over hers possessively, hungrily. She wrapped her arms around his massive shoulders, running her hands wildly through his dark, damp hair.

Lynnette felt light headed and dizzy. Her knees went weak. Jake reached a hand between their bodies finding what he was seeking. Lightly squeezing, he gently massaged her full breast through the thin fabric, running his fingers back and forth over the peak until it puckered beneath the shirt. He could feel the rapid pounding of her heart beneath his hand.

Lynnette threw her head back, moaning as Jake ran kisses down her long, soft neck. Rolling her head weakly to the side, he continued his attentions on her breast while sliding his other hand down her back to clasp her bottom in his hand, hauling her up tighter against his obvious desire.

She ran her hands over the bare skin of his muscled arms and shoulders, knowing there would be no turning back now. She wanted him as much as he wanted her, no matter the consequences later.

She was startled when Jake reached up with both hands to grasp the top button of her shirt to unbutton it. She had never been naked in front of a man before. Quickly losing patience, he ripped the shirt open, baring her breasts to his starving eyes, scattering buttons across the floor of the cabin.

Grabbing the door behind her for support, she felt her knees start to buckle. The raw hunger on his face and his sudden aggressiveness were alarmingly arousing to her. She was completely overwhelmed by his passion and desire for her. He was so sexy, so gorgeous, and yet kind of frightening at the same time.

He stood before her, staring down at her exposed body. His smoldering eyes darkened as he leaned down and swung her up into his arms, carrying her across the room and gently laying her on the bed. Standing to admire her, he swallowed, taken aback by her luscious body.

"Oh damn, Lynnette, you're beautiful," he said, his voice sounding husky.

She instinctively tried to close the shirt to cover herself but his hands stopped her as he sat down next to her on the bed. Running both hands up her body, he grasped both firm breasts, lightly rubbing the hardened tips between his fingers. Leaning down, he kissed them, taking first one aroused peak, then the other in his mouth, sucking, kissing, and teasing with his tongue as she writhed in pleasure beneath him. She tasted so sweet to him. The weak grip on his control was quickly slipping away. He had to have her now, every part of her.

He kissed her lips again, his mouth no longer gentle, but more forceful and demanding. His tongue invaded her mouth, seeking hers out. He tangled his fingers in her long, dark hair, which lay damp across the pillow, pinning her head between his hands.

Looking down at her with all of the intense passion he felt inside glowing in his blue eyes, he moaned, "I want you so much, Lynnette. I want you now."

Standing, Jake quickly unbuttoned his pants, sliding them down his legs as his eyes continued to devour her nearly naked body. She was shocked by the size of him. She had never before seen a man fully aroused and Jake was huge. This would never work, she decided, losing her nerve. She had no experience at this but could tell there was no way he would ever fit inside her.

Beginning to feel panicked, she watched as he walked over to the nightstand to remove a slim, square packet, which confused her until she realized she had not even thought about protection. Thankfully, he was prepared. She watched in fascination as he easily rolled the smooth covering down over his anxious manhood.

Grinning at her, he could see a combination of shock and wonder on her face. She had not yet spoken a word and he wondered what she was thinking. She appeared to be getting quite nervous.

"Are you sure you're okay with this, Lynnette?" he asked sitting back down on the bed, running his hand down her body in a soft caress.

She could feel the heat of his touch coursing through her and felt an overwhelming need for..., what? Something, but she wasn't even sure what. She was hot, wet and wanting, but with no experience she didn't have a clue what she should do next. She had never had sex before and she felt uncertain and embarrassed at her lack of experience.

Looking up into Jake's eyes, she said hesitantly, "I don't know what I'm supposed to..., I mean, I've never..."

Jake looked astounded at the beautiful girl laying bare beside him in sheer amazement. "You mean to tell me you're still a virgin?"

The look of embarrassment on her face was answer enough and she tried looking away. Catching her chin between his fingers, he guided her face back to his.

"Sweetheart, don't be embarrassed. I think it's wonderful and quite a surprise, but don't ever be embarrassed with me. What you're offering me is a gift, the most wonderful gift you could ever give a man. I want you more right now than I've ever wanted any woman in my life, but are you really sure of this? I won't force myself on you. I need to know that you want this as much as I do." His face showed the torture of his need as he waited, unsure of what her answer would be.

Her brown eyes smoldered with emotion as she looked up bravely at his handsome face. She answered without reservation, her voice sounding faint, yet sure.

"Oh yes, I'm sure. I want you, Jake."

Reaching up, she pulled him down over her body, her mouth demanding more of his wonderful kisses. Their lips molded together in sheer passion. His head dropped to her neck, smothering its length with light nipping bites and kisses.

Her hands moved urgently over the muscles of his bare back and down further over his body, as she closed her eyes in ecstasy. Moving lower, he kissed her breasts, teasing each nipple into a rosy peak with light flicks of his tongue, bringing her shivers of delight. Laying the strong length of his body out next to her, Jake possessed her mouth once again with his lips as he ran his hand down the soft curves of her slender body. Inching down further, he felt soft curls beneath his fingers as Lynnette immediately tensed beneath his touch.

"It's okay, sweetheart. Let me touch you there, please," he said in a low voice as he nuzzled on her earlobe.

Slowly, she tried to relax, but was uncomfortable. Running his hands up and down her smooth thighs, he gently pulled her legs apart. Finding what he so desired, he began caressing her with practiced fingers. She cried out in shock. In shock and surprising pleasure. He captured her mouth with his own. Instinctively, she raised her hips toward his touch, tossing her head on the pillow, moaning in pleasure. He watched her reaction to his touch, amazed at an unfamiliar emotion welling up inside him. She was so uninhibited, so natural. She was fantastic. And she was now his.

"Do you like how that feels, Lynnette?" His breathing was irregular as she moaned in answer. Pleasure was coursing throughout her body.

She gave herself to him so freely, he thought. This naïve beauty now looking up at him had such gorgeous trusting eyes. He never wanted this to end, this exquisite torture of going slowly, preparing her for her first time. He wished they could stay locked away together in this cabin forever.

As his fingers continued to expertly massage the moist, protective folds of her womanhood, he saw the raw, uncontrolled pleasure in her eyes. She rotated her hips instinctively against his touch now as waves of passion washed over her. She tried to breath, gasping as she rose in pleasure further and further, her mind losing all ability to think clearly. Closing her eyes, her mind spun as her desire moved her yet higher and higher until she finally cried out, finding her pleasure.

"Oh, Jake, please. I need you, …love you, oh how I want you now…," she trailed off as she quivered her release in his hand, trembling.

Her words hit Jake squarely in the heart like a fist. She just said she loved him. Pleasure filled every pore of his body. He wanted this woman more than anything.

Jake moved over her, resting most of his weight on his arms as he kissed her moist and swollen lips. Moving himself between her legs, he reached down, spreading her thighs further apart. Taking himself in hand, he slowly rubbed the moist tip of his throbbing manhood over her sensitive bud making her whimper with desire.

Inching slowly inside, he clenched his jaw as he fought for the control to hold back until she was ready to take all of him. She was wet, but very small and tight. He would have to go slowly to avoid hurting her.

Lynnette could feel him entering, his throbbing shaft invading her body. At the same time she could feel her body opening up to accept him and marveled to think she could accommodate his huge size.

Moving slowly and with the utmost control, he reached the tender barrier he'd anticipated. Using every ounce of willpower he possessed, he ground his teeth and forced himself not to thrust himself further inside her. He buried his head in the pillow next to her speaking through jagged breaths.

"Lynnette, honey, I'm going to have to hurt you a bit now, but the pain won't last long. I promise, sweetheart."

Pushing himself through, he felt her flinch as he looked down to see the pain cross her face. Looking down at her face he felt the joy of true intimacy unlike anything he had ever experienced before Lynnette. He slowly leaned down to kiss her face, ears and neck, while trying not to move until her pain finally subsided.

Soon he could feel her body relax again. She began to move beneath him, wrapping her legs around his back, inviting him deeper access. Thrilled with her response, he began moving in rhythm as she clung to him desperately. She matched his tempo with increased excitement. He filled her completely as they moved together as one, both rising to a peak of pleasure neither had realized existed.

She began to reach her pleasure again, this time bringing Jake with her. Moving with one rhythm together, they continued up and over the edge, until he groaned his release. He buried his face in the pillow next to her head. He was completely spent. He was thoroughly happy.

Used up and completely satisfied, together they slowly floated back down to reality. Jake held his body weight on his elbows to keep from crushing her beneath him. Finally, he eased out of her and rolled onto his back, pulling Lynnette protectively into the crook of his shoulder. Resting her head gently on his chest, he held her comfortably in his arms.

Listening to his rapid heart rate as it began to slow, Lynnette felt an unfamiliar warmth and protection as he held her so tightly in his strong arms. It felt so right, yet her mind said it was all wrong. He was always so in control and masculine, so protective of her since the first time they met.   Suddenly she realized she really liked his protectiveness, which was surprising. Usually, she disliked those traits in a man, but with Jake, she found herself beginning to rely on the feeling of comfort he offered. She knew now she wanted to tell him about her problem with Todd so he could help her, but she also knew she couldn't do it. How could she be certain she could trust him? These things she was feeling for him were very confusing to her. They went against everything she had always believed growing up. Yet, Jake seemed to be somehow different she suspected. She couldn't be sure, but maybe she had found a man she could actually trust. Possibly even love in time she thought, unaware she had already admitted as much to him in their moment of passion.

Jake loved the feel of just holding her in his arms as they lay there together in bed, but he could also feel the increased motion of the sea due to the approaching storm and felt torn between continuing to lie here holding her soft and naked body close to his, or of going up on deck to check on the weather again.

There was a large tropical storm quickly heading north toward them but it wasn't due to reach their coordinates until much later that night. His sense of responsibility to the safety of those onboard won out and he decided with more than a little regret he better get up to the bridge to check on things. Storms were not always predictable.

"As much as I hate leaving your temptingly soft body, I've got to get back up on deck to check the weather."

Hugging her close, Jake placed a gentle kiss on her forehead. Giving her a final squeeze, he got out of bed and went into the head. While he was gone, Lynnette hugged his pillow tightly and closed her eyes, breathing in his masculine scent from the pillowcase. She remembered the touch of his fingers on her skin, the feel of him thrusting deep inside, the feeling of his hot urgent kisses on her lips. Each new memory sent shivers down her spine. She had never known it could be like that between a man and a woman. It had been absolutely fantastic.

As Jake quietly came back into the room, now fully dressed, he stood at the edge of the bed observing Lynnette as she lay there curled up so comfortably. He realized he had never wanted a girl this much before in his life. He ached to get undressed and make love to her again, but knew she would be sore for a while, this being her first time. The fact he had been her first and only man made him feel euphoric. He would have to wait until later when she felt better. What a wonderful gift she had given him, her innocence, and her virginity at a time when it was hard to find girls who had held on to their innocence.

In the past, he had always been anxious to leave bed after sex. He didn't care for the snuggling and emotional talk women conjured up after intercourse. Lynnette made him feel different. The long moments of silence between them were comfortable and somehow, peacefully intimate. He wanted to just lie there with her all afternoon, listening to her tell him about herself. There was so much he wanted to know about her.

She rolled over, realizing he was watching her, amazed he had come back into the room without hearing him. He was smiling down at her, his gorgeous eyes intent with emotion. After several moments she spoke.

"Jake, will you turn the boat around now, please? I really need to get back to Cabo."

She watched his facial expression change and knew from the look on his face, the special time they had shared was over. He looked ready to throttle her again. She knew she hadn't timed her request well at all.

Jake looked down at her with disgust. Was that the only reason she had allowed him to have sex with her? If so, she was nothing different than the other women he had known in the past with their ulterior motives and conniving ways. The thought made him angrier than he would have believed possible.

"Lynnette, when I said we aren't turning back until you've told me the entire story, I meant it. You haven't quite yet got it through that thick little head of yours that I'm the one in charge have you? You'll need my help with whatever mess you're in and whether you like it or not, I'm involved now. Just tell me the truth and I'll turn the boat around," he demanded.

Lynnette reacted to Jake's change in mood immediately. Gone was the loving, handsome man and back was the irritatingly bossy dictator who insisted everyone do as he demanded. It got her hackles up more quickly than anything else could. She rose from the bed pulling on his shirt and held it closed with one hand. She stood facing him, her chin held up defiantly.

"I won't tell you, Jake. I can't," she insisted, raising her chin for emphasis. "You don't understand. It would only make things worse with you involved. These guys are dead serious and I don't want anyone hurt, including you."

"Don't want anyone hurt? You're the only one likely to get hurt, you little fool," he yelled back clearly annoyed with her. "You want examples? What about your dangerously stupid stunt of jumping off the boat into the ocean nearly a mile offshore, risking your life because you're too damn stubborn to answer my simple questions? What about the fact I had to jump in to save your skinny ass before you drowned?" he demanded, his anger apparent in his voice.

"I don't recall asking you to save me, Jake," she yelled back, turning away.

"Don't even start in again telling me how you can handle this mess by yourself, sweetheart," Jake said firmly, bending down to pull on his deck shoes. "Let me explain something to you in real simple terms so you can understand," he stated slowly, standing up to his full height.

He spun her around to face him, holding her firmly by the shoulders.

"You say those guys are dead serious? If they want something from you, they are going to do whatever it takes in order to get it. If you think you stand a chance in hell against them, you're wrong. You are out-numbered, over-powered and since they are the ones calling the shots, probably out-smarted as well. You need my help and I don't care if you are too thick headed to realize it, you're getting it anyway! I now care too much about you and your safety to allow you to handle this on your own," he finished, his voice loud and forceful as his eyes bore down on her.

Releasing her, he walked to the desk and retrieved his key. "You will answer my questions later. Right now I have to go check on that storm. When I come back though, we'll have dinner alone and you will answer me then. Trust me, you will answer me, Lynnette."

Turning, he walked to the door, he added, "I'm going to lock this door behind me to avoid another man-overboard drill. I've had enough salt water for one day."

"Don't you dare lock me in here, Jake. I'll break everything in this room if you do," she warned.

Turning back, he looked at her across the room through narrowed eyes.

"You break anything in this room and I promise I'll turn you over my knee again, honey."

Horrified and furious, she ran over to the bookshelf, grabbed a book and hurled it at the door just as it closed behind him, striking the door at the spot where his head had been just a moment before.

THIRTEEN

Maria was busy preparing Sunday night dinner in the galley when Jake walked in. Miguel had suggested she get as much as possible done early due to the coming storm.

Stopping next to the cutting board where she was quickly and efficiently chopping up a stock of celery, he grabbed a handful of freshly cut vegetables and tossed them in his mouth. The increasing size of the swells and increased movement of the water beneath the boat was making it more difficult than usual for Maria to use her knife efficiently. She was certainly used to cooking in a moving galley though and didn't even think to mention the motion tossing the boat around. They were all used to being on the sea. Jake grabbed another handful of celery as Maria slapped his hand away.

"Stop that. I will have no more vegetables for dinner tonight if you keep that up," she disciplined with a grin, looking up at his warm and smiling face.

"Hey, I'm starving," he defended. "I missed both breakfast and lunch. What time is dinner, by the way?" he asked, quickly grabbing another handful and tossing them in his mouth.

"You will be eating earlier than usual tonight before the storm gets to us. You seemed to be working up an appetite earlier. I heard that girl yelling her head off," Maria teased. "Were you trying to kill her or is she just angry at you?" she asked as she started chopping up the pile of carrots sitting next to the cutting board that she had washed earlier.

Maria was a strict Catholic, although not a prude. She had never understood Jake's relationships. No commitment, no love, just different women coming and going constantly. Every young woman who came in contact with him seemed to be crazy about him, but Maria had always hoped he would change his ways and find a nice girl to settle down with before he got himself in trouble or found himself alone and lonely one day. He was a really wonderful man. He just needed the right woman.

Jake, she noted, had a devilish look about him and a cocky grin on his face.

"I was just teaching her a little lesson. She's a bit feisty and has a foul temper when she doesn't get her way. I'm pretty sure she understands now," he added, looking back down the corridor toward his cabin. "It was for her own good," he added, his look becoming more serious as he thought about the danger she had placed herself and his crew in. Overboard drills could prove dangerous for the crewmembers too.

"You know this girl before today, I think?" Maria asked sweetly with her slight accent and broken English. Jake had always found it easy to confide in Maria. She was usually very helpful when he was frustrated, trying to understand women and their confusing, emotional ways. Maria also had an uncanny ability to understand him without judging him.

"Yeah, we met on the flight down from L.A. She's been getting herself into one mess after the other since I first set eyes on her. I think she is in some kind of serious trouble" he said with a frown, tossing a few more pieces of carrot in his mouth.

"Why you want to help her anyway? You just met her," Maria wisely questioned as she filled a large pot with water from the sink and started chopping up the onions and potatoes. She figured maybe it would be wise to raise some questions he hadn't even asked himself yet. It might help him think it through.

"You know something, Maria," Jake confided, knowing she would keep their conversation in strict confidence, "it was strange but when I first met her, there was some sort of feeling, an attraction, sparks or…, something between us. We both felt it. I could see it in her eyes. You know that I've never believed in that stuff before, but now even when she isn't around I can't seem to get her off my mind. And when she is around, either I want to kiss her or I'm mad at hell at her," he finished, his confusion obvious on his face. "I just don't get it. It's ridiculous. We just met and I have all these feeling going on. It's confusing."

Maria just smiled to herself, knowing Jake was probably beginning to fall in love with the pretty girl. Well, it was about time, she thought, but it wouldn't be good for him to know it just yet. It would only scare him off. She added the chopped vegetables to the heating water and began cutting up the meat for the soup.

"What I don't understand," Jake asked, "is why she would be so hesitant to let me help her? I've helped her out a couple of times already and it's obvious she's in way over her head. She'll definitely get herself hurt without help."

Maria paused briefly with cutting the meat. "It could be many things, I think," Maria spoke thoughtfully, choosing her words carefully. Her accent was strong but her meaning clear. She resumed cutting up the slab of beef. "Maybe she is independent and has had to do things for herself so she is not so used to help. Or maybe no man has ever helped her and she might even have problem trusting men. She is a very beautiful girl and I think many men just want one thing from a girl that pretty. She might not like that." Maria stopped working and looked up at Jake with a serious look on her face. "Jake, you will need to be patient with this girl. Take your time and get to know her. Tell her about yourself and gain her trust." Then adding with a teasing grin, "There are other things for you to do with a beautiful girl other than..., well, you know what I mean to say."

"Maria!" Jake feigned shock. "You mean there is something other than sex I've been missing all these years? Why didn't you tell me?

Blushing, she ordered crisply, "I didn't say anything about..., oh, never mind. Now get out of here. Dinner is at five o'clock sharp, only if you go away and let me get back to work."

Jake always enjoyed unnerving Maria. Laughing, he thanked her for the good advice and gave her a hug. Turning serious, he then gave her a stern warning.

"Be careful down here this afternoon, Maria. The seas will be getting rougher in the next few hours. There's a rather large storm coming. You'll need to fasten down that pot heating on the stove with that bracket and secure everything heavy that can fall. I don't want you hurt, okay?"

After she agreed, he headed up the stairwell and paused, turning back saying, "Lynnette and I will be having dinner in my room alone tonight. Oh, one more thing. In about ten minutes, unlock the door to my stateroom." Grinning, he tossed the key on the counter and added, "If you stick your head in the doorway though, watch for flying books. She might think it's me coming back."

Jake laughed and took the stairs two at a time to the upper deck, a satisfied grin on his face.

Lynnette stormed around the room a few times, fighting the urge to break something, remembering Jake's promise of punishment if she did. How dare he toss me over his knee and spank me as if I were a child, she fumed, remembering the horrible embarrassment she had experienced. She forced the thoughts of their shared passion from her mind. I'm not his to touch that way and never want to be, she lied to herself.

"I hate him," she murmured furiously to an empty room without conviction. "He's rude and I despise him."

The fact he would treat her or any woman like that proved she could never trust him. She tried to forget how wantonly she had given herself to him just a short while later. Then an idea struck her.

Racing to the door, she turned the knob and pulled, hoping he was bluffing about locking the door. No luck. He had actually locked her in this room as if she were his prisoner. She would get even with him for this. She walked back over to the bed looking down at the rumpled sheets, recalling what had taken place there just a little while ago and felt her cheeks grow warm with the memory. Remembering what they had done and how absolutely wonderful he had made her feel was confusing. She had lost all control and he had her begging for him, she recalled miserably. He had controlled her using her own desire for him. She wasn't sure if she were more upset with him or with the weakness of her own body. She had never dreamed a man could bring her that kind of pleasure, but felt horrible about it now.

How is it he could make her body feel so feminine and hungry for him one moment and the next, so intensely angry with him that she wanted to kick him? All these conflicting emotions were unnerving her and she couldn't seem to understand her own basic feelings anymore. This guy had her so completely confused. Oh, how she wished her best friend, Barbara, were here to talk to now. Quiet, practical Barb, who always had a way of making a situation seem simple when Lynnette couldn't make a bit of sense out of it.

Lynnette took a soothing hot shower, scrubbing her body with the scented soap, using the handrails in the huge shower since it was difficult to stand upright with the increasing rocking of the boat.

Realizing she would need something to wear when she finally figured a way out of this room, which she swore to herself she would do very soon even if she had to break down the door, she walked to the closet and peered inside. Nothing of help in there. Moving unsteadily across the moving floor of the cabin and around the bed and then over to the tall dresser, she checked inside each drawer until she finally found a pair of cut-off denim jeans, which looked like they might fit if she could just find a belt to hold them up. Jake's shorts were much too large for her, but they would have to do.

She finished by rolling the ends of the same white shirt up and tying it together above the waist, since all the buttons were now missing. She slipped her soggy shoes back on her feet and began pacing around the cabin again. She had been gone from Cabo San Lucas much too long and

Todd was sure to have done something terrible to Keira by now. She prayed silently that Keira was okay.

She wondered if Todd's two partners had told him they lost her somewhere on the docks. If so, did Todd know the two were out to rip him off, as she suspected? What a mess she had made of everything. Maybe Jake was right. Maybe she did need his help. She hated admitting ever needing any man's help, but in this instance she might just have to take him up on his offer. Then again, she didn't want Jake to get hurt either.

Reverting back to her anger she reminded herself that if anyone was going to hurt Jake, it would be her. She was reminded of his high-handedness as soon as she tried to sit her slightly sore bottom down on the edge of the bed. What was she going to do? There was a storm coming and they probably couldn't turn back, even if she could convince Jake to change his course heading.

Now on top of everything else, she'd had sex with him while she was expected to marry another man, a man she had never even met. Lynnette knew if she was to be honest with herself she would have to admit she was actually falling for Jake. Sure, he made her furious and she wanted to smack him for trying to control and dominate her, but he also made her feel so..., so..., feminine, and so..., desirable. She had never known a man to make her feel even attractive, let alone pretty. Yet when Jake looked at her with those sexy blue eyes of his, she felt she would melt with desire. She had never felt like this before and it was a wonderful, yet uncomfortable feeling. He was so extremely handsome; it was hard to believe he really wanted her. Or did he?

With sudden panic, Lynnette realized this might have just been another sexual conquest for Jake and it probably meant nothing more to him than that. And here she was falling head over heels for him like some dimwitted fool, setting herself up to be hurt. What a dope you are, she thought, disgusted with herself. You actually think a guy with looks like that, who can have any girl he wants, would want you? He had left her here completely alone not long after they had been together, hadn't he? He had just used her and she had begged him to do it. Her bottom lip began to quiver as tears started to well up in her eyes. Blinking rapidly, she tried to stop the flood of tears from coming, without much success.

Looking down at the bloodstained sheets, she realized just how stupid she had been. Here she had given him her virginity and she was probably nothing more than just another notch in the belt to him. He probably wouldn't even remember her name in a month, she thought dejectedly, as the tears poured unchecked down her cheeks. She had made such a horrible mistake. Throwing herself face down on the pillow, she began sobbing uncontrollably.

Maria stood on the other side of the door ready to insert the key in the lock when she heard the sound of the girl's heart wrenching crying through the big, wooden door. Turning the key, she softly knocked and entered without waiting for a reply. Moving cautiously, she quickly crossed the swaying room. Maria sat on the edge of the bed and rubbed Lynnette's back, offering comforting words in Spanish to soothe the crying girl, not knowing whether she could be understood.

Lynnette's tears slowed as she sat up. Looking at Maria through blurred eyes, she saw the sweet face of a plump

Mexican woman with nothing but compassion and sympathy obvious in her dark brown eyes. Maria smiled and Lynnette began wiping at her tears as she tried to gather herself together.

"You just hush now," Maria consoled. "What could be all that bad? You are beautiful, and you have a most handsome man quite nuts about you."

"Nuts about me?" Lynnette shook her head in denial. "He's nuts all right, but not about me," she insisted, sniffling loudly. "He was just showing me he can get me to do whatever he wants, and I just let him. I actually wanted him to," she admitted as the tears began to flow again. With anger she added, "But, I just learned something awful about myself and I don't much like it. I'm just another loose girl without morals. Another cheap and easy female who just can't resist this guy. And here I am, supposed to marry another man in less than a month. Oh, I can't believe what I've done," she moaned as the tears poured down her cheeks.

"Oh no, don't say those things about yourself," Maria scolded. She frowned at this new information about another man. She suspected Jake knew nothing about it and she would have to find out more about that later. Looking over at the rumpled sheets, she could see the blood was the obvious cause of the girl's distress. It was clear she had never been with a man before today and she wasn't yet married. Oh my, Maria thought. She would have to distract the girl long enough to get her to stop crying to talk with her so she could find out more information.

"Now, now there," Maria consoled with her heavy Spanish accent. "I've known Jake for many years and I know him very well I think. He does feel something like love for you, even if he isn't sure yet what it is himself. Come on now, you get up and help me strip this bed and we'll have new sheets on it in no time," she insisted as a distraction, pulling Lynnette off the bed. "Then we'll talk some more, okay?" Without waiting for agreement, she continued. "Now, my name is Maria. She moved around the end of the bed and began to pull the fitted sheet off the mattress. "I do most all the cooking and cleaning on this yacht. My husband is Miguel," she continued gabbing. "He is Jake's first mate and he is a very great skipper too. Jake taught him everything he knows," Maria beamed proudly.

"I'm Lynnette Ocean and it's very nice to meet you, Maria," she smiled shyly, wiping the remaining tears away. "I'm sorry for all the tears, I do seem to be doing an awful lot of crying lately."

Lynnette did not feel any embarrassment with Maria. She found she liked her immediately and assumed Maria was wiser and more experienced than she was if she was married. She was someone she could trust and talk to as long as Maria didn't share what they discussed with Jake, but Lynnette didn't think she would. Maria seemed genuinely concerned, didn't she? Lynnette sensed she had a female ally in Maria.

She noticed the pride in Maria's voice as she talked about her husband. It was obvious Maria loved Miguel very much and was proud of him. That was the sort of relationship Lynnette had always hoped she would have with a man someday. He would be everything she ever wanted in a man, someone she could be proud of, and someone she could love with all her heart.

"You really do not know the power you hold over Jake, do you?" Maria asked Lynnette cautiously.

"Power? Over Jake?" Lynnette laughed. Then she noticed Maria was serious. "You can't be serious, Maria. What are you talking about?" Lynnette asked curiously, her innocence on the matter surprising Maria. "I don't hold any kind of power over Jake."

Maria could tell Lynnette was sincerely honest and liked her more for it. She was very different from the other women Jake had known in the past. She was honest, open and truly a sweet person who was feeling very vulnerable at the moment.

"Lynnette, I have known Jake Hunter for years now and he is a very honorable man. He might seem overpowering at first but then he is used to being in charge. Here, sit down for a minute, I will tell you something about our Jake," Maria said pointing toward the brown leather sofa.

Once they had both sat down, Maria continued in her charming accent. "When he was a young man, his parents died suddenly and he was left alone with no family except his sisters. Such a shame," Maria said, shaking her head sadly. "He became obsessed with his computer and worked at it day and night. From what I understand, he lived alone as a young man and taught himself to write on his computer, what do they call it…," Maria became frustrated at the loss of the word she was looking for.

"A program?" Lynnette offered.

"Yes, he wrote a program and started his own company with the money he earned. By the time he was seventeen years old he was supporting himself. Miguel told me that later, Jake went into the military and worked in some kind of special force where they taught him to fight. Jake has had to do some things for his country he won't even talk about to Miguel, but I know he is a very capable man. He insists on talking care of himself and those he cares most about, which now seems to include you."

Maria gave Lynnette a moment to digest this bit of information as she watched the emotions cross her face. Then she continued speaking.

"Miguel saw him in a fight one night to back up his crew in trouble and could not believe his eyes. Jake has some special way of fighting that they taught him in that Special Forces group and he is not afraid of anything, I think. But, he is also a man with many feelings that has been hurt by women in the past too. He does not trust women easily and I think you should take the time to get to know him better before you marry this other man," Maria gently suggested.

Lynnette sat there for a long while thinking about the sad story of a young boy who had become strong and forceful out of survival as she tried to understand Jake better. Humoring Maria, she said she would think about giving Jake a chance before marrying another man and then they went back to their chore.

Together they pulled the rest of the sheets off the bed and slipped on the new ones quickly, although it was easier for Maria since she was more used to the constant rocking motion beneath their feet. Lynnette doubted she could ever get used to it. She was just relieved it didn't make her feel ill enough to be sick, so far anyway.

Maria had to get back to the galley, but suggested Lynnette take a walk up to the deck to get some fresh air.

"It will make you feel better than being cramped up down here," she said with encouragement.

Lynnette was so surprised at the sheer size of the yacht as she looked around the lower level, she got lost searching for the stairs to the upper deck. Not realizing she was headed for the crew's quarters in the stern of the boat, she turned a corner in the corridor and nearly collided with the same tall blond who had helped her out of the dinghy earlier that day.

"Oh, excuse me," Lynnette said backing away nervously. "Could you tell me how to get up on deck from here. I seem to have made a wrong turn somewhere."

Lynnette did not feel at all comfortable under Eric's direct gaze. Something about him made her feel edgy. He just kept looking her body over, up and down. Turning her back on him, she decided to go back the way she had come. She would try to find Maria to ask directions.

Eric moved quickly in front of her, blocking her way.

"Wait just a minute there. What's the big hurry?" He leered down at her, standing much too close. She knew she had to get away from him. She heard voices coming from somewhere down the corridor behind her.

Instantly, the intent look on Eric's face cleared and he offered, "Come on, I'll show you the way to the upper deck. I was just on my way there anyway."

Turning, he walked away down the corridor while she followed behind, wondering if the whole thing had just been her imagination. Yes, she decided it was probably due to the recent situation last night with Todd's buddies chasing her. She was probably still just keyed up and edgy. Feeling a bit more at ease, she tried to push the thoughts from her mind.

Once up on deck, the cool wind blowing in her face cleared her head and made her stomach feel considerably better. The motion of the boat had begun making her feel a bit queasy while moving through the hallways down below deck and she much preferred to be up here where she could see where they were going. Grabbing the handrail along the edge of the deck, she worked her way carefully toward the bow. The cool wind blew her hair straight back from her face and she clung to the railing for support as the bow rhythmically hit four to five foot swells.

Eric stood there a minute staring as Lynnette headed toward the bow, his lecherous gaze taking in her long, bare legs and the soft skin of her midriff peaking out from beneath the shirt. What he wouldn't give to yank her top off her body and have his way with her, he thought with a smirk. All in good time, he thought, all in good time. Turning toward the wheelhouse, Eric went inside to deliver Miguel's message to Jake.

Looking out over the ocean, Lynnette was amazed as she noticed how quickly it had changed in appearance. It was still Sunday, but the water looked much darker now and had turned an almost grey-green color. Angry peaks of water were white capping all around them. The ocean was definitely getting rougher, she realized with definite concern now. Turning around to look out over the stern, she could see the sky getting very dark and ominous behind them, although it was only late afternoon. Her hair blew forward, covering her face so she turned back around facing the bow again, letting it blow wildly behind her. Realizing it was much rougher out here on deck than she had thought it would be, she decided to grab onto something for support.

Holding fiercely to a mainstay, she stood upright and looked out to sea, letting her mind wander over her troubles as the movement continued to toss her about. There appeared to be no way to get back to help Keira for now. The storm would certainly prevent that possibility. She would just have to hope Todd wouldn't do anything dangerous or harmful to her before Lynnette could get back to find her.

She also realized she would need Jake's help after all. This was not something she could possibly handle on her own, she now knew. She had already botched it up multiple times and it sounded, from what Maria had said, that Jake was certainly qualified and more than capable of taking care of this situation for her. She still worried about him getting hurt since Todd's friends would outnumber him, but she planned to be there to help him out.

After giving the miserable situation with her father plenty of thought, she resigned herself to the fact she would have to marry this guy Mac had chosen for her, whether or not she like it. She had spent years learning to run Mac's business and she had always worked hard to build it up so that one day she could take it over and make him proud of her. She realized she no longer cared if he was proud of her or not, but she knew the business well and she wanted it. The only way to get it was to marry a complete stranger. It was so unfair, but she knew she would have to do it anyway. The business was all she had. If she didn't do what Mac insisted, she wouldn't have the business and would have to start over when he died. It was odd, she thought, feeling both love and hatred at the same time for a parent. Her only hope was that the man Mac had chosen would not be as bad as she imagined. Maybe he would even be nice to her or even a little good looking. But she doubted it. Funny, she had not even thought to ask her father the guy's name.

Deciding it would be easier to sit on the constantly rolling deck than standing was, she lowered herself down and continued holding on to the railing. The motion was now getting more jerky and unpredictable by the minute. At least she no longer felt queasy. The strong smell of the salt air was wonderful. She never noticed Jake observing her from the cockpit in the wheelhouse.

Now that she had decided she would marry this unknown man, she knew she would have to stop anything further from ever happening with Jake. It was not going to be easy because he was irresistible and she knew her thinking wasn't clear when he was near, but she would just have to let him know how it was going to be between them from here on out. Nothing else could happen between them since she was promised to another. She hated the thought of hurting him, especially after all Maria had told her about trusting women and being hurt in the past.

She didn't regret what had happened between them, as it had been the most wonderful experience of her life. It had been beyond her wildest imaginings that a man and woman could make each other feel so wonderfully fulfilled and satisfied, but it would have to stop there. Absolutely no more kissing or touching between them. None. Her thoughts began to wander to their lovemaking and the wonderful things he had done to her.

This was certainly going to be tougher than she originally thought. Just thinking of him made her body react. It made her long for his firm body to be pressed against hers again. It would definitely be best if they were not alone together again and she would do her best not to look directly at him. That would make it much easier. She could not think straight whenever she looked into his handsomely rugged face. If he decided he did not want to help her rescue Keira from Todd, well that would be just fine too. She would just have to do it herself then.

After sitting there awhile, she awkwardly stood and began to move carefully back down the railing toward where she thought the wheel or cockpit should be in hopes of finding Jake to speak with him right away. Better to get it over with now while her thoughts on the matter were clear.

Jake had been standing at the wheel earlier, waiting impatiently for Miguel to return from the engine room with a report on the repairs to the second engine. He sure as hell didn't want to try running in this storm with only the starboard engine working.

When he first came on deck to check out the storm on the satellite, he and Miguel had both shown some concern as they looked at its growing intensity. After tuning in to the weather channel they now realized they had already issued a small craft warning. Not only had the storm grown in size, but also it was now moving faster and was still on a direct course to their current location. Had they known, they would have stayed in port another two days to avoid confronting the storm head on. You never knew about these things, though. They would not be able to outrun it as he initially hoped. They would have to ride it out unless they got lucky and it suddenly turned either inland or out to sea. He certainly hoped they had some luck.

Jake stood at the wheel, oblivious to the compass, the heading or even Eric's entrance to the wheelhouse. His attention was directed solely on Lynnette's presence out on the deck and to her hanging on carefully to the railing as she moved unsteadily toward the bow. Damn it, what in the world was she doing up on deck? It's too rough and she could easily be tossed overboard, he thought with anxious concern.

Jake's obvious preoccupation with Lynnette didn't escape Eric's notice. Eric interrupted his thoughts saying, "Miguel said to inform you that there are gonna be delays getting the port engine problem corrected. He asked me to send you down below deck right away to explain further," Eric stated, staring straight ahead, military style. "I have hundreds of hours at the helm. You can leave me at the helm without concern. I'm fully qualified," Eric stated, all businesslike now.

Jake looked Eric over, still uncertain what it was about the guy that left him doubting him. He handed over the wheel anyway, knowing the port engine was his biggest concern at the moment, other than Lynnette out on that slippery deck.

"Hold this same heading. We don't want to be too close to shore when that storm hits. Keep an eye on the satellite for any changes in the direction of the storm. I'm still hoping it will turn back out to sea before it hits."

Jake glanced once more in Lynnette's direction and saw she was safely sitting down. He then left for the engine room walking sure-footed as if he was not in the least bit affected by the motion of the rolling deck, which years at sea had taught him. Time was short and he really needed both engines working properly. He hurried down to the engine room to help Miguel get it resolved.

Lynnette continued down the swaying deck now, heading for the wheelhouse, hanging on carefully until she finally opened the door and entered. Instead of Jake though, she found Eric at the wheel.

"Oh, I thought Jake was in here. Excuse me," she said simply and turned to leave.

"No wait. I could use your help here for a minute," he smiled coldly at her.

"I can't be of much help. I haven't spent much time on boats before," she responded, turning again to leave the wheelhouse.

Eric wanted to make her stay there with him somehow. This would be a great opportunity since Jake would probably be gone a long while.

"No you would really help me out if you would just hold the wheel for a minute. It's easy. Here," he insisted. "Just take the wheel and head straight out there," he said, pointing to some undetermined point out to sea. "I need to check the satellite over there," he pointed.

Unsteadily, she crossed the room to the wheel, trying to walk straight, taking the wheel from him. He released it, suddenly and without warning since he knew she wouldn't be able to hold it by herself with the strong pulls of the wind on the sails. As he let go, the wheel began turning quickly out of control. She squealed as she struggled with it. Eric came up close behind her reaching both arms around her body to take the wheel and steady it with his strong grip.

"No, like this, Lynnette," he coaxed gently, his breath hot on her ear. "Place your hands on the wheel where mine are," he instructed her. Placing his hands firmly over hers, he told her to spread her legs further apart to steady her footing. As he stood there gazing down over her shoulder at the view of soft cleavage offered beneath her shirt, which had come loose in her struggle with the wheel. She began to realize this was a huge mistake.

Something just wasn't right. Why would Jake leave one man in the wheelhouse if it were a two-man job? She tried to pull her hands away from the wheel, but Eric had them pinned beneath his own. She began to fight, trying to get loose of his strong grip, but he held her hands firmly with his leering gaze still positioned down her loosened shirt. She was pinned and couldn't get away. Panic began to seize her.

FOURTEEN

The door crashed open and Jake stood there filling the doorway. Seeing Lynnette in Eric's arms, his eyes became dark and glaring, the look of rage on his face deadly.

"What the hell are you doing, Eric?" Jake demanded in a rage, moving across the room aggressively toward them.

"Easy now, Jake," Eric rushed out, hoping to diffuse Jake's temper. "I was just giving Lynnette a little sailing lesson, that's all," Eric tossed back. "No harm done, right Lynnette?" he asked, looking back down at her without removing his hands from over hers on the wheel.

Still struggling, she could not move away. Her hands were painfully pinned on the wheel beneath Eric's. Looking over at Jake she immediately stopped struggling, amazed once again at the sheer size of him. She felt relieved, somewhat calmed by the fact he was there to help her. Oddly, that was not at all like her, she wondered at her reaction.

"Get your hands off her now," Jake growled. "Eric, if I ever catch you touching her again, you'll seriously regret it. Got it?" Jake warned, barely controlling his anger.

Lynnette was taken back by Jake's reaction. He appeared ready to kill if the look on his face were any indication. Not wanting to be the cause of a fight or possibly even worse, she interjected hoping to avoid any real violence between the two men.

"Jake, it's alright," she tried explaining. "He was just helping me with the wheel. It was harder to hold than I..."

"Quiet, Lynnette, and don't defend him to me," Jake interrupted. His glance at her was harsh. Turning his attention back to Eric, he barked an order. "Get out on deck and help the others reef the sails. Then get down to the engine room and help them finish up that port engine repair. Now," Jake barked. Lynnette visibly flinched at his raised voice.

"Yeah, sure thing," Eric tossed back with obvious insolence. His gaze was hard and cold as he stepped away from Lynnette. Brushing roughly past Jake's shoulder, he left them alone in the room together.

The moment Eric released the wheel Lynnette was once again struggling alone with the strong pull of the wind on the sails. It was nearly impossible for her to hang onto it. Her hands ached. She just wasn't strong enough. As she stood there fighting the wheel and trying to keep her balance, Jake stood staring at the doorway Eric had just disappeared through. He was struggling to control his temper and to understand his furious reaction at seeing Eric's arms around Lynnette.

His first thought when he saw them together was to kill Eric, which he knew was completely irrational. That reaction would have been totally overdone. Eric wasn't really doing anything that terribly wrong, he argued with himself. Nonetheless, Jake realized he could not stand the thought of any other man touching her, period. It was surprising to him, the sudden strength of feelings that he had regarding her. They had grown so strong so quickly. He would have to keep them in check.

This was certainly a new experience for him. He had never felt this type of emotion for any woman before. This must be that chemistry thing other guys had tried to describe to him in the past. Not being in complete control of his own emotions didn't sit very well with him. He had always preferred being in control at all times. He would have to really work on it, he decided.

Lynnette continued struggling with the powerful pull of the wheel until she finally cried out in frustration. "Don't just stand there, Jake. I can barely hold this wheel. Could you help me out here?"

In an instant he was across the room and took the wheel from her, holding it easily with one huge arm. She noticed that his strong grip on the wheel made his arm muscles bulge and forced herself to look away. Backing away, she grabbed the ends of the shirt she wore and yanked the knot tighter.

"Stay away from that guy, Lynnette. I mean it. I think he's trouble."

"This was all your fault," she retorted in frustration. "I came up here looking for you. Where were you anyway? You were supposed to be in here."

Jake just looked down at her curiously as one eyebrow raised in question.

"It's not my fault," she defended. "He seems to be everywhere I go."

She stood there continuing to glare up at him, and rubbed her painful hands together. Keeping one eye on the horizon as he glanced down at her, he said, "Come over here, Lynnette." Jake reached out his hand toward her and drew her to him.

Helplessly, she obeyed feeling her anger quickly melting away under the warm look in his eyes. Moving next to him, she leaned against a nearby chair for support. She needed it to steady herself due to the motion of the yacht. Jake reached down and took her small hand in his, gently turning it over to assess the painful redness of her palm.

"Are you alright?" he asked concerned.

No longer did he look ready to kill, he looked tender as he pulled her hand up to his lips, softly kissing her palm. Mesmerized once again by those blue eyes, she could only nod her head in answer. She wasn't capable of speech at the moment. What a tremendous difference in his appearance now, compared to when he had been confronting Eric. Then he had been so intimidating and frightening in his anger. Some part of her was actually pleased with Jake coming to her rescue, she admitted to herself. It had made her feel protected and cared for. Maybe Maria was right. Maybe Jake did hold stronger feelings for her than she had realized.

"Why were you in here looking for me anyway?" Jake asked returning his attention to their course heading on the large compass, placing both hands on the wheel.

"I came in here to speak with you," she answered. She was trying to quickly clear her mind, which was still spinning from the feel of his lips on her palm. Sadly, she recalled what she needed to tell him.

Moving discreetly away from him she sat down sideways in the chair at the chart table. She mentally reminded herself not to look directly at him. Her desire was to be in his arms again, but she needed to maintain control in order to successfully stay away from him. She would have to keep her distance. The effect his presence had on her body seemed strong enough to shatter her strongest resolve. As for touching him? Well, that was definitely going to have to stop altogether. It kept making her weak-kneed and helpless to stop him from doing just as he pleased with her. She needed to take definite control of this situation if it were to end.

Diverting her eyes from him, she continued her thought. "When I came in here to talk to you, Eric was in here alone and said he needed my help so he could check on a computer or satellite or something. It seemed harmless to me at first, but then I realized my mistake. I couldn't get my hands loose." Continuing to keep her eyes from glancing in his direction, she added, "By the way, thanks for showing up when you did. I appreciate it."

"No problem," he answered, realizing that must have been hard for her to say. She wanted so much to be self-sufficient. It was the first time she had ever thanked him for his help. "Again, I really do want you to stay away from Eric. I'm really not sure about him yet, but think he could be trouble. I also don't want you going up on deck again until this storm passes. It's getting too rough and slippery out there and its way too dangerous. I don't want to risk losing you over the side again, even if it's not intentional," he added with a crooked grin.

Although she hated being told what to do, she noticed the concerned look on his face, taking a moment to study it more closely. He just said he didn't want to lose her. That thrilled her. She also realized the storm really had him worried and the situation was probably worse than she knew. She was getting a bad feeling about this.

"I noticed earlier when I was up on deck that the sky is getting really dark behind us. Are we in serious danger out here?" Her voice sounded frightened. She had never been in a boat at sea before today, let alone at sea in a storm.

"It may get pretty rough out here if the storm doesn't change course before it arrives," he said, making a slight course adjustment. "We're directly in its path right now, but the Ariel is a great ship. She was engineered and built to withstand tough storms like this one."

With his eyes trained on her, he could see her nervous tension building at the news. Her eyes were wide as she stared out the window, but didn't speak.

"I've been through bad weather like this before, sweetheart. Don't worry. We'll be just fine. I won't let anything happen to us," he assured with a wink, making her feel somewhat relieved.

Deciding to distract her from the upcoming danger they faced, he asked her to tell him about the problems with Todd.

Completely ignoring his question, Lynnette commented, "This really is a gorgeous boat, Jake. I've never seen anything like it before."

"Yacht," Jake corrected.

"What?"

"It's a yacht, technically. A boat is what you were hiding in last night," he explained while suppressing a chuckle at her discomfort at the reminder.

"Whatever," she waved off his explanation. She was pleased her ploy of changing the topic had worked. Not for long though. "Is there any chance the boat will sink?" she attempted another distraction. He was on to her game though.

"Yacht," he corrected again. "And, no, she won't sink. Now, how about answering my question, Lynnette?"

"I heard you. I'm getting to it," she retorted tersely. He certainly was tenacious, wasn't he?

Looking out the window at the rough, angry water, she knew she had to tell him everything about Todd, including some things about their past. She was dreading dredging up all the trouble again. She glanced up and saw he was watching her patiently while she fretted, chewing nervously on her bottom lip. She especially didn't want to tell him she was going to marry another man. One she had never met, nonetheless.

She couldn't in her right mind choose a guy she had just met a couple of days ago over inheriting the business she had spent years of her life being trained to run. There was no guarantee that a relationship with Jake would work out anyway. She was fairly well established in business and a bit of a homebody whereas he worked on boats far away from home for weeks at a time. She also knew he was probably quite the womanizer and it would be stupid to gamble on something that would probably never work out between them in the end anyway.

"Lynnette, you're stalling again," Jake stated impatiently. Lynnette took a deep breath, and then began.

"Jake, I came looking for you because I have some things to tell you." Keeping her eyes averted, she continued. "First, I'll tell you what Todd is doing and why, but this really isn't easy for me."

Looking over at her, he noticed her discomfort and gently coaxed.

"Go on, I'm listening."

"Well, as I've already told you, Todd is my stepbrother," she began, brushing her hair back from her forehead through her fingers. Over the next fifteen minutes, she relayed the entire situation with Keira and the money as Jake listened carefully. He didn't interrupt, but his face took on a dark scowl as he looked out over the darkening ocean while she revealed her past experiences with Todd. When she was done, she answered Jake's specific questions about their childhood, telling him one story after another. Each one described Todd's horribly cruel pranks that had frightened her so deeply as a young girl.

He noticed she subconsciously held her arms protectively around her body as she told him about one time that Todd, Keira and she were at the park late one winter afternoon.

"When we were little, Todd once tied Keira and me to a tree in just our shorts and tops to leave us out there in the cold for the entire night. We were scared to death of being left alone in the dark. Luckily, a nice young couple heard us crying. They untied us and drove us home."

Then she told Jake of the incidents with his friends coming to her room and how she had finally used her tennis racket as a weapon against them. When she answered his question about why her dad had never intervened, Jake was shocked and infuriated at the callousness of the man. As she finished telling him everything, she sat there, shaken and worried yet again about her little sister back in Cabo. Suddenly, she realized Jake was the first person she had ever trusted enough to share her horrible past with and sat there amazed.

Jake on the other hand was incensed. What kind of horrible father would let his little girls go through such a living hell?

"Jake, I know a lot of what I just told you happened a very long time ago, but I think it directly relates to what is going on in Cabo now. I really didn't mean to go on about my past," she added feeling a bit embarrassed. "I just thought some of the history might help explain the problem a little better."

Jake was silent. The anger building inside him toward Todd was like a quickly spreading cancer, eating away at him. He wanted revenge for the little girls who would probably never get a chance at it themselves. Jake had spent his entire childhood defending and protecting his sisters, while this jerk had tortured his own. Jake ached to get his hands on Todd. This guy was going to someday regret ever scaring Lynnette. He'd make sure of it.

Lynnette had no idea what thoughts could be forming in Jake's mind at the moment. Just looking at him now made her hope she never made him this angry. He looked ready to kill again and she was certainly glad it wasn't directed at her. He looked downright scary as he glanced over at her from across the wheelhouse. Maybe he was disgusted with her background, she thought. She dropped her eyes to the floor and then turned sideways in the chair, looking out across the angry grey sea.

Jake felt the moment she withdrew from him and noticed again that she was continually avoiding looking at him. Whenever he looked at her, she looked away. He decided to find out the reason.

"Lynnette, look at me?"

Glancing his way briefly, she looked away again. Hoping he would let it drop, she continued to stare unseeing out the window.

"Look at me," Jake stated gently.

When she didn't respond, Jake quickly set the autopilot, knowing it would only hold temporarily in these rough seas. He moved quickly across the room to where she sat. Looking up, startled by his sudden approach, she quickly looked away again. Jake held perfect balance as the cockpit rolled back and forth. Placing both hands gently on either side of her face, he raised her chin with his thumbs. Lowering his head, he looked into her deep, brown eyes. These were the beautiful exotic eyes he loved to stare into, but they were now moist with tears.

In a rich, deep voice, he said, "Honey, I'm so sorry for what Todd did to you when you were a little girl. It was terribly wrong of him and I'll get Keira away from him safely. I promise."

A tear slipped from the corner of her eye, traveling slowly down her smooth cheek. He quickly wiped it away with his thumb.

"Lynnette, I know you're worried about her, but we can't go back until this storm either passes over or changes course. It's too dangerous now. You have my word though. Todd will pay for this, one way or another. I only wish you had told me what was going on when we were still there. I could have handled it for you by now."

Dropping a sweet kiss on the corner of her mouth, he noticed the sad look still lingering in her eyes.

"What is it, honey? Something else is still bothering you." He had forgotten all about the autopilot.

"Yes, there is something else," she answered hesitantly, hating to tell him.

"What?"

"I decided that..., um. Look, what happened between us earlier was, well..., it was absolutely wonderful. I don't regret it for a minute and I never will, for as long as I live. I'll always remember."

"Yes, I feel the same way, sweetheart. I sense a 'but' coming though."

Finding it hard to find the right words, she struggled. "My father is..., I'm supposed to..., oh Jake, I cant' tell you how I hate doing this," she exclaimed in frustration, jumping up out of the chair and turning away from him as she finally blurted it out.

"Jake, I'm engaged to be married," she finally blurted out. "I didn't tell you earlier because I hadn't yet decided if I was going to go through with it, but now I realize I must. So from here on out, you and I can't let anything else physical happen between us. It just wouldn't be right. You know... since I'm engaged."

Jake felt like he had just been sucker punched in the gut. He stood there looking at her, confused and pissed off.

After a long pause to gain control of himself, he spoke.

"What in the hell do you mean you're engaged? When did this happen? What do you mean you realize you must?

What in the hell?" His questions were coming faster as her words began to sink in.

Jake raked his fingers aggressively through his hair, knowing there was no way he wanted to let her go now. He wanted her and hoped she felt the same way. Jake had now completely forgotten he had set the autopilot.

"Jake, please don't ask me any more questions," she pleaded. Turning around to face him, she grabbed the edge of the chart table behind her back to steady herself. "It can't be changed. It's just the way is has to be." Seeing his mood change once again as his eyes grew darker, she added, "Look, as I said, I don't really have a choice in the matter. That's it. If only we had met sooner...," her voice trailed off. She began to cry and covered her face with her hands.

Pushing her way past him to walk unsteadily toward the door, she attempted to leave before she started crying openly in front of him.

Jake stepped in front of her, easily blocking her way. Grabbing her shoulders, he demanded, "This is not how it has to be, Lynnette. Not if you don't want it to be. This doesn't make any sense. You do have a choice in the matter. Just don't marry him if you don't want to. It's as simple as that," he insisted as his voice grew louder.

"You don't understand, Jake," she moaned in frustration. "There's more to it than that. I have to marry him and I don't want to keep talking about it. We have to stop what we've started."

Jake released her shoulders. She couldn't keep her balance and stumbled backward grabbing the wall for support against the rocking of the ship. Towering over her, he stared down into her eyes, his pain mirroring her own.

"Do you love him?" he asked in anger, moving forward.

"What?" she stammered, leaning back against the wall.

"If you can honestly tell me you love him, I'll let you go. But I don't think you can honestly say it, can you?"

Wouldn't he be shocked to learn she not only didn't love the guy, but she didn't even know who he was, she thought grimly.

"Say it," he pressed, knowing he would come unglued if she actually did say she loved this other guy.

Looking up at this gorgeous man towering over her, she knew this would be the hardest thing she had ever had to do in her life.

Slowly, she nodded. "Yes, Jake. I do love him," she lied. "I'm getting married to him, aren't I? Please just let it go. We cant' change it."

She jumped when his fist smashed into the wall beside her.

"No, damn it! I can't just let it go and neither should you," he yelled. "Lynnette, there is obviously something between us and you're making a big mistake agreeing to marry this guy. It's obvious you can't really love him considering what just happened between us." It was at that moment he realized he was in love with her. "Besides, where the hell is he and why isn't he down here helping you?"

Lynnette stared up at him in, her mind in complete confusion. He wasn't making this any easier for her, was he? Her feelings were all jumbled up with her thoughts and she couldn't make any sense out of anything at the moment. There was no easy choice for her to make. She either had to walk away from Jake or walk away from the family business and everything she had worked for. She wanted both.

She remembered her father telling her it was already too late for her to choose a man herself, even if she did fall in love. If she were to call home now and beg him to change his mind, she knew he wouldn't. He would probably just accuse her of trying to delay his plans. Mac knew his time left was very short now and was really pushing this on her. No, it was no use getting her hopes up now. It was too late for her and Jake. Why couldn't they have just met sooner?

"Oh, Jake," she said faintly. Looking up at him, her heart beat wildly in her chest. She desired him so much, but was terribly conflicted. "We can't continue...," she began. Suddenly he reached out and scooped her into his arms, pulling her to him with such force it nearly pushed the air from her body. Grabbing her around the waist with one arm, he backed her up against the wall to steady himself as his other hand gently cupped the back of her head. She felt herself getting weak and her resolve was quickly disappearing. Leaning down, he covered her lips with his own. The mouth that took hers was aggressive and hungry. It felt as though he were taking out his anger in the kiss.

Just then the yacht jerked hard to the port side, throwing both of them sprawling to the floor. A loud booming crash sounded just outside the wheelhouse. Jake cursed and looked up to see the wheel spinning wildly out of control.

FIFTEEN

"Shit!" Jake hollered. Springing to his feet he raced toward the spinning wheel at the helm.

Lynnette could feel the yacht tossing back and fourth out of control in the rough water, throwing her sprawling back and forth across the floor. She couldn't gain her footing to stand and wondered how Jake had made it look so easy to get to the other side of the wheelhouse so quickly. The motion was jerking her around like a rag doll.

"Damn it, that was stupid of me," he loudly cursed himself. He had been so distracted by Lynnette that he hadn't even been thinking of the potential danger he was placing his crew and the yacht in.

As Jake spun the wheel around correcting the course heading, there was a loud slap as the huge sails above them quickly filled with air again. The room once again assumed a steady, although crooked angle beneath them.

Lynnette finally gained her footing and leaned against the wall for support. Just then, Miguel burst through the doorway with a worried look on his face. His eyes narrowed as they darted from Jake to Lynnette, then back to Jake again.

"What just happened?" Miguel asked nervously. He could see Jake looked mad as hell and he didn't want that anger directed at him. He tried not to provoke him.

"Damn it! I had the autopilot set and knew it wouldn't hold in this weather. The water is just too damned rough out here. It was stupid of me to try it," Jake answered brusquely, still angry with himself.

A knowing grin slowly spread across Miguel's face as he realized the cause of Jake's distraction. Glancing over at Lynnette, he smiled at her with a knowing look in his eye. Quietly, he said, "If you two really needed time together, you should have asked me to take the wheel. I would have understood," he taunted.

Turning a frown on Miguel, Jake introduced the two of them.

"It's a pleasure to meet you," Lynnette said politely. "I've already met and spoken with your wife this afternoon. I like her, she's very nice."

"It is my pleasure to meet you, Senorita." Oddly, Miguel's accent sounded thicker than usual to Jake. "It is such an honor to finally meet a beautiful woman that can distract this man from his magnificent yacht," Miguel grinned. Jake frowned. Lynnette's face flushed at the compliment, not catching the fact Miguel had just referred to the yacht as Jake's.

Jake noticed though. He grunted, interrupting them with a harsh voice.

"Miguel, I need an immediate count of the crew. If someone was up on deck when the wheel let go, they could have easily been caught off-guard and thrown overboard. It'll be dark within half an hour and if anyone is in the water we'll never find them then, so let's get on it."

"Good point, boss. I'll do it now," Miguel responded with all seriousness and quickly left the wheelhouse.

Lynnette walked unsteadily back to the chart table feeling terribly guilty. If only she had not come in here to talk to Jake, this would have never happened. She should have waited until later to talk to him, when he wasn't working. What if someone had been thrown overboard? Then she thought, with a panic, if someone had fallen overboard and drowned, it would be all her fault. Looking over at Jake, she saw the raw look of concern on his face as he leaned forward to look up at the mast and sails through the glass. He needed to ensure everything was alright with the rigging.

Quietly, she said, "Jake, I'm really sorry. I should never have come in here. I distracted you. This is all my fault and I'm so sorry."

Miguel burst back in the door stating, "Matthew's missing. I have everyone else looking for him now but no one knew where he was at the time it happened."

"Damn it," Jake swore. "Is anyone hurt?" he asked harshly.

"No, everyone's fine. Maria had some trouble in the galley though. She's going to have to do some clean up and then start dinner over again," Miguel answered.

Just then Eric walked in. "We found Matt," he announced. "He was just in the head taking a lea...," he stopped short, noticing Lynnette. She quickly looked away.

"Good," Jake replied, relieved everyone was accounted for again. He noticed the silent exchange between Eric and Lynnette, observing her becoming noticeably uncomfortable in his presence. He decided to keep a closer eye on the guy.

"Miguel," Jake said, "take Lynnette down to help Maria out with dinner. Get yourself something to eat and then rest up for a few hours. I'll need you to take the nine to one shift, and then I'll take it from one o'clock until dawn. The worst of the storm should hit after one in the morning." Turning his attention to Eric, he asked, "What progress have you guys made on that port engine?"

As Miguel led Lynnette out of the wheelhouse, she looked over at Jake, noticing he never even glanced her way as she left. Was he really that angry with her? She had apologized, hadn't she? He seemed intent on hearing whatever Eric was telling him. Feeling dejected, she silently followed Miguel below deck.

Jake could feel Lynnette's eyes boring into him as she left the room. Although it had been his mistake, he had put everything and everyone else at risk because of her. He knew it was best to keep his distance from her for a while. At least until after the storm was past them. He did not need any more distractions and she was one hell of a distraction to him. Whenever she was around, he couldn't keep his mind off her. Mistakes out here could be deadly though. He needed to give their safety his complete and undivided attention now.

Jake issued orders to the crew to reef the main sail again and drop the headsail completely. The winds were getting too strong now. He told the men to take turns heading below deck for dinner in shifts. He wanted two guys up on deck at all times in case of any trouble. He was just asking one of them to bring him back a quick bite when a ship-to-shore call came through from his uncle.

"Hey, Uncle Elliot. It's good to hear from you," Jake said with sincere enthusiasm. He motioned for Eric to take the wheel from him. "You sure picked a fine time to call though. We're about to ride out a major storm down here off the tip of Baja." Jake moved around the chart table to sit down.

"Jake, are you sure you're okay down there?" Elliot asked with real concern in his voice. "I saw the storm on the Sunday news just this afternoon and it looks rough. Do you need me to send you help?"

"Oh, no. We'll be just fine. Don't worry yourself," Jake assured. He was well aware that his uncle actually had the international contacts to get the Coast Guard dispatched to assist if he said he really needed them.

There was no man in this world Jake loved and respected as much as his Uncle Elliot. Following those difficult years after Jake's parents died, his uncle had been there for him whenever he needed a mentor or some good advice. Elliot had always offered Jake guidance and was his male role model during his youth. His Uncle Elliot had taken special interest in Jake as no one else could. Elliot was the one person responsible for Jake's high confidence level, his strength of personality and most of all, his ability to trust and love those closest to him. He loved his uncle like a son loves his father.

"You're sure you don't need some assistance out there, son?" Elliot pressed.

"No cause to worry," Jake reassured his uncle. "I've been in storms like this one before and this new yacht I picked up is outstanding. It'll handle this storm just fine."

"Very well then, but please just report in with me when it's over, okay? I need to know you're alright."

"You got it. So, how the hell are you anyway? Seems we haven't talked in weeks," Jake inquired.

"Oh, I'm just fine boy, just fine." After an uncomfortable pause, he continued hesitantly.

"So, Jake, I know you've got your hands full at the moment and this is a really bad time to bring this up, I need to pull in that favor you promised me years ago. Never thought I would do it and I really hate to ask this of you, but I'm afraid I must," he warned.

Jake laughed into the phone. "Hey, you trying to talk me out of it before you even tell me what it is?"

"Yeah, it must sound like that to you," Elliot smiled uncomfortably.

Jake kept one eye on the heading and the other on Eric at the wheel. He was doing fine, but there was just something about this guy he disliked.

"So, you're finally going to let me pay off my enormous debt to you, huh?" Jake continued. "I thought you'd never give me the opportunity."

"Now Jake, this is nothing to take lightly," he answered, sounding very serious. "It's a hell of a request I'm about to ask of you."

"You know I owe you my life. Hey, if it wasn't for you, where would I be now?" he asked not really expecting an answer. "Just tell me what you need me to do and I'll take care of it."

As Elliot began to explain his strange request, Jake's expression hardened. He couldn't believe it. His uncle actually wanted him to marry his friend's daughter? And this just so she could inherit her family's business and avoid being written out of his will? It sounded crazy.

"That's nuts!" Jake exclaimed. "What kind of father would do something like that to his daughter? This is outrageous."

"I know and it's a long story, Jake, but know this. She is a sweet girl, she's smart and she is absolutely beautiful. She is beautiful both inside and out." He hoped to spark some slight interest in Jake. "Trust me on this and please just consider coming over to meet her in person," Elliot concluded.

Jake could not believe his ears. He had finally met a woman he really wanted to be with and his uncle wanted him to marry someone else. What a cruel twist of fate. What in the hell was he supposed to tell his uncle? He had promised to do whatever was asked of him years ago, hadn't he? No matter what the request was, he owed it to his uncle. He had given his word. Damn it. There had to be a solution without letting his uncle down. He tried reasoning with him.

"You can't really be serious, can you? You're asking me to marry a woman I've never met and you think that's acceptable? Look, think about it if things were reversed and you were in my shoes. Wouldn't you resist a request like this too? Please, Uncle, ask anything else of me, but not to get married. I'll do anything else for you, man. Just name it."

Elliot felt more uncomfortable by the moment. It was pure hell asking Jake to honor his word with such an outrageous request, but knew he had to do it. It was Mac's dying wish and in Elliot's heart he really thought the two kids would be perfect together.

"Who is this friend of yours anyway?" Jake asked, trying to keep the misery he now felt out of his voice. "This is a hell of a favor you're doing for him." Jake was curious to know who could get Elliot to actually ask something like this of him. Elliot obviously knew how serious this particular request was and seemed uncomfortable asking him.

"You may not remember my friend, Mac Ocean, but you met at a couple of my social gatherings in Newport Beach years ago," Elliot answered. "Well, he's dying of cancer now and it's his daughter, Lynnette, that you're being asked to marry. I've known her since she was a little girl and I love her as if she were my own daughter, Jake. She's a wonderful girl and I know you'll love her."

Jake couldn't speak. He sat there frozen in the cockpit chair staring unseeingly past the deck of the yacht and the white-capped seas. All thoughts of the approaching storm were forgotten for the moment. The phone lay limp in his hand. His thoughts were racing ahead of Elliot's conversation. Could it really be the same Lynnette? It had to be. What a coincidence. He had to think. He needed to make sense of it. If he was just now being asked to marry her, she didn't yet know whom she was engaged to. Jake's mind raced. And here he had thought she had cheated on her fiancé by being with him. She didn't even know who her fiancé was yet. It's not really considered cheating if you don't know whom you are cheating on. That's odd though. She had told him she loved the guy. Then it dawned on him what she had done. She had lied about that part, probably trying to make it easier to break it off with him. The irony was incredible. In reality, she had already met her fiancé, Jake realized in disbelief. She just didn't know it yet.

Jake quickly decided he couldn't tell his Uncle Elliot that he already knew Lynnette. If Mac ever found out he'd slept with his daughter, he would want to kill him or worse. No, Jake decided. He needed more time to think it thru. This was an incredible coincidence. Elliot and Mac couldn't know about his relationship with Lynnette until he figured out how to handle the situation. He now recalled meeting Mac years ago and remembered just how intimidating and irritating the man could be, even to a man like Jake.

How a father could even threaten to write a child out of his will, especially a daughter as sweet and kind as Lynnette, was beyond him. Not only had Lynnette dealt with being raised by a callous, overbearing father, she had also grown up with a horribly evil stepbrother with no good example of a mother figure at all. It tore at his heart to know the pain she must have gone through in her childhood. He had always thought he had it tough losing his parents when in reality; Lynnette had lived through much worse by still having hers. He intended to make it up to her somehow. He didn't know how, but he knew he would forever try.

"Jake? Jake, you still there?" Elliot asked into the static on the line.

"Yes, I'm right here. I was just thinking, that's all," Jake answered quickly, raising the phone back to his ear. "When is all this supposed to take place anyway?" he asked.

"The engagement party is set for a week from Friday night. That's where you're supposed to meet for the first time. Will you be back in town by then?" Elliot asked, sounding relieved Jake seemed to be going along with the plan so far.

"Barely, but don't worry. I'll be there. I said I'd do anything for you, Uncle Elliot, and I meant it."

"I know this is asking a lot from a confirmed bachelor with women waiting in the wings. I really do appreciate it, son. And I think someday, you'll be thanking me. She's a terrific woman."

"Don't mention it," Jake replied. "I do have a couple questions though. Has his daughter agreed to marry a guy she's never met? And if so, why?

"Jake, the honest truth is, she doesn't think she has another option. She runs his business and has worked hard for years to build it up to what it is today. Her father has given her an ultimatum. It's a terribly sad truth, especially for such a lovely girl. I've openly disagreed with Mac on the matter, but he just won't budge. He wants her married before the cancer takes him," Elliot finished with a heavy sigh. "Again, I really do appreciate this, Jake."

They agreed to make contact as soon as Jake arrived back home. Finishing up their conversation, they said their good-byes. Jake hung up heavy in thought. He was going to have to spend some time thinking about the situation. It looked like Lynnette was unknowingly going to marry him one way or the other. The fact that he was already beginning to think of her as his future wife was amazing, but he knew he didn't want to be forced on her by her father. He much preferred she choose to marry him. How could Lynnette's father be such an ass? Somehow, he would need to get her to defy her father and agree to marry him by her own choice. Jake concluded that was the only way he wanted Lynnette to be with him. Not by force, but by her own choice. Jake walked across the wheelhouse and took the wheel back from Eric.

Later, after dinner had been served to the crew and everything was cleaned up, Lynnette quietly entered Jake's stateroom. She was let down that they didn't get to have dinner together in his room tonight and was disappointed to find the room still empty. She had hoped and expected him to be in bed sleeping since she heard him say he would be taking the one o'clock shift. Surely he would need to sleep sometime before that. Maybe he had decided not to use his own room since she was there and he was still mad at her for the incident earlier in the day. He had seemed so upset with her after the accident, but she had apologized and no one was hurt. Surely he wasn't still blaming her for the accident was he? As she remembered, she had tried at one point to leave the wheelhouse and he had blocked her way.

She felt uncomfortable and unwelcome in his room but assumed this was where she was supposed to sleep for the night since this was the only stateroom she had ever been in. On the other hand, she had told him they couldn't continue their relationship, physically anyhow, so maybe he was sleeping elsewhere. That was dumb of him, she thought. This was his room and there was a perfectly good couch right there for her to sleep on. Surely she wouldn't disturb him if he wanted to sleep in the bed.

Being honest with herself though, she knew she just wanted him here because she missed him. That and the fact she felt safer when he was around. She wasn't about to let him know that though. If he were here she probably would disturb him just like she had in the wheelhouse earlier. She didn't necessarily mean to, but nonetheless it wasn't likely he would get any sleep at all with her around.

Finding one of Jake's oversized t-shirts in his dresser to sleep in, she washed up in the head, found an extra blanket in the closet and pulled a pillow off the bed. She decided to leave the bed empty for him to sleep in, just in case he did come in later that night. Curling up on the couch, she lay her head down on the pillow. Breathing in his scent deeply, she hugged his pillow closer to her body. Closing her eyes, she let her thoughts wander to the handsome man she would miss so much when this trip was finally over.

Lying there, she thought back over the evening. Due to the accident, their Sunday night dinner had started out to be a bit of a fiasco but thanks to Maria's talents it had turned out fine in the end. After helping Maria clean up the food that dumped all over the galley floor when the autopilot broke loose, they had quickly gone about preparing another tasty meal. There hadn't been much time for conversation and it was just as well. Lynnette didn't feel much like talking anyway. She was too depressed.

Maria asked Lynnette to peel the potatoes, instructing her to cut them up into tiny pieces in order to cook faster. Dinner was already late and she had to make up time. Rough water on an empty stomach was a bad thing, so Maria had ended up serving seasoned ground beef with hot bread, mashed potatoes and gravy. She always had dessert for the crew and tonight she had baked a nice fruit pie, served with a scoop of ice cream on the side.

Lynnette had figured Jake would come down to dinner at some point during the evening like everyone else onboard. Each time another one of the crewmen walked into the dining room, Maria noticed Lynnette anxiously look up, then look away. She obviously was hoping it was Jake.

He never showed up. Just seeing him standing there in the room would have lightened her black mood, even if he were still mad at her.

Lynnette hadn't had much of an appetite, despite Maria's comment that she was too thin and must eat. The thought of Jake being upset with her had her feeling down and she couldn't eat. That and the knowledge that they would never get a chance to develop a relationship together saddened her. Maria tried to get her to talk about what had happened to upset her so much, but Lynnette just said she wanted to go lie down.

After several miserable hours of lying there in the dark, Lynnette finally drifted off to sleep.

Without warning, Lynnette's head hit the edge of the coffee table as she was thrown from the couch onto the floor and rudely awakened from a sound sleep. No sooner had she landed on the floor, the room then tilted the other way, sending her rolling backward into the base of the cold leather couch. Once again, she was thrown back against the coffee table, smashing her shoulder against the leg. Terrified, she knew she had to get out from between the two pieces of furniture immediately before being beaten to death. While trying to protect her head, she raised herself up on all fours and crawled out to the center of the dark room. She remembered Jake telling her all the furniture was fastened down so she hoped there wasn't much of a chance anything big would come crashing into her.

It was pitch dark in the stateroom and she couldn't see the smaller objects being thrown across the room at her.

Waiting momentarily with her breath held, she was relieved to notice most everything seemed to be on the floor now so it wasn't likely she would be struck in the head, although the yacht was being tossed violently back and forth in the water. Crouching there alone on the floor, she could hear the eerie creaking and groaning of the wood as the large yacht was twisted by the storm's waves.

She supposed it was probably well after midnight by now and this must be the worst of it. Jake had mentioned the storm would hit them after one o'clock in the morning, though this was much worse than she had ever imagined. She was suddenly tossed onto her side, sliding across the floor. She prayed the boat would not break into pieces under the constant strain of the angry seas.

Figuring the bed would be the softest and safest place for her to be for the remainder of the storm, she crawled on hands and knees across the floor until she found the base of it. Standing carefully, she fell sprawled across the bed as the next wave hit the hull from behind her.

The bed was softer than the floor, but she found it was no easier to stay on than the couch had been. Scooting over to the edge against the far wall, she tried to brace herself to keep from rolling back and forth. She continued to hit the wall next to the bed with her side. Her shoulder still ached from where she had hit the coffee table, so she placed the pillows between herself and the wall to cushion the blows. She couldn't remember being this scared before in her entire life.

Lynnette lay there alone in the dark for hours, terrified for herself and for everyone else onboard. She prayed for all of their safety. She felt knots in her stomach each time the boat rose up on a swell, only to then come crashing back down into a trough. Each time the water pounded loudly against the hull, it threatened to unnerve her completely. She heard strange noises throughout the night and hoped the boat was not cracked and leaking. What if it snapped in two and she was down beneath deck, trapped? She worried that maybe she should try to find her way up on deck to locate a life jacket. Then again, she remembered Jake said it was very easy to be thrown overboard. She probably couldn't find her way up there in the dark anyway. So she continued lying there crying, scared for hours, getting more and more frantic each time another huge swell hit the yacht. Finally, after what felt like an eternity, she began to see the faint light of a new day dawning through the window across the room.

Hours later, after the storm had begun to quiet down, Lynnette was roused from a wonderful dream she had been having of a very tall, handsome man whose face she could not quite make out in the thick mist. By the way the dream had left her feeling though, she was well aware whom it had been she was dreaming of just then.

Suddenly, she realized it had been the light touch of a hand on her body that had awakened her from her deep slumber.

"Jake, I was hoping you would come to...," stopping short when she finally opened her eyes she realized it wasn't Jake. There was Eric standing above her, leering down at her. In the dim light from the window she could see the crazed look of hunger in his eyes. Fear overcame her.

As she tried to sit up, Eric pushed her back down as she began kicking and hitting him as hard as she could. She screamed for him to get out. Backhanding her brutally across the face, she fell back against the bed in shock that he had actually struck her. She had no idea whether or not anyone could even hear her scream from up on deck.

"Don't be such a prude, you bitch. Why should Jake have all the fun?"

She realized, with regret, she had not locked the door in hopes that Jake would come in sometime during the night. She never imagined Eric would intrude in Jake's stateroom, especially after Jake's recent threat.

Eric's leering gaze took in her entire body, as she lay there in front of him, wearing only a thin t-shirt that had now ridden up around her hips in the struggle. Feeling a lust he could not control, Eric was unable to stop himself as he reached out to touch her. Lynnette screamed at the top of her lungs as she smacked him in the side of the head with her closed fist.

Just then, the door burst open banging hard against the wall as Jake stormed across the stateroom and grabbed Eric by the neck. He pulled Eric across the room, slamming him hard against the far wall. Miguel ran into the room. He quickly took in the situation noting Jake holding Eric against the wall with both fists with Eric's feet several inches off the ground. He then spotted Lynnette across the room in the bed against the far wall looking wide-eyed and horribly frightened.

Jake growled, "Miguel, get her out of here. Now!"

Miguel grabbed the blanket and helped Lynnette down out of the bed as he carefully covered her body.

"No, Jake," Lynnette said, "I don't want to leave you with…"

"Now!" Jake yelled between clenched teeth.

"Come on, Lynnette," Miguel said, guiding her firmly out of the stateroom. "I'll take you to Maria."

Lynette turned back in time to see Jake kick the door shut with one foot. She allowed Miguel to lead her away, wondering what was about to happen back in the stateroom.

"What the hell do you think you're doing?" Jake demanded of Eric.

Eric cringed, cowering from the wrath of Jake. "I didn't mean anything by it, man. Why are you getting so pissed off?"

"I'll tell you one last time, you little shit. Don't get anywhere near her again or you'll seriously regret it. Got it!" Jake yelled.

"Yeah, yeah, I got it. Didn't know you had such a thing for the bitch." Eric mistakenly blurted out.

Just as Jake's fist connected squarely with Eric's jaw, Miguel raced back into the room. Eric crumpled in a heap on the floor. Jake reached down hauling him up by the collar to take a second punch just as Miguel stepped in to stop him.

"Hey, Jake. No," he reasoned with him. "Don't do it. I can see that look in your eyes and this jerk just isn't worth it. Let me get him out of here and you can cool down. Okay?"

Eric moaned half unconscious. Jake stared down at Eric a moment, then let go of his collar dropping him to the floor.

"Don't ever call her a bitch again, you little bastard," Jake ordered and then stormed out of his stateroom.

SIXTEEN

Late Monday morning Lynnette and Jake shared breakfast together up on cool deck. The storm had passed and they sat outside in the bright morning sunshine at a large dining table located directly behind the wheelhouse, which also served to block them from the wind. The seas were much calmer now and Lynnette thought it was an absolutely beautiful day. The winds were light, there were seagulls and pelicans flying peacefully overhead, and she could once again see the shoreline of Baja, Mexico. Only now, it was on the other side of the yacht. Jake had obviously turned Ariel around and they were now headed back to Cabo San Lucas.

"So, what did you end up doing with Eric last night?" she asked taking a small bite of toast.

Jake looked at her, the light breeze blowing her long, dark hair back over her shoulders, exposing the light pink bruise on her cheek where Eric had smacked her. The thought brought a scowl to his face. Taking a deep breath, Jake looked out to sea and controlled his temper. After a short while, he once again looked at her with his face now relaxed as he smiled.

"Well, I considered throwing his ass overboard," he joked, "but Miguel talked me out of it. So instead, I shackled his arms and legs to a wall in the hot engine room until we reach shore."

Laughing, she said, "No, I'm serious. What did you do with him?"

Little did she know the strength of character it took for Jake to avoid crippling Eric last night after hearing her screaming. The scene he'd witnessed when he busted into his stateroom was almost enough to make him lose it. He had been trained not to ever lose control and he knew he needed to keep a check on himself. He had come close to letting himself go due to the intense anger he felt and intended to give that further consideration when time allowed.

"We did lock him up, but only in a small room where the mechanic usually sleeps. The mechanic has been moved to the main crew's quarters until we reach the harbor. Eric obviously can't be trusted to wander about the yacht with you onboard."

Lynnette took a long sip of the deliciously hot coffee from the thick, steaming mug.

"Jake, I noticed you've already turned the boat around. Thank you," she smiled sweetly. Their eyes connected for a moment, then she quickly looked down at her plate and took a small bite of eggs.

"Yacht," he corrected her patiently yet again.

"Hmm?" she mumbled taking a bite off the corner of her toast.

"Technically, this is a yacht, Lynnette. Not a boat," he explained yet again with a grin. If he had told her once, he'd told her a dozen times. Would she ever remember?

"Whatever," she answered absently as she swallowed. She found herself completely distracted, watching him while he ate his breakfast. She liked to observe him, especially when he was preoccupied with something else and wasn't noticing her. His dark, wavy hair blew freely around his suntanned face. The morning sun reflected in his dark blue eyes. He looked up at her suddenly and then smiled when he caught her watching him so intently. Her insides melted when he smiled at her the way he was doing right now. He was so masculine and protective, yet sensitive and concerned for others too. He also had a great sense of humor. Oh, how she wished they...

With a heavy sign, she realized she was just wasting her time wishing for something that just couldn't be. Not now, not ever. She had made her decision to marry the guy her father had chosen and she must stick with that decision. She had always wanted to inherit and run the educational aspect of the family's businesses and had great ideas of expanding the private schools, establishing teacher training centers and opening a chain of school supply locations. She had planned to present the business plan she had prepared next month until this new situation came up. Walking away from what she had built up and had positioned for such potential growth just wasn't an option. She might end up in a loveless marriage, but she would be productive and fulfilled in her work.

Determined to keep things friendly with Jake this morning, yet uncomplicated, she asked him, "How did you get into sailing anyway?"

Jake swallowed the last of his breakfast and pushed his empty plate away. Sitting back in his chair, he took a slow sip of coffee and looked straight at her. She wished her stomach would stop fluttering every time their eyes met.

"When I was a little boy in Chicago, my uncle bought me a little Sabot, which is a small sailboat. I'd sail it all over the lake we lived near. Whenever I visited him in California, he'd charter a sailboat for the weekend and we'd take off for Catalina Island. I've always loved sailing, even back then. We used to watch all those old swashbuckling pirate movies and I knew even then I wanted to be out on the sea. Sure, sailing is not the same today as depicted in those old movies, but that's what got me started anyway. Then in high school, I worked as crew with a group of my buddies. We would fly to Hawaii in the summer to sail someone's yacht home. We had a great time and I got weeks of open ocean experience," he finished. Sliding his chair closer to hers, he placed his arm over the back of her seat.

Enjoying his closeness, yet uncomfortable with it at the same time, she slid further away from him.

"Sounds like you had a fun childhood. I kind of wish I had spent more time playing instead of being so serious all the time. Even as a little girl I was that way." Looking up at the huge sails full of wind, she sighed.

"Sailing looks so peaceful," she commented. "I've always loved looking out at the ocean to watch the sailboats. They're so calming." Grinning she looked over at him. His eyes were studying her face intently.

"There's this one special place on a cliff overlooking the mouth of the harbor where I go sometimes when things are bothering me and I just sit there, looking out at the sailboats for hours. It always makes me feel so much better."

Jake realized just how many things in this beautiful woman's life must have bothered her. She had likely spent many hours over the years sitting on that cliff above the ocean. He knew she hadn't had it as easy as some people might think, being raised under Mac's controlling thumb.

Lynnette found herself staring at Jake's mouth. Unable to stop herself, she slowly raised her hand to his chin to gently outline the thin white scar with her finger. "How did you get this scar, Jake?" she asked, slowly stroking his chin with her soft fingertips.

"Do you find it ugly?"

"Oh no," she answered too quickly and then smiled as color flooded her cheeks. "What I mean to say is that it makes you look sort of…, well, you look kind of ruggedly dangerous. It somewhat reminds me of a pirate," she finished grinning up at him, unaware she was still touching his face. He held himself carefully in check knowing he would scare her off if he made any move just now.

"So, how did you get it?" she repeated.

Enjoying her uninhibited touch immensely, he answered. "In a bar fight."

"Why were you fighting?"

"A woman," he replied.

"What happened?" She dropped her hand back in her lap, not liking the thought of Jake fighting a guy over another woman.

If he had to guess based on her body language, she was experiencing a little taste of jealousy. It was just fine with him. It was a good sign as far as he was concerned and hoped it said a bit about her growing feelings toward him.

Lynnette realized she was going to have to dig the story out of him. Growing impatient, she coaxed him. "But, why were you fighting over a woman?"

With a heavy sigh, he knew she wasn't going to let up on him until he told her the entire story. Choosing the shortened version, he explained.

"I wasn't fighting over a woman. It was more like fighting for a woman. It's different. Back in college I was dating a girl named Carrie who happened to be a huge flirt with every guy in sight. I was either naïve or stupid to think she was into only me. One night she and I were in a bar. A guy got a bit overly excited by her flirtation so I ended up stepping in to help her out of trouble."

"Oh," Lynnette simply stated with raised eyebrows. She thought about it awhile and then asked, "Was she worth it?"

"No. We broke up the next morning. I protected her knowing I was going to break it off simply because she needed my help. As a girl, she wouldn't have been able to fend off this guy, even though she was the one asking for trouble by flirting with him in the first place. Regardless, he should have backed off when she said no."

They sat in companionable silence for a while looking out to sea, each one savoring their quiet time together. The sun sparkled off the beautiful blue water all around them. The breeze was light and refreshing on their skin. Reaching over, he lightly brushed the backs of his fingers down her neck, then her shoulder.

"Have you ever been sailing before?" he asked casually.

"Hmm?" she mumbled, her eyes closing as she felt his fingers gently stroking her skin.

Looking over at the dreamy look on her face, he grinned knowing she was just as lost in their circumstances as he was. Although she had said it was over between them, she seemed to have forgotten that fact, at least for the moment. Neither of them could resist the other and he knew it. She was only fooling herself. If she was melting now at just the touch of his fingers, he was thrilled to think what he could make her feel again using his entire body.

She felt him taking her shoulder in his hand and he began pulling her closer for a kiss. Finally, she came to her senses and pulled back. She scooted away from him with one hand pushing firmly against his chest.

"Jake, no. We can't," she stated sternly. "I said we have to stop this from happening between us and I meant it. It's wrong. If you want, we can be friends, but we can't continue with anything physical. Now that I've decided I'm engaged, we can't go there. I am not a cheat. It just wouldn't be fair to him."

This was nuts, Jake realized. He was in competition for her against himself and she didn't know it. He acknowledged it would never be the same to be with her if she had been forced. Damn, this was frustrating. He had to make her want him before she found out he was the one being forced on her. Time was short and he was going to have to move quickly, yet carefully. Leveling his look at her, he replied more aggressively than he intended.

"Lynnette, I don't want to be just friends and I'm not giving up. We haven't even had enough time together yet to know if what we're both feeling towards each other is real. I'm thinking it is, but we have to give ourselves time to find out. I don't really give a damn about what's fair to this other guy or not."

They sat staring at one another. She raised her stubborn chin and he could see the determination on her face.

Upset, he tried reasoning with her. "Look, you say you're getting married in less than two weeks, right?"

Her eyes narrowed in suspicion.

"How did you know that?" she questioned. "I never mentioned when I was supposed to marry."

"I thought you told me earlier," he answered quickly, mentally kicking himself for the slip up. It was Uncle Elliot who had given him the timetable. He rarely made such a blunder when he was working under cover. Then again, he had never been emotionally connected while on assignment. Rushing on, he continued.

"Look, let's just focus on getting your sister back for now. We don't have to resolve anything between us. Things have a way of working themselves out."

Jake reached for her, his fingers tangling in her hair as he wrapped his hand around the back of her neck pulling her closer. His lips brushed lightly across hers in more of a caress than a kiss. Her breath escaped in a small whimper.

"Come on, Lynnette, you know you want me as badly as I want you," his deep voice accused. Pulling back, his deep blue eyes delved into hers for an answer. She admitted to herself he was right. She did want him. He was making this very difficult and her resolve was quickly slipping away. She honestly wanted to be his.

It was then that the reality of all that she would be giving up hit her like a wave. She closed her eyes. She had to do it. She had to give him up. Fighting off the urge to cry, she slowly opened her eyes and pulled away. Getting up, she rushed to the edge of the deck and held the rail for support. Looking out toward the coastline, a tear slipped down her cheek as she tried to gain control of her thoughts.

She had known that being near him this morning would be tempting, but she didn't anticipate being so overwhelmed. She wanted him to touch her body again the way he had the other night down in the stateroom. Was she that weak? True, what she and Jake felt for each other was very strong, but she would not be a cheat. Or rather continue to be a cheat, she acknowledged. She thought she had made that very clear to him. It would be considered cheating on her new husband even if they hadn't yet met because of the fact she had definitely decided to marry him. That alone should stop her from having anything further to do with Jake. No, she corrected, it would stop her.

What if Jake was the right man for her though? What if she walked away from him without ever finding out? She might regret this decision for the rest of her life. Her thoughts were churning around in her head and she was in complete turmoil.

Jake silently approached her from behind as she stood at the rail. She sensed his presence, rather than heard his approach. Turning, she faced him.

"Fine, I admit it. I do want you, Jake, but that doesn't make it right. I'm engaged to another man and I just won't betray my fiancé. Put yourself in his position. If he were you, you wouldn't find it alright, would you?"

He ground his teeth in frustration. I am he, Jake thought, his mind screaming the words he couldn't say aloud. What an impossible position he found himself in. Damn it!

"Alright. I'll give you that one. I wouldn't like it."

She looked away. Was she doing the right thing though? Would if feel so right if it were truly wrong? This was so difficult. She looked down feeling dejected.

Jake softly took her face in his hands, forcing her to look up at him. "It pleases me to know you wouldn't cheat on me or any man you're with for that matter. That's a wonderful trait in a woman. Just promise me you'll keep an open mind about our relationship, Lynnette. Although you've given your word to your father, that doesn't mean it's written in stone. This entire idea of a prearranged marriage is ridiculous anyway. What your father is forcing on you is wrong and maybe he'll come to realize it and change his mind. People change their minds all the time."

"Not my father," she said. Knowing they had to move past this impasse, she agreed.

"Okay. Friends?" she asked.

"Friends," he conceded, but only for now. They would be a lot more than that, he knew.

SEVENTEEN

Lightening the mood, Jake bent down and kissed Lynnette soundly on the lips with a loud slap to her bottom. Squealing, she punched him in the arm.

Laughing, he asked if she wanted to learn how to sail. Willing and eager to learn, she spent the entire day with Jake, either watching the crew work the rigging or helping to pull on the sheets. She helped pull in the headsail as they came about, changing their tack. He carefully instructed her on trimming the sails, choosing a course or holding a heading while steering until her arm muscles literally ached. She loved every minute of the day as he taught her. She recalled how it felt each time his arms reached around her as they cranked in the main sheet together or as he stood beside her while she turned the wheel, changing their course heading for a new tack. He was a patient teacher and very knowledgeable. She found she enjoyed his company and found him immensely pleasurable to be with as she learned from him.

Miguel and Maria exchanged knowing glances throughout the day as they observed the two together. The budding relationship growing between the two was as obvious as a perfect sunrise. They were truly pleased it seemed to be working out for Jake. They had never seen him this happy before and new it was directly due to the time he was spending with Lynnette.

By late Monday afternoon, Lynnette's hair and skin felt sticky from the salt air and sea spray, so she went below to shower and change clothes. She was smiling and humming happily to herself as she entered the galley on her way to Jake's quarters. Maria looked up from a pot on the stove, a look of question on her face.

"Oh, Maria, what a terrific day I just had."

"Yes, you look to be very happy together," Maria said pleased. "You make a lovely couple, I think."

A couple? Lynnette smiled but felt a nagging feeling at the brief thought of the other man she had decided to marry. Pushing those thoughts from her mind, she sat down at the table.

"I wish I had my suitcase. It's still back in the motel and I don't have anything left to wear. I've resorted to searching Jake's closet and everything in there is way too big."

Maria walked around the galley counter and began sizing up Lynnette's trim body.

"I think I have a very nice, clean dress for you to wear tonight. It will be too big here in the middle," she stated, pointing to Lynnette's small waist, "but no mind. We will get a sash to belt around it and it will look most lovely on you."

Lynnette responded by jumping up and throwing her arms around the short woman, hugging her tightly.

"Oh thank you, Maria. You've been so nice to me. I'm so glad you're here. I'd be completely lost without you. Thank you," she said, spinning happily away and heading down the hallway to the cabin. She didn't realize in her excitement that she had forgotten to wait for Maria to fetch the dress.

Lynnette stood in the shower smiling to herself letting the hot water run down her body. Letting the spray hit her face she turned and rinsed the shampoo from her hair thinking back over the day with Jake. She knew it would always stand out as one of the happiest days of her life.

In a low measured tone, Jake's voice broke into her thoughts.

"We only have so much water stored on board, woman. Are you planning to use it all up yourself?"

Lynnette jumped nearly a foot, almost falling on the wet, slippery surface. Naked, Jake stepped into the shower with her.

"What are you doing," she squealed, whirling around to face him. Her attempt at covering herself with her arms was futile.

"Get out of this shower and wait your turn."

"By then all the hot water will be gone," he insisted. The teasing grin on his face was unmistakable. "By the way, taking a shower together would conserve the precious water you're wasting so freely."

"Get out," she squealed. "Now!"

Jake was fully aware of her persistent resolve to avoid having anything further happen physically with them and sensed she had a high moral standard she tried to live by. He really liked that about her. He liked her naked and wet much more though.

Lynnette stood there shocked, frozen in place, unable to move or speak. There he was, standing in front of her completely and comfortably naked. Modesty was apparently not an issue for him. How had she lost control of the situation again so quickly?

"Relax," he chided. "I'm just helping you shower so we can get to dinner sooner."

"Jake Hunter, you are such a liar," she accused as she stormed out of the shower and grabbed the closest towel to quickly cover herself. Flustered, she moved across the room and sat on the edge of the bed to collect her thoughts.

After he dried off and quickly got dressed, he said, "I enjoyed our shower, sweetheart." He looked down in intrigue at the thin towel she had wrapped around her. He considered pulling it off then and there. He was feeling hungry for more of her. Mustering up all his strength, he decided to let it go for the moment.

"I'll see you later at dinner, sweetheart."

"Jake?" she asked.

Turning back with one hand on the doorknob, he answered, "Yes, sweetheart?"

"It's Monday and Todd told me that Monday was my deadline or he was going to do something awful to Keira.

The fear in her voice was real and the anger inside Jake toward Todd was palatable. As much as he tried to hide his feelings, you could read the hatred in his eyes whenever he thought of the guy. He controlled his anger and knew his first priority was appeasing Lynnette's concerns for her sister.

Returning to her side, he took her hand in his. "Everything is going to be just fine, Lynnette. We'll get back there tomorrow and take care of it. Remember that Todd wants that money of yours more than he wants to hurt his stepsister, so he has no gain in doing anything to her now. He was just bluffing, sweetheart. Trust me. I've dealt with his type before and they're cowards for the most part. Keira is going to be just fine, honey," he finished, hoping his words sounded more comforting to her than they sounded believable to him. He looked down again and noticed the towel slipping away. She grabbed it just in time, but he was nearly undone by then.

Kissing the top of her head, he left the room immediately wondering where he was drawing his willpower from at the moment. He had never before had to fight sexual desires this strong with any other woman. Lynnette made him crazy with desire even though she didn't even try. Heaven help him if she ever actually started trying. He wouldn't stand a chance then.

Lynnette answered the door with relief when Maria brought her the dress and some makeup. With a big hug, she thanked her. She enjoyed taking the time to fix herself up a bit before dinner using the things Maria had so nicely lent her. Lynnette had not worn any makeup or done anything with her hair since she had come aboard and thought it would be a nice change for this evening.

Convincing herself that it was just because she was in the mood to primp and not because she wanted to impress Jake, she carefully applied light makeup to her eyes, finishing off with a pale pink lipstick she had stashed in the front pocket of her backpack. She didn't usually wear face makeup and didn't even have any with her. Then again, she had never needed it. She lightly pinched her cheeks for the look of blush high on her cheekbones.

Picking up Jake's blow dryer and brush, she took a moment to smell the bristles, enjoying the scent of Jake's hair. He had such an attractive, natural scent, uniquely his own. She was glad he didn't wear any cologne or aftershave. If his masculine scent could be bottled, she knew it would sell. She was more than happy to hoard it all to herself though, at least for the meantime. She smoothed out and dried the curls of her long dark hair and then using her fingers, twisted portions around her fingers for just the effect she was after. Long, loose waves cascading down around her shoulders.

Smiling into the mirror at her reflection, she felt happy, happier than she could remember feeling in years. Thinking of Jake trying to convince her not to marry this other man, she wondered again what he would say if he found out she had yet to even meet him. He might be thinking that he was up against someone she had dated for a while and had strong feelings for. Interestingly, Jake didn't realize that in her estimation, there wasn't a man who stood a chance against him in any comparison. The only reason for the dilemma in her decision was because of the potential loss of her inheritance and entire life plan she had so carefully laid out years ago.

Thinking back over the day again, something came back to mind that continued to nag at her though. How had Jake known she was supposed to marry in two weeks? It didn't make any sense. She was absolutely certain she hadn't told him. Something wasn't quite right, but she couldn't put her finger on it yet. There was definitely something amiss though and she would have to figure out what it was.

Lynnette walked into the galley just as Maria was finishing up preparations for dinner in the dining room. Looking around the room, Lynnette noticed the table was set for eight people. It appeared that they would be having dinner with everyone else tonight, she realized with a little regret. She had really enjoyed having Jake all to herself at breakfast that morning.

Maria saw Lynnette enter wearing the dress she had loaned her, a white, Mexican style peasant dress that fit a bit too large on her slight frame. Cinched in tightly at the waist with a colorful sash though, the result was a lovely, feminine effect that was much more than acceptable. The short, puffy sleeves tended to slip off Lynnette's shoulders, but she had tested the problem in front of the mirror earlier making certain the dress would not slip completely off. The elastic seemed to hold it in place for the most part. She pulled the long, silky curls of her hair up around her shoulders and was thankful she as least wasn't still wearing her black slacks and sweater. The air was balmy and tropical tonight so Lynnette felt this dress would do wonderfully. She was pleased to find she actually felt pretty tonight.

Maria approached, saying, "Oh Lynnette, good, you are here now. Oh my, don't you look so lovely. Come now, come on in."

Most of the crew had been milling about the large room waiting for dinner and at Maria's loudly spoken comment, all eyes turned toward Lynnette. Some of them just stared mutely at her, wide-eyed and dumbstruck by her amazing beauty, while others made polite comments on how pretty she looked. She heard one long, low whistle from one of the guys, but wasn't sure from which one. Embarrassed by all the attention she was getting, Lynnette's cheeks turned a deep rosy pink that just added to the lovely look on her face as she shyly smiled back at them.

It was at that moment Jake's long legs appeared on the stairs as he descended from the deck above. She new it was Jake because of the sheer size and length of his legs. Her heart began beating double time. His presence was so overwhelming that the room suddenly seemed much smaller.

He wore black jeans and a short-sleeved t-shirt that molded nicely to his muscled torso and upper arms. It was a shade of blue that almost matched the deep blue of his expressive eyes.

"Okay guys, that's enough now," he announced possessively, leveling his look at her as he reached the bottom rung. Only the darkening of his eyes as he stared at her expressed his approval to her appearance. He forced his body not to show any outwardly physical reaction in front of the other men.

Lynnette sensed Jake's thoughts at that very moment and wondered if anyone else in the room could guess them as well.

Jake thought Lynnette looked absolutely stunning standing there across the room dressed in white. She stood tall and proud, despite her obvious discomfort at all the attention she was getting. Her face glowed with a natural radiant beauty, her eyes sparkled, her hair hung down around her shoulders in smooth, soft waves. She reached up, nervously flipping her hair back over one side, exposing a soft, bare shoulder. He longed to lean down and kiss its softness. She pulled the sleeve back up in place abruptly and looked away. Moving quickly to Maria's side to help finish with the dinner preparations, she looked nervous and unsettled.

Jake moved over to talk with the guys gathered in the corner, asking if any of them would be willing to take their dinners up to the cockpit to eat in order to relieve Miguel at the wheel so he could come down to join his wife for dinner. They rarely got the opportunity to eat together and he thought it would be a nice change tonight. Two of the guys agreed in hopes of pleasing their boss and left to eat in the wheelhouse after loading their plates with food. Jake also sent one of the other crewmembers off to take a plate of food down to Eric.

Jake continued stealing glances at Lynnette, observing her as she moved gracefully back and forth across the room, positioning plates and bowls of food carefully on the table. Every now and then, Lynnette would briefly look over at Jake, intensely aware of his dominant presence in the room. She could feel his gaze on her now and then as she finished setting the table, his eyes making her body feel warmer. He towered over the other men he was speaking with and looked incredibly handsome tonight. The wind had blown his hair dry, back away from his face, and the effect was distracting. The vivid image of his square jaw, blue eyes and wide shoulders continued to play in her head even when she wasn't looking at him. She tried to clear her mind of the thoughts and purposely started up a conversation with Maria about cooking.

When dinner was ready, everyone moved to sit down at the table. Jake moved to her side, asking her to sit at the opposite end of the table from him. He moved behind and pulled out her chair seating her politely. It felt somehow significant to be sitting directly across from him at the head of the table, but she had actually hoped to sit at his side.

Jake went to a cabinet, removing a couple of dusty bottles of red wine he had been saving for a special occasion in order to celebrate how well the Ariel had fared the storm. Miguel came down the stairs just then, walking over to where Maria sat, he placed a loud kiss on her cheek.

"Hello, my sweet. I see you outdid yourself again with this meal. This smells terrific," he said with gusto, gesturing to the table full of food. He placed another kiss on her face as Lynnette looked on smiling. Jake's joking interrupted their sweet exchange.

"Hey, Miguel, save it for later. Stop mugging on your wife and sit down so we can all eat," he joked, looking down the length of the table straight at Lynnette, one eyebrow lifted suggestively. "I'm hungry," he emphasized with double meaning. The guys all laughed, knowing exactly whom he was hungry for at the moment.

The dinner was a delight. Everyone took turns sharing interesting stories of previous sailing trips they had been on with Jake, unknowingly offering her tidbits of information about the amazing man sitting across the table. They all seemed to like Jake, as well as respect and admire him. Through their stories, she learned he had seen them through other dangers in the past and they had the utmost confidence in his abilities as a captain. Jake was a charming host as he poured everyone more wine, offering a number of humorous stories about each of the crewmembers, their first trips out in the open ocean or their first time seasick. Everyone laughed as he playfully embarrassed each one in turn. It was a wonderful exchange and Lynnette laughed in pleasure throughout the evening.

Once dinner was over, Lynnette stood and began picking up the empty dishes, but Maria and Miguel urged her to leave it for them to do. It was under the guise they wanted to spend some time alone in the galley.

"Spend time alone doing dishes?" she questioned suspiciously at Maria. She suspected they were really trying their hand at a little matchmaking, but Jake just winked at Maria and took advantage of the opportunity by grabbing Lynnette's wrist, leading her to the upper deck before they changed their minds.

Her hand held snugly in his, he led her slowly in the warm breeze along the length of the deck to the stern where he turned and leaned back against the wooden railing. Opening his arms, he invited her to rest against him within his arms. She hesitated.

"Come over here, Lynnette and look up at the sky. I want to show you something very special," he urged quietly.

Unable to stop herself, she moved into his embrace. He turned her around, settling her back against his body as they both looked up at the night sky. The air was warm and pleasant on her skin as the breeze lightly blew her hair back over Jake's arm, teasing his skin with its silkiness. He wrapped his arms loosely around her waist and she laid her arms over his comfortably. Breathing in the wonderful thickness of the salt air that she had come to directly associate with thoughts of Jake, she began to relax.

The night sky was clear and dark, void of any moon resulting in a backdrop for the multitude of bright, twinkling stars, looking much like a curtain of black velvet. She heard the sails as they lightly luffed in the evening breeze. The slow, rhythmic motion of the boat was comforting as it cut slowly through the Pacific, causing her to rock back and forth slightly in his muscled arms as he held her steady.

"Remember I told you I was interested in pirates and such as a boy?" he asked. "Back then, the captains only had rough, inaccurate charts to follow and no compass to guide them. These guys were tough and determined to get where they were going and they did so using only celestial navigation at night for direction."

She looked up at him over her shoulder. "How could looking up at the stars help them figure out where they were or where they were heading?"

Jake took his time explaining the rudiments of celestial navigation to her while enjoying the feel of holding her in his arms as she leaned back against him so comfortably and naturally.

Lynnette was not in the least bit interested in learning how to direct a ship in the night, but she was completely lulled by the low timbre of Jake's deep voice as he continued talking. She could happily stand here all night listening to his rugged voice.

Jake finished his explanation and bent his head low to inhale the sweet lavender smell of her skin. Resting his chin on the crown of her head, he looked down the length of the Ariel and knew he'd never been so content before in his life. If they headed out to sea forever and the Ariel never met shore again, he would die a happy man with Lynnette here in his arms.

Pulling free of his embrace, she turned around to face him, asking something that had been a curiosity to her now for days.

"Jake, why is it that you aren't married already or have you ever been?"

Looking out over the water into the darkness, Jake hesitated and crossed his arms before answering. "No, I haven't but I was engaged to be married once. It was to a girl named Rachelle." He clenched his jaw in reflex at the memories her name drummed up.

"I'm sorry," she quickly apologized, seeing his discomfort at the subject. "I shouldn't have asked something so personal. Forget I asked."

"No, Lynnette, it's alright. I have no problem sharing this with you if you want to know. I don't want there to be any secrets between us," he replied, feeling a tug of guilt at the fact he actually knew the truth of her engagement. That and the fact he couldn't tell her he did Special-Ops work for the government. He couldn't speak about that with anyone.

He would be honest with her later about knowing of this bizarre marriage arrangement, but first he would try to convince her to change her mind, choosing to get to know him first. Very odd, he thought, having to compete with himself. It was also very strange he was considering settling down with one woman so soon. Pulling his thoughts back to their conversation, he continued.

"I always thought of Rachelle as my first love, though reflecting back on it now I'm not sure what I was feeling then. Anyway, I unexpectedly came home from work early one afternoon and found her naked on the couch with my best friend."

There didn't seem to be anything appropriate to say, so she remained silent. Lynnette felt a slight stab of jealousy at the thought of Jake with another woman, realizing she was being silly. She was well aware he had probably been with plenty of women before she came along. She just didn't care to think about it.

"I guess it's been difficult for me to trust women after that experience. Anyway, I allowed Rachelle to save face by saying the breakup was her choice and told her I never wanted to see her again after that," he stated without emotion. "That's why it means so much to me when I hear you say you couldn't cheat on this other guy."

She looked out to sea and thought about what he had just said. She then asked, "So there's never been anyone else since Rachelle that you've been serious about?"

"No," he answered. "I recently broke it off with a girl in Long Beach, but it wasn't ever serious. Sharon was so overbearing and jealous I would never have considered her for a long term relationship." Deciding to tease with her in order to lighten up their conversation, he jokingly added, "Yeah, I've tried to date casually, but I'm such a great catch that the women just get way too serious." The humor in his voice was unmistakable. "But then again," he added mischievously, "I really am quite ruggedly handsome and irresistible."

She rolled her eyes and turned away with a grin.

"My, my, Jake Hunter, you're sounding awfully cocky, aren't you?" She was completely unaware how seductively she strolled away from him across the deck.

Leaning back against the railing, he crossed his arms over his chest again and he let his gaze slowly tour up and down the curves of her slender, inviting body.

"Well, there is the simple fact that you can't seem to resist me," he tossed back, raising one eyebrow up devilishly.

Turning around to face him, she leaned back against the mizzenmast and crossed her arms in front of her. Both sleeves dropped away in the balmy breeze, baring her shoulders seductively. Here in the starlight, she looked more beautifully inviting to him than any other woman ever had before. He mentally embedded this picture in his memory for safekeeping.

"Resist you?" she replied with a challenge in her voice. She was enjoying their verbal exchange. "Of course I can resist you. What makes you so sure that I can't?"

Jake pushed off the railing and started toward her, moving slowly and purposefully. His smoldering eyes never left hers for a moment. He looked so handsome it took her breath away. She shivered in anticipation as he drew near, knowing she shouldn't have teased him so. He looked like a wild cat on the prowl, closing in on its prey. She dropped her hands behind her, reaching for the support of the mast, her breathing deepened. She watched as his eyes dipped to the low cleavage of her dress. She could feel the labored rise and fall of her chest with each deep intake of breath. She noticed his Adams apple rise and then dip in his wide neck as he swallowed hard, the muscles in his jaw working at the same time as he fought for control.

He took a final step forward, touching one finger to her cheek, then softly ran it down her neck, down over the hollow just above her collar bone, stopping at the curve at the top of her breasts. Breathing in deeply he enjoyed a tantalizing hint of her intoxicating perfume. He could feel goose bumps on the soft skin beneath his finger. He watched the rise and fall of her cleavage and it was driving him nearly insane with desire. Yes, he'd been right, he thought with satisfaction. From the look on her face, she couldn't resist him.

He leaned down and kissed her then, deeply and thoroughly. She moaned and reached up, sliding her arms up around his neck. She ran her fingers through his hair, enjoying its thickness.

Pulling back with difficulty, he lifted her face up and they stared into one another's eyes.

Jake stood to his full height, stepped back and grabbing her by the hips he set her away from his body. He cooled himself down and teased, "So, Lynnette, I see you can resist me after all. I love the way you resist me." He was joking, yet his eyes still burned with passion as he looked down at her.

Embarrassed at her obvious lack of control, she frowned and smacked him hard in the chest. He laughed. It was at that moment a hatch on deck mysteriously opened up slowly and they began to hear the sound of smooth jazz music from below deck. Smiling to himself, Jake realized it was either Maria or Miguel attempting to help him out, so he took immediate advantage of the situation.

Taking Lynnette's hand in his, he pulled her into his arms and they began to dance. As the comfortable night breeze blew across the deck, they moved together to romantic music under a blanket of sparkling stars poised against the endless sky above. Jake held Lynnette's body close as they slowly swayed together, feeling one another's bodies moving as one, alone in the comfort of a perfect evening.

Jake wondered as they danced if the feeling he felt was in fact love. Was this the love of his life here dancing in his arms? She made him laugh, she made him care, and she filled his life with emotions. She was an amazing woman. At the same moment, Lynnette was wondering how she could ever marry another man after this wonderfully romantic experience in Cabo with Jake. It was completely impossible and entirely unimaginable. He seemed to be the man of her dreams. He made her furious, he protected her, then could make her blush too. He was perfectly wonderful.

As the song ended, Jake looked down into her eyes and said, "Lynnette, I'm falling in love with you."

Time stopped. She was shocked. He loved her? They stared intently into each other's eyes. She felt so confused and conflicted inside. She desperately wanted to reply back, but yet they had only known each other for a few days. How can you know something like that in just a few days? Then again, she didn't want to say nothing either. What if he was the right man for her and she just had not thought everything through clearly yet? She felt like he could be, but was he?

Jake sensed her dilemma.

"Lynnette, I want you to seriously think about what you are doing with your life. You don't have to marry someone just because your father told you to. There isn't much time left to decide, but this decision will affect you for the rest of your life. Only you can decide what's right. Nobody else. Not me, not even your father."

Walking away, Jake gave her space to think and seated himself across the deck in the darkness at the same table they had enjoyed breakfast at that very morning. He leaned back and reached across the table absently fingering the sand-filled ashtray left on the table. Reaching for a light in his pocket, he lit a cigar and stared out at the ocean without another word, looking deep in thought.

Leaning her elbows on the rail, Lynnette rested her face in both hands as she looked out to sea. She knew it had upset him that she had not responded in like manner, yet she couldn't tell him she loved him after only knowing him a few days, could she? How could he be so sure about something like this already? Besides, her decision to marry had already been made for her. There was nothing she could think of to say to him. She felt awful and needed some time alone to think. They both remained alone in their separate thoughts for several minutes until Jake finally broke the silence. He roughly raked his hands through his hair.

"Lynnette, come sit down here with me a minute. We need to discuss Todd," he stated in a very matter-of-fact tone.

Looking over at him, she realized this had been such a perfect day for them and now everything had been ruined. He was withdrawn and she was feeling depressed. A part of her was thrilled with the fact Jake said he loved her and the other part of her wished he had never admitted it at all. It certainly made things much more complicated.

Jake asked her to tell him every single thing Todd has said that could pertain to the current problem. Taking the seat opposite him, she carefully relayed everything Todd had said to her on the phone Friday morning, what he had said in the bar the following day in Cabo and anything else she could think of that might be important.

"So that's the reason you were looking into fishing boats at my hou…, my friend's house? That's the business Todd plans to finance with your fifty grand?"

"Yes, she answered, suddenly wondering if that seemed like a lot of money to a man who worked onboard boats. It never dawned on her before to be in the least bit concerned with his income. It didn't really matter to her what his income was.

"Do you have any idea what the name of the fishing boat is? He asked intently, leaning forward. "It's very important you remember if he did, Lynnette."

Thinking for a moment, she shook her head. "No, he never told me. I think those guys chasing me the other night though were his supposed partners and were intending to steal the money before I got it to Todd. From what I could understand of what they were saying, it sounded like they were going to double cross him and cheat Todd out of his share of the boat.

The beginnings of a plan were already formulating in Jake's mind as he sat back and gave the situation some thought. Lynnette observed him in the dim starlight as he sat there thinking, absently rubbing his chin between his thumb and forefinger before she interrupted his thoughts.

"Jake, were you really in the military? Maria mentioned it to me earlier."

"Yes, I was, for a while," he answered looking out over the moonlight sparkling on the water. "I was with a special group in the navy for a number of years."

They reverted back to silence. Lynnette started to speak, then stopped. Beginning again, then pausing uncomfortably, she finally blurted out what was on her mind.

"Jake, I'm really worried. I don't want you to get hurt. It's my fault you are even involved in this at all."

She could make out the grin on Jake's face in the starlight as he responded with some pleasure.

"It's good to hear you're concerned about me," he answered with a smile. "It's unnecessary though. Don't worry yourself, sweetheart. The government trained me thoroughly to do this particular type of job and not to sound too boastful; I'm damn good at it. It's really Todd you should be worried about, honey. By the way, what do I have your permission to do to him when I find him?

"Do to him?" she answered weakly. "What do you mean?"

Deciding whether or not to try buffering her from the specific details, he chose to be direct.

"Well, do you just want him to stop extorting you in the future or do you want him punished for all the crap he put you through all these years?"

Catching her breath, her complexion paled and he realized her answer before she said anything.

"Just stop him, Jake. Don't hurt him, not seriously anyway. Not unless you're trying to protect yourself," she added quickly.

Maybe she would forgive him if he hurt Todd just a little.

"Alright. I'll want to borrow a picture of Keira and Todd if you have one with you. We're going to reach Cabo sometime early tomorrow afternoon. When we get there, I want you to stay onboard below deck the entire time we're docked until I return with Keira. There's no telling if Todd's partners are still out there looking for you since they know you still have the money they're after."

"No, Jake. I am going with you to help..."

"Absolutely not," he insisted, interrupting her. "You would only hold me back and distract me from what has to be done. Besides, I'm used to working alone."

She persisted. "But, I could at least go get my suitcase from the motel and checkout while you're..."

"No. It's too dangerous. You are staying onboard the Ariel, below deck," he ordered harshly. "I don't want anything to happen to you while I'm gone, understood? I'll go get your suitcase after I bring Keira back."

She really hated being told what to do. She looked away from Jake without agreeing, so he patiently repeated himself.

"Lynnette? Do you promise to stay below deck and out of sight until I get back to the yacht?"

"Yeah, alright," she mumbled.

"It's probably time you got some rest now," he said almost dismissing her.

Standing up, Lynnette felt a strange mixture of emotions. She was still miffed at being ordered about by him, yet her heart felt heavier than it ever had in her life. She didn't want to go below alone.

"Jake?"

"Yeah," he answered looking up at her.

"I know I've hurt you tonight," she began, looking down at her hands, which were trembling. "You really caught me off-guard."

When he didn't answer, she continued. "There are some embarrassing reasons why I can't say I love you back. It's not that I don't want to. Anyway, I really do appreciate you helping me out with this problem with Todd, but you don't have to, you know," she said.

He sat quietly looking at her.

"Lynnette," he finally answered standing to face her. "You don't get it do you? I'm doing this because I care about you."

Raising her chin up in an effort to boost her confidence, she continued as her eyes misted over. "Well, Jake, if it's any consolation, I think I'm in..."

Standing, he quickly placed a finger gently over her lips to silence her. "No, don't say it, Lynnette. Make damn sure of your feelings before you ever say those words to me. If and when you do ever say it, I want you to really mean it, sweetheart. There will be no taking those words back," he warned.

Tracing his fingers back along her cheekbone, he ran his fingers through her hair, grasping the back of her neck and pulling her face towards his. Stopping a few short inches away, he studied her eyes intently, then lowering his gaze to her moist lips, he gently brought his mouth down over hers possessively, letting her experience the full intensity of his feelings for her in that one kiss.

Pulling back, she felt cheated that their kiss had not lasted longer. She wanted more of him, the feel of his arms around her, his mouth on hers again, devouring the uncertainties that possessed her. Standing upright, she took one last look at the man who would most certainly haunt her dreams that night and then turned and walked away.

EIGHTEEN

Lynnette had a horribly fitful night sleep, tossing and turning on the couch in Jake's stateroom until daybreak when she had finally fell soundly asleep until late morning. It was Tuesday morning and her head ached. She couldn't push the nightmares out of her thoughts. The most recent one had to do with being left alone stranded on a deserted island as she watched Jake sail away into heavy fog. She screamed for him not to leave her there, but he disappeared from her view without hearing her cries.

Hoping it would make her feel better, she swallowed two aspirin she found in Jake's medicine cabinet and took a quick hot shower. She wondered where he had slept again last night. His bed had not been touched.

Joining Maria in the kitchen, she poured herself a mug of strong black coffee and asked if she could help.

"The crew seems to have also slept in late this morning," Maria replied. "I don't need help but I would enjoy your company."

Maria was happily mixing a large bowl of pancake batter and opening a container of bacon, bustling around the galley. She finally noticed the haggard look on Lynnette's face.

"Oh my, you look like you didn't sleep at all. What is wrong? You look upset?"

"Yeah, you're right. I didn't sleep very well last night. Things have gotten so complicated between us," she said sitting down at the table and propping her chin up in her hand. "I'm so confused, Maria," Lynnette admitted.

"What's wrong? Everything was going so good just yesterday. Tell me what has happened," Maria's voice conveyed her sincere concern.

Lynnette confided to Maria that Jake had revealed his feelings for her, but that she'd already made the final decision to marry the other man. Lynnette wasn't prepared for how much this news would upset Maria.

"Why?" Maria demanded angrily. Her accent became stronger the faster she spoke. "Why do you not love Jake? He loves you so. Anyone can see it. A blind man could see how he loves you. We never thought he would trust a woman again, then he tells you he loves you and you reject him?" she continued getting even louder. Maria shook her head in frustration. "I cannot believe this."

"Maria," Lynnette defended, "I'm engaged to be married to another man in a couple of weeks, remember? Besides, we just met. We don't really even know each other yet. How can he think he truly loves me? Maybe he'll change his mind in a month and then where would I be?"

"Maybe you don't know him, but I do. He does not do something without thinking it through and he does not change his mind. When he is set on something, he never lets go of it. He is a very stubborn man," Maria insisted shaking the wooden spoon at her.

Lynnette stood and walked over to stand next to the stove.

"Maria, I just wish we had met sooner before all these other plans were set. It's too late for us now," she added sadly.

"Do you love him, Lynnette?" Maria asked bluntly.

Forgetting she had told Jake she loved the man she was to marry, she answered Maria honestly not noticing Jake quietly enter the room behind her.

"I've never been in love before Maria. I'm not certain what it feels like exactly, but I do know that I think of Jake all the time. When I see him, I get all fluttery and nervous in my stomach and I feel all warm and excited in his presence." Looking dreamily over Maria's shoulder she continued her description. "When I'm not with him, I can't stop thinking about him. Then when he looks at me or kisses me, I feel like I've died and gone to heaven. I know all that probably sounds silly, but if that's what love feels like, then, yes, I guess maybe I do love him," she finished quietly.

Lynnette didn't notice Maria's glance at Jake nor the smile and wink he returned before quietly backing out of the room again.

"Maybe if you are falling in love, you should not go through with your plans until you give Jake a chance, you think?" Maria suggested.

"No, Maria, it doesn't matter if I'm falling in love with Jake or not. Regardless, I have to marry this other guy," she said, looking as if she wanted to cry.

"Why in the world would you do that?" Maria exclaimed in frustration as she laid the bacon strips on the hot griddle as they sizzled and popped.

"If I tell you, you have to swear you won't tell anyone, not even Miguel and especially not Jake. You promise?"

Maria looked up at Lynnette's face with a frown. "I don't usually keep secrets from Miguel, but if you insist. Go ahead. Tell me. Why?"

Lynnette explained the situation about her controlling father, her inheritance and the business she stood to lose if she did not do as her father demanded. Maria took the information in, her eyebrows drawn together in worry. She took her time turning over each sizzling strip of bacon, and then began pouring small circles of pancake batter on a griddle on the stove. Looking up at Lynnette, she pursed her lips as she shook her head in disbelief at the messed up situation.

"I am going to give you advice and you can take it or not, but you will hear what I say. Sit down with me over here."

Maria led Lynnette over to the dining table as the smell of hotcakes and bacon filled the room.

"You say you spent your life under the thumb of your overbearing, demanding father and you do not like to be told what to do. You also said you always tried to prove yourself to your father, right?" Not waiting for a response, she continued. "This will probably be the last time in your dying father's life you will have the chance to prove to him you can make your own decisions. This is the last chance you'll have to stand up to him by refusing to do as he tells you. If you lose your inheritance and gain true love, I say you would come out better in the end."

Maria reached over to pat Lynnette's hand and then stood to move back to the stove to flip the pancakes as Lynnette sat alone at the table contemplating Maria's words. Her thoughts were all jumbled up in her mind and twirling around in her head. Nothing made sense anymore and she wished desperately to be back in the mundane routine of her daily life. She just wanted to wake up in her own bed, take her normal morning run and have a nice boring day at work with nothing major to decide and no family members to concern herself with.

Maria tried but could not talk Lynnette into staying for breakfast. She said she wasn't really feeling hungry and just wanted to be alone for a while. Not wanting to run into Jake up on deck until she had more time to think, Lynnette went back to his quarters. Pulling an interesting looking book down from the shelf, she snuggled up on the couch to read. After staring at the first page for several minutes without reading a word, she resorted to just staring blankly out the window as she thought about Jake and their situation.

A few hours later, Lynnette was still sitting lost in her thoughts when Jake suddenly walked into the room. Seeing her there, he froze with one hand on the doorknob. It seemed so right to come in here with her in his room. She looked beautiful sitting there and his first instinct was to go to her and take her in his arms. He refrained from his desire as they looked at each other uncomfortably, each unsure of the other's mood or how to act after what happened the night before.

Jake opted to stick to business for now. He smiled and moved inside, quietly shutting the door behind him. In his hand he had a small black duffle bag that he laid on the bed. Moving over to the dresser, he pulled out black jeans and a black t-shirt, shoving them both inside the bag. Then he pulled out a snorkel, mask, fins and binoculars from the closet and placed them in the bag as well.

"Do you have that picture of Todd and Keira for me?" he asked, all business now.

She opened her wallet that was sitting on the coffee table and pulled out a couple pictures, handing them to him.

Going to the desk, he slid open the bottom drawer and pulled out a gun and a long wooden club. Walking across the room, he checked the ammunition, checked the safety on the gun and placed them inside the duffle bag.

"Jake, what are you doing with a gun?" she asked tensely as she nervously bit on her lower lip. "I didn't realize you were going to take a gun with you." She always reacted nervously at the site of a weapon and she especially hated guns, mainly because they scared her to death.

"I'm taking a weapon in case I need it," Jake answered directly. "I don't intend to use it, Lynnette, unless I absolutely have to."

She jumped up from the couch and began pacing across the room, nervously wringing her hands. Jake watched for a moment as she began working herself into a frenzy. Setting everything down on the bed, Jake moved in front of her, blocking her way and took hold of her elbows stopping her in her tracks. Tilting his head to the side to get a better look at her lowered face, he tried teasing to ease her worry.

"Lynnette, you're going to walk a hole right through the bottom of this yacht and sink us if you don't calm down." Setting a finger under her chin, he lifted her face, seeing the attempt at a smile there. "Now stop your worrying. It's going to be just fine. No one is going to get hurt, so stop fretting and let me take care of this for you, alright, sweetheart?"

She felt chills run down her spine all the way to her toes. He was so sweet and his gentle words were comforting. She was still worried though. "I just want this to be over so we can all go home," she said. "I'm so afraid something terrible is going to happen. Jake, please promise me you'll be very careful," she pleaded, looking up into his deep blue eyes.

Pulling her into his arms, he answered with a wide grin and a kiss that sent the tingles back down to her toes. It was too late by the time she realized she had determined not to let him do that to her anymore.

"Yes, I'll be careful," he answered. "It'll be over soon. We're docking in about thirty minutes. Just stay put and I'll be back with Keira, safe and sound.

Lowering his head back down, his mouth captured hers in a final kiss. Jake pulled away from her with all the strength he could muster. God, she smelled good. This wasn't the time though. His intense desire for her was killing him, but he needed to focus on his task ahead. They were due to dock shortly and he wanted to take the helm while docking Ariel.

"I'll be back with your sister just as quickly as I can." Turning, he grabbed the duffle off of the bed and left the room without looking back.

Lynnette began slowly pacing back and forth again across the room, wringing her hands nervously. With a heavy sigh, she turned again and started back across the room, biting her lip and thinking about Jake and the fact he loved her. Did he really mean it? They had only met less than a week ago. He might think he loved her, but he was sure to have second thoughts and back out of it sooner or later. He'd probably leave her and break her heart in the process. No, she was better off not setting herself up for that kind of pain. A guy as charming and gorgeous as Jake would certainly come to his senses and realize he did not really want to get tied down to a simple girl like her when he could have any woman he wanted. She would just have to say her goodbyes when he returned with Keira, before they left for the airport to go home. She knew she would miss him terribly. He was so wonderful. He was masculine yet sensitive, self-assured but giving, sweet though rugged, and aggressive but tender. Just looking at him made her heart race. She felt so alive whenever they were in the same room together. Things just looked brighter, smelled stronger and sounded better when he was a part of it. Jake made her body crave things she was not even aware of before she met him. But it wasn't to be. She had to be realistic. She would marry this other guy and in time, try her best to forget about Jake, hopefully. Not likely though, she admitted to herself.

The minutes slowly ticked by as she worried. Minutes felt like hours, and she continued waiting until she thought she would scream. The walls began closing in on her and she felt she would go insane if she didn't get off the boat. She knew Jake would be upset but she would deal with his anger later. She just wanted to run over to the motel real quickly to retrieve her bag and check out. She was still being charged for every additional day since she had checked in. She would just have to keep her eyes open and be very careful, she thought as she stepped off the Ariel and onto the dock, heading for the center of town without anyone noticing.

* * *

The first stop Jake made was the Harbor Master's office in the corner of the marina. Having no luck finding out anything about Todd's whereabouts there, he headed over to one of the two most popular bars in town. Most every vacationing fisherman or hired fleet crewman hung out and drank beer after an early morning of fishing. It was mid-day and the Giggling Marlin was packed as usual. Jake started at one end of the huge room filled with people, mostly men, and proceeded to make inquiries. He showed Todd's picture around hoping it might jog someone's memory, but had no luck other than the occasional interesting proposal from intoxicated females on the prowl, looking for a good time. Smiling with his usual charm, he easily declined each invitation without any real interest and moved to the next table to ask more questions.

He was getting thirsty, but refused to get frustrated. He would find Todd, even if it took him a week, which it wouldn't, he was sure. He was doing this for Lynnette and he would find Todd and stop these damned extortion schemes once and for all. Jake headed over to the bar to speak with the bartender and to get a cold beer.

The bartender, Jake learned shortly, had overheard Todd bragging one night when he was drunk, which was a common occurrence according to the guy. Setting a cold bottle of beer down on the bar in front of Jake, he explained.

"Yeah, I remember the guy," he said after taking a closer look at the picture. "He was a real pain in the ass. Typical ugly-American. A real big talker. Must have bragged for hours about his new fishing boat and how he was going to get rich."

Jake took a long swig from the chilled bottle of beer and calmly asked, "Did you happen to catch the name of his boat?"

"Yeah, I did. Let me think a minute," he paused, rubbing the stubble on his chin. "It was a catchy name. Oh yeah, I remember. He called it Reel-Em-In. Yeah, that's it. I thought it was fairly catchy, but...,"

Jake dropped some bills on the counter for his unfinished drink and was out the door before the bartender could finish his sentence.

* * *

Sneaking away from the Ariel with only enough money in her pocket to pay off the room, Lynnette didn't mention to anyone onboard where she was going or when she would be back. She did not run into anyone as she left the docks so she hoped they wouldn't even be aware she was gone until she returned. She would be back in no time at all. Definitely before Jake returned. He would probably toss her over his knee again since she was doing exactly what he had told her not to do, but interestingly, she found the thought intriguing. It conjured up an image in her mind of what had happened in his quarters just after he had spanked her the last time.

Walking faster, she realized she wanted to be back on the Ariel when he and Keira arrived so she could comfort her little sister. Todd and his two Mexican goons had probably scared Keira half to death.

Remembering the two Mexicans who had chased her up and down the streets of Cabo had her suddenly wary, looking behind to make sure no one was following her. She had been carelessly daydreaming and not paying attention to her surroundings. She would have to be more careful in case they were still looking for her, as Jake suspected.

Arriving at the motel, she went to the front desk to settle the bill, then to her room to gather up her belongings. She pulled the key out of her pocket and unlocked the door. Everything in the room was just as she had left it a few days ago. Gathering up her clothing, she quickly laid them inside her suitcase. Closing the case, she headed for the door.

She was suddenly grabbed from behind. One dirty hand covered her mouth, silencing her scream. The other filthy arm reached around her and pinned her arms to her sides. She screamed frantically, but the smelly palm over her mouth muffled the sound to a mumble. She tried to bite down but that only resulted in her teeth sliding over the stinking, sweaty palm. It disgusted her to the point of nearly vomiting.

Fighting with all her strength, she tried everything to get away from her attacker. Kicking him in the shins, stomping her heel on the top of his foot and attempting to unbalance them both to get his grip to loosen enough to escape. Nothing worked. In the reflection of the mirror across the room, she recognized the guy restraining her as one of Todd's partners. She began to scream again, but the look on his face and the huge fist he warned her with was enough to silence her. She had noticed most of the rooms in the place were empty so nobody would likely hear her anyway.

Finally, exhausted from her struggles, Lynnette stopped fighting and went still in his arms. It wasn't fair, she thought furiously. Men are stronger and can dominate women anytime they please. She hated being of the weaker sex. It meant having no sense of control over her life. He dragged her roughly to the bed in the corner of the room. He tied her hands to the headboard over her head and her ankles together and to the leg of the bed frame. He then stuffed a gag in her mouth and tied a bandana around it to hold it in place.

She lay there glaring up at him as he sat down across the room to wait for his buddy to return from searching town for her. Jake was right, she realized. They had been looking for her. She was really scared and wished she had listened to Jake.

* * *

Jake sat completely still on the hot sand near the edge of the water, the ocean lapping at his feet as he concentrated on a particular fishing boat as it rocked back and forth in the water. It was moored in the furthest row out directly in front of him. Taking his binoculars out of the duffle bag, he verified the name, Reel-Em-In, painted on the transom. He watched carefully for any sign of movement onboard, hoping to find Todd there alone. Better yet, he hoped this is where Todd was holding Keira and he could finish the job now. He just hoped the two Mexicans were not onboard with them. He would be far outnumbered, which wouldn't make his job easy.

Two stunning young girls on the beach wearing tiny bikinis and big smiles approached Jake asking blatantly if he was vacationing alone. They were obviously trying to find out if he brought a wife or girlfriend along. He talked with them awhile, continuing to keep an eye on the fishing boat. After a few minutes he still had not shown any real interest in either girl, so they turned and stalked away, convinced by his lack of response to his advances that he must be gay.

"What a waste," he could hear one remark. "All the best looking guys are gay."

Jake had to laugh at his own strange reaction to the two gorgeous females. A week ago, that same situation would have gone down much differently, he thought with a grin. Ever since meeting Lynnette though, he seemed to be unaffected by other beautiful women. Very strange, this recent change he was noticing in himself. He continued to observe the Reel-Em-In through the binos.

Once he felt relatively certain Todd was onboard with only one other person, Jake sealed up his waterproof bag, pulled it on over his shoulder and silently entered the warm turquoise-blue water. Gracefully and controlled, he quietly swam straight out to the Reel-Em-In and listened carefully as he raised his body up out of the water slowly so he would not cause the boat to rock. He could see over the back transom. Todd was pacing back and forth in the boat, a half empty bottle of booze hanging in one hand and a gun in the other. He sounded angry, talking loudly, but making little sense. Jake knew a drunk could be much more dangerous than someone sober who was thinking rationally. It wasn't clear whom he was speaking to. Knowing Todd was unpredictable, he decided to take extra precautions.

Easing his body gently back into the water, Jake moved to the bow of the boat and pulled his body up the mooring line to the edge of the bow. With one arm, he held himself up as he used the other to pull the bag off his shoulder and fasten it on a cleat. Carefully, he pulled his body slowly up onto the deck without causing any noticeable motion to the boat. He efficiently pulled his bag up on deck, unzipped it and pulled out his gun. Tucking it into the back of his shorts, he pulled out his money clip from his front pocket knowing money would get Todd's attention faster than anything else in his bag. It would serve as an effective distraction.

Staying low to the deck, Jake eased his way down the starboard railing toward the back of the boat, listening carefully to the heated conversation within.

"Todd, would you put the damn gun down before you shoot yourself in the foot," a female voice harped. "You're a drunken fool with a stupid plan. She's not going to give you the money."

"Oh yeah? What do you know you stupid bitch?" Todd slurred. "If it weren't for me, you wouldn't be getting any of the inheritance money, now would you?"

It only took a moment for Jake to realize things were not at all as Lynnette thought. Knowing he would get further to the truth with a little deception of his own, he made a quick decision. Just then, Jake tossed the money clip into the cockpit where it landed with a loud thump. As expected, Todd headed up the stairway and onto the back deck to see what the noise was. Quickly, Jake ducked down to peak into the window, knowing he would find Keira inside. Sure enough, he recognized her from the picture Lynnette had given him, but she wasn't restrained and there was nobody else inside the boat. Taking in the situation quickly, he confirmed it had been her voice speaking to Todd. Realizing she wasn't being held against her will, he decided to proceed for the moment as if he were actually rescuing her from Todd and pretend he hadn't heard their conversation. He knew she would likely deny the fact that she and Todd had hatched this plan together, yet she had no way of knowing Jake had heard their previous exchange.

Jake needed to secure a drunken, gun wielding Todd before he could do anything else.

Keira looked up in surprise at seeing Jake's face in the window. Putting a finger over his mouth he effectively communicated for her to stay quiet. Once he knew she understood, he gave her a quick nod. She slowly nodded, not knowing who he was and whether or not he was with the authorities. She needed to think fast on her feet in order to appear the victim here.

The next moment Jake was behind Todd in a flash. Grabbing both arms Jake swiftly restrained him as Todd dropped the bottle of tequila. Pulling out the lengths of cord he had tucked in his pocket, Jake quickly tied Todd's wrists together behind his back, enduring Todd's scathing curses.

"What the hell is this? Let go of me you bastard," Todd slurred, stumbling sideways, trying to look behind him to see whom it was.

Jake spun him around and pushed him backward into the seat behind him. Todd's unfocused eyes widened the moment he recognized Jake from the bar in town. Todd began to get up until Jake grabbed his neck in one hand and warned him not to move a muscle if he valued his pitiful life. Even stinking drunk, Todd saw the wisdom in obeying when he saw the intensely fierce look on Jake's face. Jake stood to his full height and turning around, he ordered Keira to join them on the aft deck.

Keira had no idea who this guy was, but she instinctively knew it was critical that she appear the victim in this situation until she had it figured out. She had never seen anyone like this before. He moved with amazing speed and she was completely undone by his good looks.

Jumping up, Keira ran over and threw her arms around Jake's neck.

"Thank you so much. You saved my life," she drawled out.

Unwrapping her arms from around his neck, he set her back a step. She continued to go on about how scared she had been and how awful Todd had been treating her. Jake raised an eyebrow as he realized her game. She carried on with her fabricated story and his eyes narrowed in disgust as he recognized the ease of her lies and the conniving way she was able to weave an even more complex tale the longer she continued. He was disgusted by the knowledge of what she was trying to do to her own sister as he recalled how terribly worried Lynnette had been. Lynnette obviously had no idea of just what level of deception Keira was capable of carrying out.

Lowering her lashes, Keira seductively asked, "Who are you anyway and how did you know I was being held captive out here?"

Ignoring her, Jake turned away to nudge Todd with his foot. Todd had passed out and looked like he would be out for a while. Jake slapped his cheek, but Todd didn't move a muscle.

Keira was undeterred by the fact that Jake was ignoring her. Seductively, she slinked toward him with a suggestive grin. He noted how blatantly obvious she was, but Jake had to admit to himself this girl could probably be a real handful. He found her attractive, but not nearly as much as her sister. He realized that fact probably wasn't lost on Keira either. Combined with her father's favoritism toward his firstborn child and knowing the control of the family trust was going to her older sister, this young woman had likely become very hateful and a convincingly deceitful liar. She had conceived a clever plan with her ex-stepbrother to extort money from her own sister. Well, at least she had been stopped in time. Jake certainly didn't want to be the one to break the news to Lynnette. It would break her heart. He wouldn't reveal his knowledge of their plot against Lynnette, not just yet anyway. He was curious how Keira would handle the situation when she saw her sister.

Keira continued her attempts to engage Jake in conversation with constant chatter and by flirting until he finally couldn't bear listening to another word.

"Enough with your lies, Keira. I know damn well that you and Todd are extorting Lynnette," he charged.

"What are you talking about?" she cried out. "That's not true. I was being held for a ransom, you idiot."

"Give it up, Keira. I just heard your conversation with Todd and I know you are trying to extort Lynnette," Jake stated, shaking his head in disgust at the situation.

Keira's demeanor changed instantly and her face contorted in her fury.

"That's not true and how dare you accuse me of such a thing! Who the hell are you and how do you even know us?" she demanded angrily.

"I'm a friend of your sister's. You've got some explaining to do, don't you?" he insisted.

"I don't have to tell you anything," she threw back.

"Not me. You're going to tell your sister. Look, you have a simple choice here, Keira. You either tell Lynnette what you've been up to or I will. It's your choice, but my advice is that you come clean with it," he threatened.

"I didn't ask for your advice, now did I?" she said curtly. "You know what? You just go ahead and do that," she retorted. "Just which of us do you think she's gonna believe, huh? You, her 'new friend' or me, her loving little sister?" she challenged.

Jake glared down at her in anger. "You're a real piece of work, aren't you?" She disgusted him and he couldn't resolve how she could even be related to a sweetheart like Lynnette.

"Come on. Let's get you out of here," he barked. "Your sister is really worried about you. She's waiting onboard my yacht. Go get your stuff together," he ordered. He didn't realize he had just referred to Ariel as his own.

Keira was furious she had been caught and that this guy hadn't responded to her flirtation, yet she had not missed the fact he owned a yacht. That and the fact he was handsome. Really handsome, she thought as she wondered what was up between him and Lynnette. She went below to gather her few things.

Turning his attention back to Todd, Jake decided to leave him lie where he was rather than drag him back to shore for a couple of reasons. One, it wouldn't be easy to explain the situation to the authorities for one and secondly, Todd was one of her family members. He might be an ex-stepbrother and a jerk, but a Mexican jail was the absolute worse place to land in, even for a guy like Todd. Jake reached down next to Todd to pick up the money clip he had thrown as a distraction. It had been a graduation gift from Uncle Elliot and he carried it with him at all times. Jake pulled away quickly, utterly repulsed by the stink coming off of Todd. The combination of Todd's cheap cologne and the disgusting stench of booze emanating from his skin were disgusting.

Jake decided to use Todd's dinghy to get Keira back to the Ariel. As Keira stepped into the dinghy, her bad attitude was obvious.

"You never answered my question. Who are you anyway?"

"I'm Jake Hunter. I met your sister on the flight down from Los Angeles last Friday." His answers were brief and he refused to look at Keira as he climbed into the small dinghy.

Keira was curious about Jake, but didn't trust herself to ask any more questions at the moment. She would get the information she was after out of Lynnette later.

"You're just going to leave Todd here like that?" she questioned.

"Yep," Jake stood in the dinghy to retrieve his bag from the deck of the fishing boat and then sat down and started the engine.

Keira felt unsettled, knowing she would have to really think about how to best handle this situation before it all came unraveled. She certainly wasn't going to let Lynnette get control of all of the family trust and then have to ask every time she wanted some money of her own. No, she wanted what was rightfully hers now, no matter how she had to get it.

It was a quiet ride back to where his yacht was docked. Keira was deep in thought, concocting her plan. Jake cut the engine on the dinghy when he pulled alongside his yacht. Miguel came out to meet them. Maria and a few other crewmen closely followed behind Miguel. Keira climbed up onto the deck, followed by Jake. Jake introduced Keira to Miguel and Maria. With fresh new ears to hear her tale, Keira took the opportunity to share with them an exaggerated version of her horrible experience. Jake closed his eyes as he massaged the bridge of his nose. Her story sounded even more horrific than the tale she had told him earlier.

Maria, who was always compassionate toward others, was taken by her tall tale. She reached out to console Keira, gently patting the back of her hand. At first, it caught Keira off guard. She had been getting so involved in her story telling, she was surprised at the passionate response her acting was getting from Maria. She smiled smugly to herself, knowing she had pulled off the lie.

Jake asked Miguel to bring Eric up from the locked room below deck. It was time to get rid of Eric for good. "Pay him for his few days labor in cash and get him out of here." "Where's Lynnette, Maria?" Jake asked. He was curious to see Keira's initial interaction with her sister. "I thought she'd be the first one out here by now to greet her long lost sister," Jake stated, giving Keira a sideways glance. She had not yet even asked for her older sister.

Maria suddenly looked concerned. "Oh no, Jake. I have not seen her since we docked." Watching the concern on Jake's face, Maria also noticed how Keira looked up at Jake with such odd interest on her young face. It seemed strange that the talkative young woman would be standing so close to him. They had just met. Was she trying to flirt with him? Maria noted that Jake paid no attention in any event, but where was that scared girl of a few minutes ago?

Maria offered to take Keira below deck to find Lynnette. Taking a firm hold on Keira's unwilling arm, she firmly led her away from Jake's side. He nodded in thanks to Maria. "Maybe she does not know you are here yet," she added as the two women headed across the deck toward the stairs.

"No, Maria, that's alright. I'll just wait up here with Jake until she..."

Keira resisted, but it was futile. Maria continued down the stairs, Keira in tow frowning.

Jake waited impatiently up on deck. He had a bad feeling and wanted to see Lynnette for himself. Miguel escorted Eric off the yacht and Eric's eyes pierced Jake as he brushed past him. Jake thought he heard him issue a low warning sounding something like, "Watch your back, asshole."

As Maria and Keira arrived back up on deck, they heard Jake's assertive, yet controlled voice threatening Eric as he secured him by the collar in one large fist.

"...now, go on, Eric. Get the hell out of here and I don't ever want to see you again. Understood?" Jake's voice sounded deadly. It was enough to intimidate the toughest of men.

Jake waited. No response, although Eric looked frightened enough. Jake's voice rose as he shook Eric briefly. "I said, you got it?"

Eric finally agreed and Jake pushed him aside. Eric stumbled backward barely catching himself before falling.

Keira leaned toward Maria to whisper, "What did that guy do to make Jake so mad?"

"He tried to force himself on your sister last night and I think Jake is quite taken with her," Maria added with a contented smile.

Keira looked over at Maria in amazement. How had this all this happened to Lynnette so fast? It was always Keira that had all the guys, not Lynnette. Lynnette never attracted guys. She never even dated.

"Maria, is this yacht really his?" she asked taking it all in.

"Yes, it's the newest one of his fleet," Maria innocently answered.

Keira continued without taking a breath. "I just can't believe Lynnette could have ever landed a guy like him in less than a week." Jealousy was overtaking Keira at the realization of what Jake offered. Lynnette had all the luck. Why couldn't this have happened to her instead? She was now fuming inside. Lynnette gets the hunk, control of the estate and the family businesses. This was just so wrong.

Jake turned and approached the two women. Keira couldn't get over how gorgeous Jake was and thought she might go after him if Lynnette didn't want him. Hell, he's rich, good looking and that combination always interested Keira. He stopped in front of them, doing a quick double take at the odd expression on Keira's face. Strange, yet comical somehow. Disregarding it, he turned to give Maria his attention.

"Where's Lynnette?" he asked.

Maria knew delaying would not help matters so she just came straight out with it. "We cannot find her onboard, Jake. Maybe she just took a walk to get her land legs back."

"Shit, she's done it again," he cursed under his breath, spinning away and punching his fist into his other hand. He stormed across deck to the port facing railing. "She knew I didn't want her to leave Ariel and she did it anyway." His eyes quickly scanned the shoreline. No sign of her anywhere in site. "Todd's two goons had probably been waiting for her and she walked right to them. "Damn it," he exploded in frustration, "if she isn't the most stubborn, head-strong, frustrating woman I've ever met in my life."

His sudden outburst startled Maria and Keira down to their toes. Jake's temper would be intimidating to the bravest of souls, but to the two women, he sounded downright frightening. They were each quite pleased at the moment that his anger wasn't directed at them.

"Miguel," Jake called out sharply to his first mate. "Get us provisioned for the trip north again and be ready to leave in two hours time. I think I know where to find Lynnette. I'll be back as soon as I can. Keep a close eye on Keira for me, will you? Don't let her leave and don't trust her for a minute. Believe me, she's not what she appears."

With that, Jake was off the boat and running up the docks past the parking lot. He was headed for the center of town, leaving Keira at the rail watching him disappear as she schemed how she might get Jake interested in her and away from her sister.

NINETEEN

Lynnette was frantic as she continued to pull at the rope around her wrists hoping to slide her hands out of the bindings. The Mexican had dozed off about ten minutes earlier and in that time she had already rubbed her wrists raw. She knew she had to get out of here soon or the second guy would show up. Then they would demand the money from her, which she didn't have with her, it was aboard the Ariel. She certainly didn't want to lead them back there. They could hurt someone or worse. She couldn't get her hands loose and was more frightened than ever.

The sudden banging on the door startled her as did the sound of the second Mexican yelling loudly to open the door. Her captor woke from his sleep and stood, looking over to check on her. She glared at him. Opening the door, Todd's second partner sauntered in with a six-pack of beer and a look of satisfaction on his face as he spotted Lynnette tied up on the bed.

The two goons argued in Spanish, but Lynnette got the basic idea of their disagreement. The newcomer was angry her feet were tied together and wanted the other guy to let him have some fun with her. The first guy kept pointing at his watch and saying "no" repeatedly.

The first guy finally backed down and went into the bathroom.

Lynnette's eyes went wide in alarm as the second Mexican approached the bed with a knife in his hand. She was frozen in terror. She never expected things could go so wrong. Would he violate her and then kill her or would he just kill her quickly? How many times would he stab her before she couldn't feel it any more? No, that didn't make sense. First, he would want the location of the money. That was her only hope. Oh, why hadn't she listened to Jake and stayed on the boat?

She held her breath as he came at her with the knife. She watched him cut the bindings on her ankles and then he laid the knife on the nightstand. She exhaled loudly. It was a complete shock to her as he then climbed over her body. She must think, fast. When he straddled her, she instinctively brought her knee up as hard as she could into his groin. He cried out in intense pain, bringing his buddy flying out of the bathroom to see what was the problem.

The second guy might have been in incredible pain, but not so much as to keep him from retaliating. He struck Lynnette in the face as hard as he could. She saw it coming and deflected as much of the blow as possible by shifting her head quickly to the side.

Jake edged carefully up to the window of Lynnette's hotel room and heard male voices shouting inside. He recognized the sound the instant he heard a fist making contact with flesh. He heard her muffled moan and his hands curled instinctively into fists. His jaw clamped down hard as he attempted to control his raging anger. One of them had just hit Lynnette and would seriously regret it shortly. Knowing there were two men in the room with her, he knew he would have to work quickly and accurately to keep Lynnette from being hurt any further.

Moving quietly to stand in front of the door, every muscle in his body was on the ready. He stepped back, reached out with one foot and in a moment kicked the door open. Inside the room in an instant, he quickly disabled the closest guy by reaching around his neck and choking off his oxygen supply. Easily tossing him aside unconscious, he saw in the mirror the second guy coming quickly from behind holding a broken off beer bottle.

Jake shot a quick glance over at Lynnette. He could see her gagged and tied up on the bed across the room, both scared and pissed off, all at the same time. Damn, he loved her spunk. He would release her in a bit, but first he had to take care of this idiot trying to kill him first.

Turning to face the guy, Jake noticed the sharp edges of glass as the guy held the neck of a broken bottle in his right hand. He also noticed the goon was a whole foot shorter than he was. Knowing he didn't have the arm length to reach his body, Jake knowingly grinned down at him. The first swing of glass at his torso was surprisingly quick. Jake jumped back in reflex, realizing he couldn't underestimate his opponent. Reaching out with his right hand, then grabbing the guy's wrist holding the bottle with his left, he squeezed tightly enough to get him to release the bottle. As it dropped to the carpet, he felt a powerful punch in the rib cage. He was certainly strong enough, Jake had to give him that. Each hit from then on was solid. He hit like an Irish boxer, but after awhile all it resulted in was to piss Jake off. He wondered which one of these two punks had struck Lynnette and his anger grew more intense. What kind of man hits a woman in the face? Glancing over, he could see the dark bruises rising on Lynnette's cheeks even in the dimly lit room.

Jake turned to the stout Mexican. His patience was gone. He reached out and punched him squarely in the nose and heard it break instantly. Continuing his assault with a series of body punches, Jake finally sent a hard blow to his jaw, knocking the guy out cold. Damn, this guy went down hard.

Shaking out his fist, which was now a bit tender from over use, he rushed to Lynnette's side. He quickly untied the bandana and removed the gag from her mouth, all the while telling her how angry he was at her for disobeying him.

"Oh Jake, I know I should have listened to you. You were right," she cried holding him tightly around the neck. "They were waiting for me, just like you said," she sobbed in relief as a nervous rush of tears flowed down her bruised cheeks.

"Damn it, Lynnette! When I told you to stay put, I meant it. You scared the hell out of me. You could have been raped or killed if I hadn't shown up when I did."

Lynnette felt the change in mood come over her in a wave. No longer was she crying. She was getting really angry with him.

Noticeably withdrawing, she brusquely requested, "Enough already. Would you please just untie me now? I already said you were right."

As he effortlessly untied her wrists, he continued. "Well, if you aren't the most stubborn, ungrateful..."

"I really don't want to hear it, Jake. I was wrong and you were right," she frowned.

"Shut up and let me finish my rescue before you get angry with me again, alright?"

He finished untying her, amazed at her constant change in moods. Just a little while ago, she sat there looking scared and shaken, yet now she was acting as stubborn as ever. Oddly, he admired her all the more for it. At least she wasn't playing the mousy, useless victim. She certainly was a strong and resilient woman.

"Lynnette, I guess I'm just destined to be the guy who rushes around behind you, protecting you from each dopey mistake you make. I suppose this is just my fate," he finished, standing to his full height and reaching down to take her hands to help her off the bed. Looking down at her wrists, he frowned at the redness where she had struggled to get free of the bindings.

"Hey, wait a minute. Are you sure you're all right, sweetheart?" he asked while gently examining her wrists. She noticed the deep concern in his voice.

"Yes, I'm fine," she answered, looking up at him. She admittedly still loved to hear him call her sweetheart. "I was just scared, that's all. Did you find Keira, Jake? Is she all right?

Frowning momentarily at the reminder of Keira's deceit, he hesitated in answering since he didn't think he should be the one to tell her. It really should come from Keira, so he answered as honestly as possible.

"Yes, she is fine. She is with Maria on the Ariel. Come on. Let's get you back so you can see her." He was more curious than ever to find out how Keira would respond to Lynnette now that her extorting scheme hadn't worked out as planned.

As Lynnette turned to leave, Jake added, "Hold on a minute. I want to tie up these two jerks and call the Mexican Policia."

Once Jake had them both secured and gagged, he called down to the front desk to summon the authorities. Grabbing Lynnette's suitcase in one hand and taking her hand securely in his other, they headed downstairs to load her bag into the rental car. After they finished speaking with the authorities, Jake drove them back down the streets of Cabo, winding his way toward the docks. It was a bright and sunny afternoon and after being stuck in the cool, dark room for so long, it took Lynnette's eyes awhile to adjust. She was satisfied to trust him to get her there without a worry. It was amazing how he made her feel so angry one moment and so trusting of him the next.

"Lynnette, I've decided I want you to sail up the coast back to California with me," Jake announced suddenly, glancing over at her in the passenger seat. "Your sister can sail back with us too, if you like. We could use more time together to get to know each other better and I know we'll have a good time. It makes the most sense in order to give me time to change your mind about marrying this other guy," he added.

He knew he was being a bit deceptive considering he was the other guy, but it was for Lynnette's own good. Not only did he need to determine from Keira if she and Todd would cause future trouble, but he also knew without a doubt Lynette would be absolutely furious when she found out that he was the one her father had chosen for her to marry. He only had a short time to be certain she loved him in return and to get her to realize they were right for each other. Once she admitted it to herself, then he could come clean with the plan and tell her the truth. But first, he needed more time alone with her and sailing north nine hundred or so miles would give him that time.

Lynnette cringed inside. She had no intention of sailing back home with him, but how should she tell him? Admittedly, she knew she wanted to be with him more than anything else in the world, but she also knew she had already decided to go on ahead with her father's plans. Knowing she was probably falling in love with him, there was just no way of knowing for sure if it would last. It was too new to be certain. Was it just infatuation? If it didn't work out with him, she would have gambled and lost everything for naught; her business, her inheritance, everything she had worked so hard for these many years. If she didn't give them a chance though, she might never feel this way about any man again. Her draw to him was stronger than any attraction she had ever felt before and there was no denying the chemistry between them was nothing short of fantastic.

Jake stopped the car in the intersection and turned to face Lynnette. The fact she had not answered was her answer. She glanced over at him knowing he was still waiting for her to answer. He just stared at her as she chewed on her lower lip. It was a nervous habit she had, he noticed.

Lynnette glanced up at him again trying to figure the best words to use. Oh, why did he have to look so handsome? It made it so much harder to do this. No, she couldn't do it. Avoidance was the best answer.

"Jake, I promise to think about it. Right now, I really just want to get back to see Keira. What happened with Todd, anyway?" she asked hoping to change the subject.

Angry now, Jake was aware but unconcerned that they were blocking traffic in both directions on the dusty main road through town.

"You've already made up your mind, haven't you?" he accused accurately. His eyes held her frozen in place as other cars began honking in impatience. His lips were a thin line on his angry face.

"No I haven't," she hedged, looking down. She was unable to look him straight in the face.

Knowing the truth, he continued. "Yes you have, Lynnette. Don't sit there and lie to me. If you are already so sure of your answer, then there is no reason to delay you from leaving any further. Let's go," he snapped. "You and Keira can drive to the airport tonight."

As he depressed the clutch and put the car in gear, she suddenly realized that angry drivers on both sides of the car were furiously honking at them. She hadn't even heard their horns blaring until now.

Disturbed and upset, Lynnette held on to the dashboard as Jake drove a brisk pace back to the Ariel. Wishing she could say what he wanted to hear, she knew it was too late. He would never calm down until she agreed not to marry the other guy and to give them a chance, but she just couldn't do it. As much as she might want to, she couldn't. Maybe it would be for the best if she just left so they could each get back to their normal lives again.

Racing along the docks back to the Ariel, it was all Lynnette could do to keep up with Jake. He was pissed off and walking fast, his long legged stride impossible to keep up with without running. She could see Keira up on the deck of Ariel even from this distance and was pleased to see her safe and sound.

"Jake, thank you for bringing Keira back safely," she called ahead to him as he continued along the line of boats. "I really do appreciate it."

"No problem. I said I'd do it," he replied curtly over his shoulder.

"Jake, stop!" she implored. "Please don't be so angry with me and just try to understand this from my point of view. It's a really difficult situation."

Jake stopped walking and turned to face her. Looking down at her, he could sense the distress she was feeling and softened a bit towards her.

"You're right. This is complicated," he replied, rubbing the back of his stiff neck. She didn't even know the half of it yet. "Just promise me you'll not make any hasty moves once you get home and stay open minded about us. I'll get back in to Long Beach harbor late next week and we'll get together to discuss this further, alright?"

Lynnette hesitated and then finally nodded in agreement.

"Yes, I'll try to wait until you're back, but my father will put a lot of pressure on me by next Friday. He planned an engagement party and I don't know if I can delay it much later than that."

"Give me your number and I'll call you when I'm coming in."

"Okay. I'll write it down when we get back onboard," she suggested.

"You can just tell me and I'll remember. I'm fairly good with numbers," he modestly answered. He could still remember the combination to his junior high locker even to this day. She said the number, he made a mental note of it and then he gently kissed her, as they stood on the dock in the afternoon sunshine. It was a long, sweet, passionate kiss and they savored the moment. Taking her hand, he smiled down at her and then led her the remaining length of the gangway to his slip.

No one noticed Keira still standing nearby on the deck above, glaring down with overwhelming and barely controlled jealousy. The cold look on her face was telling of her anger. The depth of her intense desire to take what was now her sister's was immense and she wanted to be in Lynnette's place at that moment, more than anything. It just wasn't fair. Things were going to change though, she'd see to it.

As Jake helped Lynnette up the stairs and on to the deck, Maria hurried ahead of Miguel to greet her first. Hugging her tightly, she then took Lynnette's hands.

"Oh my, Lynnette, you had us so worried. Jake was furious when I couldn't find you onboard and we had no idea where you went," Maria rushed on. "Are you okay?"

"Yes, I'm fine now," she answered, glancing back at Jake, whispering a 'thank-you' to him. He grinned down at her.

"Where's Keira?" Lynnette asked in concern. Jake's face hardened as he looked directly at Miguel. Miguel knew Jake was concerned she had fled. He nodded at Jake, letting him know it was fine and that she was still onboard. Maria held back any comment, already realizing something was amiss with the girl.

Just then, Keira appeared on the aft deck.

"This yacht is so gorgeous," Keira exclaimed in excitement, already imagining herself in this lifestyle. "I can't wait to see the others in your fleet, Jake."

Jake frowned. Miguel let out a groan and Maria glanced over at Lynnette for a reaction to the fact Keira had not yet even greeted her.

"Keira?" Lynnette said, curious why her sister didn't look upset by her recent ordeal.

"Oh, hi, Lynnette," Keira responded. "Thanks for sending Jake out to save me. It was just terrible, Lynnette," she began again with a fabricated story of her own making.

The fact she hadn't hugged her sister yet wasn't lost of the three of them watching. Lynnette looked somewhat surprised, but handled her discomfort well. As Keira expanded on her version of the story, Jake stepped forward and loudly cleared his voice, reminding Keira of his warning about telling her sister the truth or he would do so.

Cutting her off short, Lynnette told Keira she was glad it had turned out so well and that she needed to collect her things from Jake's stateroom. Keira was seeing red, angry at being cut off, but hid it as best she could. Following Lynnette down the main companionway, Jake glared at Keira as he brushed past her. She fixed her eyes defiantly on him, but didn't budge.

* * *

It was now hours past sunset, Tuesday night, and the sky was completely dark. The night air was chilly in California in late October in comparison to the daytime heat of the Baja desert. Even as they landed at LAX airport, Keira continued harping on Lynnette about Jake. As they exited the plane, Lynnette walked briskly ahead of her following the overhead signs to the baggage claim area on the lower level.

"I still can't believe you, Lynnette," Keira exclaimed in confusion hurrying to keep up with her sister. Lynnette had so far successfully refused to discuss Jake with her sister the entire trip home, but Keira was seemingly relentless on the topic. Lynnette was getting exasperated.

Keira had figured out her angle. She assumed if Lynnette thought she might lose Jake to her sister, she might want him all the more and if Lynnette decided to be with Jake, she would anger their father to the point of losing her position with the family trust. Keira figured she would possibly then get her portion instead of Lynnette. So, Keira simply planned to get Lynnette to choose Jake and possibly lose her position as executrix of the trust when their father passed. It was a perfectly simple plan.

"Just tell me how in the world could you not want to be with him, Lynn? He's a hunk. He's so dark and handsome, so masculine and I think he's rich besides. Any woman would dream about nabbing a guy like him," Keira continued relentlessly, obviously expressing her own personal desires for Jake. "Maybe I could nab Jake if you don't want him," she said cunningly.

Finally losing her patience, Lynnette stopped in her tracks and turned to face Keira.

"No you can't, Keira. Don't even go there. Look, I know all of that is true of Jake, but I can't be with him," she exclaimed as she continued on to the baggage carousel. "You already know that Father made other plans for me. And women don't nab men, Keira, they're supposed to fall in love and marry them. I don't know where you get all these ideas. Oh, and not that it matters, but Jake is not rich. He's a hired hand on that boat. It's not his."

Keira smirked and followed Lynnette through the sliding glass doors and over to the baggage carousel. It was slowly revolving, but there were no signs of any luggage unloaded from the airplane as yet.

"No, I don't think he's a hired hand on the yacht and I really think he owns it," Keira responded. "I heard him mention twice that it was his yacht and I think he's probably just as rich as he is handsome."

Lynnette rolled her eyes heavenward.

"Personally Lynn, I think you're nuts," Keira continued harping on the matter. "You're certifiably crazy. Why, I'd just die to be with a guy like him. He's such a hunk," Keira sighed with a dreamy look on her face.

"Keira, you're acting like a little drama queen. Knock it off. He's not right for you, so don't even think about it."

Keira just glared at the back of Lynnette's head as she pulled her bag off the carousel. If Lynnette didn't want him, then he was fair game as far as she was concerned. He was certainly better looking than that other handsome guy she had met in the Cabo airport bar before boarding their flight. He had approached and introduced himself as Eric while Lynnette had been in the ladies room and although he was somewhat charming, he hadn't been nearly as attractive as Jake, nor probably as rich. She had given him her number anyway. You never know. Now that Keira was aware that the plan with Todd had failed, she would have to come up with another one, an even better one. She needed a perfect plan that didn't involve Todd, the stupid, drunken idiot. He had screwed everything up and now she still had nothing.

She would have to beg to Lynnette for anything she wanted. Well that was going to change and she would most certainly see to it.

She needed to make sure Lynnette didn't find out she was in on the extortion plot and must also think of a way to keep Todd silent. Then she could work on ensuring her position in the family trust.

TWENTY

Jake had been on a north-northwest heading for several days, heading back up the coast to Long Beach. He allowed for only two short stops coming north. One was at Bahia Tortugas, a lovable, dusty little fishing village known as Turtle Bay where they fueled up, and another quick stop at Bahia Santa Maria, a gorgeous bay in the middle of nowhere. He felt pressed to get home, but the crew needed a break. They had been lucky with consistent moderate-to-strong head winds and small-to-moderate seas.

Jake had spent long hours at the wheel, doing some serious thinking and had drawn some conclusions. One was a realization that in a very short time, Lynnette had changed his outlook on life. He had not previously felt about any other woman the way he did toward Lynnette. He had felt more exhilarated and alive in those four days with her than he had felt in years. She was an intriguing woman and although she could be a pain in the ass, he ached with desire to be with her again.

Jake had also decided it was best not to inform his Uncle Elliot just yet that he had inadvertently met Lynnette. He had come to the realization that he could not go ahead with marriage to Lynnette under these circumstances. He felt it was horribly wrong for Mac to force his own daughter into marriage, even if it was to him. He knew he had to quickly resolve the situation before she learned from someone else that he was the unknown groom. He wanted to be the one to explain it to her.

Thinking back to how they had parted on Tuesday afternoon, he had to admit he was anxious to get back home. They had not had much chance to speak in private before she left for the airport except for the few minutes as she was collecting her things in his stateroom.

Jake had opened the door and found her stuffing her few belongings in the backpack full of money. They had stood there in awkward silence.

"Well, I guess this is goodbye," she'd said weakly.

"Yes, I suppose it is, for now anyway."

Lynnette had looked down at her feet uncomfortably.

"Jake, I really thank you so much for getting Keira back safely for me and for everything else too."

"Sure thing" Jake quietly responded.

Standing there in his stateroom, the vivid memories of all that had taken place between them the past few days had been overwhelming. Their goodbye had been so terribly awkward.

"Jake, I..., I need to go now," she had stated uncomfortably.

"Lynnette, you're acting like we'll never see each other again," he had stated. "Like I said earlier, I'll call you when I get back."

She simply nodded.

"Pending unforeseen weather conditions," he said, "I should be there by next Thursday."

Everything had felt so awkward. Jake had reached down, kissing her on the forehead and then gave her a hug.

Walking away, he had left the room realizing she was too confused at the moment for any more input just now. What a mess they were in. Well like he always said, things have a way of working themselves out. He suspected this would be no different. It was time to get tough with himself, this wasn't an easy situation he was in.

As he sat at the helm, heading north just off the coast of Huntington Beach, he recalled when she had left with Keira for the airport. As they drove away destined for the Cabo San Lucas airport, Jake had thought to himself how odd it was just how much it bothered him to see her go. He had just met her the Friday before. It was amazing how someone can impact your life so quickly and unexpectedly. Either way, he would be seeing more of Lynnette Ocean once he got back home.

Now, days out at sea, he was feeling bored. Now that she was gone, there were no unexpected surprises. There were no emotional outbursts or things flying at his head. There were no stolen glances across the room as he thought of what he would do to her once behind closed doors. Meals were now just food for the empty hole in his gut. His bed was a place to flop for rest. His sense of humor was gone and he was short-tempered to boot.

* * *

Once Lynette got home, she returned the cash to the bank, caught up on errands and then tried to get back into her daily routine. She hoped to take her mind off of Jake. As usual she set her coffee maker to go off each morning before five o'clock. She then took her morning run before work along the cliffs over the beach along Corona Del Mar. Each night she came home to watch her favorite television shows. She tried to keep busy, but by Thursday, she was only thinking of Jake getting home within the week. When she got home Thursday night, she cooked a quick meal and then sat down next to the fireplace to read more of a romance novel she had started a few days before. Curled up in her favorite overstuffed chair, she tried to focus on the same page for five minutes without successfully getting into the story. It was no use. Just as everything else had that week, it all felt empty and unfulfilling. Everything reminded her of Jake and she continually wondered where he was at that exact moment and what he was doing.

During her morning runs, she looked out over the Pacific remembering how it felt to stand at the railing of Ariel and look out to sea with Jake there beside her. Now being back home, she was miserable and to top it off, she felt like she was catching a cold. Walking into the kitchen, she made herself a cup of hot tea and chewed on a couple vitamin C tablets.

She jumped, startled as the phone suddenly rang next to her on the kitchen counter.

"Hello?" she answered.

"Hi. It's Barb."

Lynnette paused, confused for the moment by her distraction. Lynnette only now remembered it had been her turn to make the weekly call. Every Thursday night for nearly two years they had both curled up with a glass of wine and talked on the phone three thousand miles apart, Barbara living in Maryland and Lynnette in California. They loved their weekly chat and never missed it.

"Hey, what's going on with you? Barbara asked. You didn't call tonight and now you sound distracted. Is everything alright?"

"No. I mean yes. I'm sorry, Barb. I spaced out and I forgot to call. I'm just not myself this week."

"What's going on out there?"

"I can't slip anything past you, can I?" Lynnette smiled into the phone. Barbara was smart and savvy, always aware of everything before Lynnette even shared with her.

"Are the girls asleep yet?" Lynnette inquired about Barbara's two daughters, five and two years old.

"Yes, sleeping like little angels."

"Then let me pour my glass of wine and get settled in first. What are we having tonight, red or white?" Lynnette asked.

"White, chardonnay," Barbara responded.

"Okay. Hey, Barb, you won't believe what I have to tell you."

Much later, Barbara had been informed of everything that had transpired, from Mac's demand that Lynnette marry a stranger to her trip to Cabo San Lucas and all that had happened including meeting Jake. Barbara was nearly speechless.

"Are you making this stuff up?" Barbara accused. "I can't believe after all the months, no wait..., after years of your routine life, you mean to tell me this much has happened since we spoke last week?"

"I know. It's been a whirlwind and I'm overwhelmed by it all. What do you think I should do, Barb?" she asked.

"Well, I know what I would do, but you're not me. Tell me this though. What has been foremost on your mind this week at work, at home and during your run in the morning?" Barb asked.

"Honestly?"

"Of course, silly. You want my help or not?"

Lynnette thought back over the days since she had been home and realized Jake had been on her mind constantly. Everything reminded her of the short time they'd had together. She awoke in the night clinging to her pillow as if it were his lean body next to hers. Lying in bed at night waiting for the peace of sleep to overcome her, she wiggled restlessly under the covers in remembrance of Jake's passionate kisses and the feel of his strong hands on her bare skin. She shared as much with Barbara.

Taking a long sip of wine, Barb answered with her usual wisdom. "There's your answer, Lynnette. It appears the only right decision for you is to give this guy, Jake, a chance and not to agree to marry this stranger."

"You really think so?" Lynnette asked again for confirmation of what her heart was telling her.

"Of course. Your father is such a jerk to try to make you marry a guy you haven't even met," Barbara added. She had never liked Lynnette's father anyway and couldn't feel badly about his demise. He wasn't a pleasant man and never had been.

"But, Barbara, we just met. What if I'm giving up everything and it doesn't work out between us?" Lynnette groaned in dismay. She took a sip of wine and moved down on to the carpet to get closer to the fireplace.

"I think you're really over thinking this. There are no guarantees in life or in relationships, but you should follow your heart, Lynnette. Forget about this stupid idea of you father's. Seems like an easy decision to me."

"Well, there's also the business I'll lose. I've worked hard for so long to build it up to what it is now. I have some really exciting plans for expanding it into some new related areas too. I'll lose everything," she moaned.

"It doesn't matter. You're smart, capable and can start your own new business from the ground up if you have to and I have all the confidence in the world you'll be just fine without your father's inheritance. Lynnette, it's just wrong for him to hold that over you and you've been sick and tired of his control anyway for years, so why not finally show him your independence. Who knows, maybe your dad will change his mind before it's too late. People do, you know," Barbara reasoned, although not convinced Lynette's stubborn father would ever come around.

"How strange, that's just what Jake told me," Lynnette recalled, deep in thought. She could remember the deep timbre of Jake's voice and the confident look on his face as he firmly expressed his opinion. He was so sure of himself and his choices. Why couldn't she be that way too instead of being so undecided all the time?

"When does Jake get back anyway?" Barbara asked.

"Well, I don't know exactly, but he said he would call me as soon as he got into Long Beach harbor. He thought he would get here by next Thursday. What if he changed his mind about me and doesn't call when he gets here?"

"I seriously doubt that, Lynnette. Now you're just being silly. Just be patient, he'll contact you when he can. In the meantime, why don't you phone your dad to call off the dinner party next week and then call Jake to leave him a message? Do you have his phone number?"

"Yes," she answered, her stomach turning flips at the thought of calling Jake. "I'm getting all nervous and excited just thinking about it. Oh, Barb, do you really think I should do this? It's crazy and completely not me."

"Yes, I do and no it's not. Just go for it. Women dream of meeting men like Jake. After everything you've just told me, he sounds terrific and I think you'd be a fool not to give it a chance with him. Just relax and let it happen naturally. It's going to be fine, Lynnette. You'll see."

Sipping her chardonnay, Lynnette stared into the fire amazed how Barbara could make everything so clear and decisions so simple. How did she do it?

"You're amazing, Barbara. I really appreciate your advice and wisdom. I'm so glad to have you as my best friend," the quiver in her voice revealing her emotional state. "Okay, enough about me. How is everything out there with Richard and the kids?"

"Well, that's actually why I was trying to reach you. Everyone here is fine, but I need to come out there next Friday to see my mom. She's scheduled for an unexpected surgery and I want to be there with her. Can you pick me up next Friday afternoon at John Wayne Airport at about four and then run me over to her house?"

"Sure," Lynnette replied.

"I'm coming in on Southwest, flight 472."

"Of course, but what's wrong with your mom?" Lynnette asked with concern.

Barbara explained the blockage in her artery and the possibility of a bypass surgery if a stint wasn't enough. After more conversation and another glass of wine, Barbara finally admitted it was getting late.

"It's been great talking with you, but it's almost eleven o'clock here and I've got to get some sleep."

"Yeah, okay. Hey, Barb. Your mom's going to be just fine," Lynnette consoled.

"Of course she will," Barbara replied confidently.

"Love you. Bye," Lynnette said quietly before hanging up. Lynnette decided it would be great if she could be as confident and self-assured as Barbara was, rather than to second-guess every decision in life.

Taking a deep breath, Lynnette picked the phone back up and called her father to cancel the engagement party.

*   *   *

After many long days out at sea, motoring into Long Beach was a welcomed sight. They had dropped the sails earlier when the wind had died and from quite a distance off, Jake could make out the majestic city skyline of the variously shaped tall buildings lit up in the night. He could see the white dome he knew housed the world's largest wooden airplane built by Howard Hughes and named the Spruce Goose. Next to it, the Queen Mary was docked proudly where she had been positioned as a Long Beach landmark for years and would hopefully be for years to come. She was a romantic and historical beauty that he always enjoyed touring when visitors came to town. Yes, he had grown to love this town. Although it was a big city and major seaport for the west coast, he was always surprised it had such a small town feel to it.

Without having to say a word, his crew appeared on deck with fenders and dock lines in hand, working together tying them off to the starboard cleats. The closer they came to the dock in Rainbow Harbor, the more excited Jake became at arriving home. Jake's excitement was a strangely unique feeling for him and he expected it mostly had to do with the anticipation of seeing Lynnette again. He would go home and call her tonight. Maybe they could still get together, although it was Thursday night and she would have to work tomorrow.

The night air was calm, but cold. Looking out across the marina, the lights from the high-rise buildings reflected in the small ripples. Jake could see clearly the most prominent building along the waterfront, where he had purchased a penthouse flat on the upper level. They lit up the unique green copper roof at night, making it stand out dignified from all other buildings in the city, whether day or night. His flat in the fantastic historic Villa Riviera, a landmark built back in 1928 as a hotel and then recently converted to condos and flats. When he had first looked for a property in Long Beach, he had toured many of the other newer luxury high rise condos, many that also offered commanding ocean views, but Villa Riviera clearly stood out from the others with the 10 foot high ceilings, remarkable architecture and large, open floor plans. It was also within walking distance to any number of fine restaurants, movies, entertainment, as well as the docks. Jake loved it here.

Leaving Miguel in charge of the yacht for the night, he gave quick instructions to begin preparations for the charter north and then took off at a brisk pace up the hill toward his flat. He had an important phone call to make.

*　　*　　*

Thinking back to the week before Lynnette realized that the phone call with her father had not gone as badly as she had expected. Sitting on the couch to calm her nerves before calling Jake's number, she warmed herself next the fireplace. She shivered thinking back to the conversation with her father. It could have been worse, she knew, but when he had finally stopped yelling long enough to listen, she had explained her reasoning to him. She had been proud of the fact she had stuck to her guns. She was just as proud of the fact she had not started crying until after she hung up. It felt somehow liberating to have finally stood up to her father. After awhile, he had finally agreed he would cancel the dinner party and then asked her to come up to the house to visit him a week from Saturday for lunch. That was certainly different. He hadn't ordered her to be there, nor summoned her to his office. He had actually asked her to come over for lunch. Amazing. Sitting there in complete wonderment, she tried to take it all in.

It was Thursday night and getting late, but she hadn't heard from Jake yet. Barb had made her promise to call him tonight. She always made it a point never to call anyone at home after nine o'clock at night, so she quickly found Jake's phone number in the entry table where she had placed it last week for safe keeping and sat down to dial his number.

*　　*　　*

Sharon rode up the elevator to Jake's penthouse suite, digging in her sequined bag for the key. It had been a couple of weeks since she had seen him and had put up with his temper long enough. Now it was her turn to be upset. He hadn't even had the decency to call her since their big fight. She thought going away to Palm Springs for two weeks would make him come find her or at least she would come home to a string of messages from him wondering where she was. He didn't even call once, she fumed, unlocking his front door and slipping inside.

As expected, he wasn't home and the lights were all out. The room wasn't dark though, for the city lights reflected through the windows with an elegant glow. Sharon loved his place. It was so richly impressive and masculine. She could faintly smell a hint of his tastefully refined cologne and made her way carefully across the polished hardwood floor in her spike heels to his desk. Turning on the desk lamp, she began to flip though his mail looking for anything that might give her a clue that he was seeing another woman. Sure, he had broken up with her and asked for his key back, but she knew he was just angry with her. It wasn't enough of a reason to break it off, was it? So, she had gotten really upset with him for leaving her yet again to go on one of his trips? So what? She didn't like to be left alone. Then he had also been angry about her reaction during his friend's dinner party when Jake had been speaking to that horrible blond his buddy brought along, so she yelled at him and they left the party. Couldn't he tell the bimbo was flirting with him and embarrassing her in the process? God, men were thick.

Not finding anything of interest on the desk, she considered listening to his messages on the answering machine, but didn't know how it worked. Undeterred, Sharon then stalked into Jake's bedroom to search his nightstands and dresser for anything she could use. Just then the phone rang. Pausing a moment, she decided to answer. It certainly wouldn't be Jake calling his own place, right? Her curiosity made it impossible not to answer his phone.

Lynnette heard it ring for the third time and began to quickly formulate in her mind the best message to leave him. She was so nervous. What should she say?

"Hello," a sexy female voice answered.

"Hi," Lynnette hesitated in confusion. Why was a woman answering his telephone? "Is Jake there?"

"No, he isn't home yet. Why do you ask?" the female voice accused. "Who's calling anyway?" Sharon added more aggressively.

"Ummm, I'm Lynnette," then stalled, trying to figure it out, "uh, well Jake gave me this number..." her voice trailed off weakly in confusion and disbelief. Who was this woman?

"Honey, I'm certain Jake didn't mean to hurt your feelings," she drawled out in condescension, "but I'm afraid I have to inform you he's already taken. He's in a committed relationship with me. You see, I'm Jake's girlfriend and I would really appreciate it if you would lose our number, okay? Please don't call here again," she finished in anger as she slammed down the phone.

"Who in the hell were you just talking to, Sharon?" Jake's loud voice boomed behind her, causing her to jump and nearly fall off her four-inch heels. What was he doing home already? Hadn't he said he would return next week? Maybe she hadn't really been listening when he told her. He had accused her of that several times in the past. Collecting herself, she thought fast and turned to face him. His anger was obvious, he was absolutely furious. She would just have to distract him somehow.

Using her most seductive moves, she began to slink over to him in the doorway. He stared at her in disgust, almost as if seeing her clearly for the first time. She was a gorgeous woman with long black hair and a perfect body, but as she moved toward him in her tight red cocktail dress and ridiculously tall heels, Jake's mind flashed to the night on the deck of Ariel last week as Lynnette leaned against the mizzen-mast in a white dress that was much too large for her and slipping off her soft shoulders. She was even barefoot. She was the perfect, sexy woman without even trying. Shaking his head to clear the image, he was shocked by the stark contrast with this woman now standing in front of him. Whatever he had seen in her at one time was completely gone now. Her perfume was so strong it was already beginning to give him a headache.

Putting up one hand in front of him, he told her, "Stop it! Your attempt at seduction is not going to work on me, Sharon, so knock it off. I asked you who you were just talking to on the phone. Now tell me!" he yelled, causing her to jump.

"Fine," she answered snidely. "It was some woman you gave your number to, okay?"

"What did you say to her, Sharon? Exactly?" he asked slowly, his voice low and measured.

Pushing past him, she slinked across the great-room, over to the bar to pour herself a drink. Following her, he took the glass and bottle from her hands, returning them to the shelf.

"Don't bother, you're not staying long enough," he stated coldly pulling her from behind the counter by the wrist.

"Babe, why do you want to fight with me? Huh? You just got home and we haven't seen each other in weeks.

Come on, is that any way to greet me," Sharon asked in her sexiest tone. She tried to run her hands up the front of his shirt, but he knocked them away angrily.

"A name, Sharon," he demanded. "Who was it?"

"It was Lynnette, you bastard," she blurted out. "She said her name was Lynnette. So who in the hell is she anyway?" she demanded.

Glaring through narrowed eyes at her, Jake replied curtly.

"It's none of your damn business. I broke it off with you weeks ago, Sharon."

Grabbing her shiny bag off the desk, he took her by the elbow and forced her toward the front door.

"Now get out of my place and stay out of my business. Don't bother keeping a copy of the key this time. I'll have a locksmith here tonight. You're becoming disgusting to me so it would be best for you if I never see you around here again. Do you understand me?" he demanded.

"Go to hell, Jake Hunter," she spat out. Turning on her heel, she stormed down the hallway toward the elevators.

Closing the door, he quickly raced across the room to the phone to call Lynnette back.

* * *

Lynnette sat there stunned in utter shock and disbelief. After what she and Jake had shared together last week, she would have never guessed he had a woman living with him. He was such a convincing liar, so believable. But he was already in a relationship and said he wanted one with her too? What was he thinking giving out their number knowing this woman could answer? How cocky was he?

Oh my gosh, she realized with a horrible, sinking feeling. I cancelled all Father's plans and gave up my entire inheritance to pursue a relationship with Jake only to find out he was already with someone else? He was a total liar. That was the one thing she had told him she couldn't abide. He could have come clean then. He didn't though and he had lied to her. It was all a lie. Now it was over. She didn't know if she felt more hurt by him or more anger toward him at the moment.

Jumping up, she began to pace back and forth across the room. She felt closed in and was in dire need of some fresh air at the moment. Not really knowing why she did it, she turned off her answer machine, pulled on a coat and then pulled the front door firmly shut behind her as she left for a walk along the beach.

Jake must have let it ring twenty times before acknowledging the message machine was not going to pick up his call. Damn it! He should have changed the locks before leaving for Cabo. Sharon would not have been able to get in then. Calling the front desk, he requested the locksmith be dispatched, and then poured him self a dirty martini. Rubbing his forehead, he thought about the situation from Lynnette's perspective. Knowing how Sharon could be, he could only guess the lies she had told her. Yeah, right about now Lynnette probably wanted to kill him. Rubbing his eyes, he took another drink, and then dialed Uncle Elliot. He would certainly know how to get in touch with Lynnette. Jake needed to explain everything soon before it was too late. No answer, so Jake left a message to contact him immediately. They needed to talk.

Taking his drink out to the balcony, he stood in the cold night air looking up at the stars wondering why Lynnette had called in the first place. What message would she have left for him if Sharon hadn't screwed it up by picking up the phone? Could it be she had made her decision and wasn't going to go through with the wedding plans her father had hatched up? He couldn't wait any longer to talk with her; he needed to find her now.

Knowing his Uncle had a live-in housekeeper, Anna, who never answered the phone when she was there alone, Jake decided to drive over to ask her where Elliot was. It was better than sitting here helpless and drinking. Stopping by the front desk to inform them not to let Sharon upstairs again he took the elevator down to the subterranean parking garage, jumped in his Ferrari and drove the thirty miles to Elliot's house. Getting behind the wheel of his red machine worked to improve his mood somewhat. He knew he would find a way of working things out, he just hadn't figured out how yet. Finding Elliot's Tustin Hills house completely dark and apparently empty when Anna didn't answer the bell, he headed down the 55 freeway to the 73, exited MacArthur Boulevard and then drove down the hill to the coast highway, turning south to Corona Del Mar. He wasn't entirely sure why, since he didn't have Lynnette's address, but as he drove slowly through the quaint, narrow streets of small cottage-like homes, he found himself wondering if she were inside one of them.

At the same time just a short block away, Lynnette unlocked her front door in the dark and slipped back inside, still feeling alone and miserable. After taking a short, hot shower to warm up again, she went to bed and lay there for hours, softly crying.

Jake noticed the answer machine light was flashing the moment he got home. It was a message from Elliot saying he would be in meetings the next afternoon and that Jake's little sister was coming to town for a short visit. Could he please pick up his little sister, Melody, from the airport in the afternoon? He could join them for dinner at Elliot's house tomorrow night. Also in the message, Elliot said he was really sorry not to inform Jake in person, but had to let him know that Mac's daughter had called off the engagement and they would discuss it further tomorrow night over dinner.

Jake hit the delete button on the machine and sat down hard in the chair at his desk. Lynnette had likely called tonight to tell him herself, but now thought he had a girlfriend living with him. That would be just like Sharon in her jealousy to lead Lynnette to believe such a lie. Crap. He needed to speak with her and make her understand. Lifting up the receiver, he dialed her number by heart.

Slightly groggy from the beginnings of sleep, Lynnette lifted the phone to her ear. "Hello." Attempting to turn on the light to check the time on her bedside clock without dropping the phone, she caught her breath at the sound of Jake's deep voice.

"Lynnette, it's late, I know, but we've got to talk," Jake spoke earnestly willing her to listen. The silence in his ear was deafening.

"Look, I know you're upset, but you have to listen to me," he implored.

"I do, huh? And just why would I want to listen to a liar, Jake? Just how long have you been back anyway? Wouldn't your girlfriend let you call me when you got home to her?" she added sarcastically.

"She's not my girlfriend, Lynnette. Listen to me. She let herself into my place with her key…"

"How handy for this girl who isn't your girlfriend to have a key to your place," she added harshly.

"She was my girlfriend, but we recently broke up. Remember, I told you about Sharon when we were on the Ariel," he added trying to get her to understand. "I threw her out when I got home tonight. Sweetheart, I want to see you, now, tonight. Can I come over to talk with you?"

Not sure if he were telling the truth or not, she decided against it. Walking into the bathroom with the handset, she turned on the light to a horrific reflection of swollen eyes from crying and a bright red nose. She knew she looked like shit and absolutely didn't want him to come over now.

"Jake," she said, "hearing a woman answer the phone and say what she said to me, well it hurt me. I've told you I can't stand lying and I really just don't know what to believe. I just need some time to think about things."

"Believe me, Lynnette, I don't have a girlfriend and I wasn't lying. She kept an extra key and let herself in against my wishes. I broke it off with her last month and we weren't together long anyway. She's nothing to me, honestly," he explained.

It sounded reasonable, but she wasn't completely convinced.

"Honey, you called me for a reason tonight. What was it?" he coaxed, yet not wanting to admit he already knew about her decision. He really would have to get the truth of his role out in the open soon though. He wanted her to know the truth now that she had made her decision.

Hesitating, she wondered if she should even tell him now. "It was really just nothing, Jake," she hedged. "I've got to go now. We'll talk later, alright?"

Not waiting for his answer, he heard the soft click of the phone as she hung up on her end. He sat there at his desk a long while wondering if she had believed a word he had said.

TWENTY-ONE

By four o'clock sharp, Lynnette had already circled John Wayne airport twice in her excitement to see Barbara and was now looking for a space to pull up to the curb in front of the terminal. Barb's flight had probably already landed, she figured, so she decided she would just wait outside the area designated for arrivals. It had become their routine every time Barb flew into town.

Getting out of the car, Lynnette went around to the other side and leaned against the front fender so airport security would know she hadn't left her car unattended. It appeared to be all right, since the uniformed security guy just walked by without even questioning her. Taking a deep breath, she calmed her excitement, recalling the reason Barbara had flown home. Barb's mom was a very sweet person and Lynnette prayed her surgery would be successful.

As Lynnette waited, she observed the people arriving and being greeted by their loved ones. She enjoyed observing the happiness on the faces of travelers as family and friends embraced with huge smiles and hearty welcomes. How nice it is to fly somewhere where someone was waiting and excited to see you.

"Hi Lynnette," Barbara cried out coming toward her, pulling a single bag on wheels.

"Hi," she replied. "Wow, you look terrific, Barb," she said sincerely, hugging her close and then stepping back to take a better look. "Honestly, no one would ever guess you have two little ones at home," Lynnette exclaimed enthusiastically.

"Thanks, Lynn. You look gorgeous as always," Barb replied.

Suddenly emotional, Lynnette said, "Barb, I'm so glad to see you, but nowhere near as much as you mom will be. She's going to be just fine, you know."

"Yeah, I know she will. She's just a little scared of going under the knife, that's all. She just needs a little comfort right now."

"Do you think she'd be up for a visit with me when I drop you off?"

"Oh, I'm sure she will. She always loves to see you, hon," Barb answered her with a hug. "Thanks for being so sweet, Lynnette."

"Let's get moving and go see her then. Come on, my car is right here."

The girls worked together to stuff the suitcase in the small trunk of Lynnette's sports car, giggling the entire time at their silly attempts.

"Okay," Lynnette laughed, "that's it. Either you need a smaller suitcase or I need a bigger car."

Finally getting the bag shoved inside, she stepped onto the curb to unlock the passenger door for Barb when Lynnette spotted him. She couldn't believe her eyes. A double take confirmed that it was indeed Jake. He was coming out the sliding doors of the terminal directly in front of her, arm-in-arm with another woman. A very beautiful woman too, Lynnette observed with a frown. They were laughing easily together as they headed right for her. Jake hadn't noticed Lynnette standing there just yet.

"Lynnette, what is it?" Barb asked concerned, coming up next to her. "You look like you've just seen a ghost." Barb's eyes followed the direction of Lynnette's obvious concern.

Lynnette didn't answer, but just stood there in shock. Hadn't Jake just told her he didn't have a girlfriend and had kicked her out of his place? And now, here he is picking up yet another girlfriend at the airport. What a liar. And how many girlfriends did this guy have anyway? She wasn't at all rational and her fury toward Jake grew as she watched them coming closer. The woman he was with laughed just then at something Jake said, looking at him with obvious admiration. Lynnette wanted to scratch his eyes out.

It was at that moment that Jake looked up and saw Lynnette. He stopped dead in his tracks. He glanced briefly at the woman at his side and then at Lynnette again knowing how this must look to her. She was close now and by the look on her face, he knew she was pissed off.

"Lynnette, this isn't what you..." he began to explain.

"Save it," she interrupted angrily glaring at him. "I should have known! I trusted you when you said you don't have a girlfriend and then this? You pig!" she exclaimed loudly. She turned on her heel and headed to go around the front of her car.

The female stranger looked over at Barbara in obvious discomfort at the awkward moment. Barb on the other hand was suppressing a grin. They each suspected quite a scene was coming.

In a flash, Jake moved in front of Lynnette, blocking her path.

"Lynnette, just stop and listen to me a minute," Jake demanded aggressively. "You're drawing the wrong conclusion. She's not my girl..."

"I don't believe you, you..., liar!" she shouted. "I should have known not to trust you."

Jake controlled his frustration and tried to reason with her, although his temper was getting short.

"And just why would you think you couldn't trust me, Lynnette? What have I done to make you think I'm not honest with you, huh?" he yelled back, feeling a little anger of his own.

Jake's sister stepped forward to try to interject. The angry young couple was standing toe-to-toe in heated disagreement, ignoring her. She was hoping to diffuse the situation.

"He really is my brother," she offered cheerfully, looking so absolutely beautiful to Lynnette that it only resulted in making her even angrier. She wasn't going to listen a moment longer. Her mind was made up. She didn't trust him.

Utterly exasperated, Lynnette pushed roughly past Jake to go get into her car. Jake took a quick second to ask his sister to stay put where she was, stating he would be right back. Looking back, he realized his mistake. Lynnette had already circled the car and jumped in the front seat. She slammed the driver's door shut and started the car.

For the moment, Lynnette had forgotten all about Barb, who was still standing by grinning. She had watched with curious pleasure as the entire scene enfolded before her, knowing without a doubt that there was only one reason a woman would act the way Lynnette was acting now. Lynnette was hopelessly and emphatically in love with this guy, Jake. This was certainly going to be a very interesting visit, Barb thought as she moved up next to Jake's sister for a little chat.

Lynnette threw the car into gear and began to pull away from the curb just as Jake jumped in front of it, slamming his hand down hard on the hood. She hit the brakes immediately, jumping at the sudden sound of his palm contacting metal. By now, they had drawn the attention of everyone at the terminal in the immediate vicinity. There was a small crowd forming to see what would happen next.

Fully resolved to control the situation, Jake leaned down pressing both palms on the hood of the car, aggressively hollering through the windshield at her.

"Lynnette, stop a damn minute and listen to me," Jake shouted. "You're being ridiculous. She's not my girlfriend, you little dope, she's my little sister."

"Oh come on," Lynnette yelled back. The open car windows allowed everyone within earshot to hear their heated exchange.

"You really expect me to believe you now? I just caught a woman in your place last night and now you're with another woman. Just get out of my way and let me go. I don't trust you, Jake," she shouted.

"Just give me a damn minute to explain," Jake yelled coming around to her driver's side door.

Looking up at him in impatience, she rolled her eyes. Why did this have to be so difficult? Why couldn't he just let her leave? If she stayed, she knew he was going to hurt her feelings.

"Lynnette," he directed at her, "I'm not lying to you. She is my sister and we need to talk. There's something else I need to tell you."

"Just terrific, Jake. There's more, huh? What? You're married? You have a wife and children? No, I'm done," she answered decisively. "I'm leaving now."

Just then, a police officer stepped up to her car window behind Jake asking if there was any trouble. She quickly looked at Jake and answered with a sigh.

"No, Officer. Everything is just fine. I was just leaving, thank you."

She nearly pulled away from the curb without Barbara. At the last second, Barb opened the door and jumped in just as Lynnette sped away from the curb.

"What in the world was that all that about?" Barbara exclaimed.

"That was Jake, the guy I told you I met in Cabo!" she replied, still angry.

"Well, yeah, I sort of gathered that, Lynnette, but why all the theatrics? That's not like you at all," she replied suppressing a grin.

Lynnette turned right and entered the onramp to the freeway, merging smoothly into the flow of traffic. After awhile, Lynnette took a deep breath and slowly answered, feeling calmer now.

"It's just that I keep finding him in lies, Barb," Lynnette answered in frustration. "I know I'll get hurt by him, so I'm afraid to go any further. I just don't trust him and don't know that I ever will."

Barb was well aware that Lynnette's trust issues stemmed from her relationship with her father and stepbrother, so she tread lightly as she helped her friend explore the cause of her deepest feelings of distrust.

"What was the lie Jake told you that made you not trust him?" Barbara asked directly.

"Well, when I called him last night after I spoke with you, a woman answered the phone saying she was his girlfriend. She told me to leave them alone, that he was taken. After awhile, he called me back and said she was an ex-girlfriend who broke into his house and answered his phone. He told me he kicked her out after she and I hung up and that he doesn't have a girlfriend. Then I see him picking up yet another woman at the airport," she exclaimed, sounding aggravated again. "Yeah, like I'm gonna believe that was his sister back there. Does he think I'm stupid?"

"Well, you sure showed him alright." Barb baited her. Lynnette glanced away from the road to look over at Barb.

"What do you mean?" she asked.

"You dope. That was his sister, Lynnette. He was telling you the truth. She told me herself. Her name is Melody and she just flew in from Chicago to visit her uncle and see her brother, Jake."

"No way," Lynnette replied unconvinced, but losing her conviction.

They transitioned on to the southbound 405 freeway. Barb gave Lynnette some time to let the news sink in, but smiled to herself. She was pleased Lynnette was finally falling in love. The happiest times in Barb's life were after she met Richard and they started their family together. He and their two daughters were her world and there was nothing more fulfilling in life than family. Barb wished that same fulfillment for her dearest friend and truly hoped this fellow, Jake, would be just the man who would make Lynnette happy.

They rode along in silence a while until Lynnette finally looked over at Barb.

"Do you think she was?" she asked hesitantly.

"His sister, you mean?"

"Yeah."

"Yes, I do. And if the gal on the phone last night was in fact his ex, broke into his place and answered his phone, which isn't completely unreasonable, then he wasn't lying to you at all. What else happened between you two that's made you so distrusting of him?" Barb asked patiently leading her to the truth of her feelings of distrust.

Lynnette frowned and didn't answer. They drove quite a distance in silence, Barb giving Lynnette time to think it through. She knew Lynnette would give it some serious thought and they would get back to it before she left town.

A short while later, Lynnette pulled into the Laguna Hills neighborhood where Barb had grown up. They had enjoyed many sleepovers here as little girls and seeing the house again brought back good memories.

She parked in the driveway and turned to face Barb.

"Before you go in, Barb, I just want to apologize. I feel like such a jerk. Your mom is going in for surgery and here

I am being selfish and full of my own problems instead of being sensitive to yours. I'm sorry," Lynnette finished, her voice cracking and her eyes welling up with tears.

"Oh, stop it now," Barb consoled. "The words, 'you' and 'selfish', just don't belong in the same sentence. You're the most giving person in the world, so forget about it. You don't owe me an apology and if anything, your antics back there were an entertaining distraction from my reason for being here," Barb joked with a smile.

"I love you," Lynnette smiled.

"I love you too."

"You want me to come in now or wait a bit?" Lynnette asked as they struggled removing Barb's bag from the trunk.

"Let me first go in first to check on her and see if she's up to a visit now. I'll just be a minute," Barb replied, finally wrestling her bag free.

Following a brief and emotional visit with Barb's mom, the phone rang. It was Barb's aunt. Before taking the call upstairs, Barb's mom thanked Lynnette for bringing Barb, giving her a tight hug.

Lynnette found Barb in the kitchen cutting up a plate of apples, Parmesan cheese and olives. Handing Lynnette two glasses of wine to carry, the girls took their snack out onto the back patio.

Sitting in the last of the day's sunlight near the water fountain overlooking the garden, the girls enjoyed the view and the smell of the flowers in bloom as they talked about the upcoming surgery before continuing their earlier conversation.

"You know what?" Lynnette began, taking a slice of apple. "You're right. There isn't anything Jake has done to deserve my distrust. Logically, my mind says to trust him and move ahead, but my heart is warning me not to get involved and set myself up to be hurt by him. What's wrong with me?"

"Lynnette, there is nothing wrong with you," she smiled. "Each one of us goes through things in life that make us who we are and guide our decisions. Your particular experiences in life, especially pertaining to men, haven't been the most pleasant, so it stands to reason you're distrusting of them."

"You mean Todd and my dad?"

"Yes, exactly. But there is one thing you have to remember, Lynnette," Barb advised sipping her wine.

"What's that?"

"Jake is not your dad, nor is he Todd. He's a unique individual who deserves to be judged on his own actions and not those of others. Do you think you can separate the two?" Barb asked.

"I can try, but it's not easy for me. I suppose I am prejudging Jake just because he's a man and that's not fair to him."

"Good girl. Let me know how it goes, okay?"

"Yes, call me Monday after your mom's surgery to let me know how she's doing," Lynnette suggested.

"I will. Mom will be just fine. She's not going to let a little surgery keep her down long," Barb stated.

Lynnette loved Barb's positive attitude.

As Lynnette drove away, she thought back to just what a great friend Barbara had been over the years. She was lucky to have such a close friend with sound council. Not feeling in the mood to stop for dinner, nor in the mood to go home just yet, she decided to drive up to Tustin Hills to talk with Uncle Elliot about everything that had been going on lately. Elliot always made perfect sense and she desperately needed his help sorting it all out. How was she supposed to trust a man when she didn't trust men in general (other than Elliot), she admitted to herself? Her mind was in a confused jumble of thoughts and she was having difficulty making sense of it. Her mind said to get away from Jake and her heart said to go be with him. Or was it the other way around with her mind telling her to trust him and her heart afraid of being broken? Was he a liar? Was he really who he said he was? Keira said she had been told he owned the Ariel, but he said he only worked on it. The woman on the phone said they were a couple, yet he adamantly denied it. The beauty at the airport didn't appear very sisterly at all, but he said she was his sister. As a matter of fact, they made a very attractive couple together, she thought frowning.

Pulling up at Elliot's house, Lynnette was pleased to find his interior lights on. She knew she should probably have called first, but he never minded when she dropped in on him. Elliot didn't often date, so it wasn't likely he was entertaining a lady tonight. She looked forward to sitting in front of a warm fire by the hearth and talking over hot tea, as they often did when she was having trouble with life. Coming here always felt a bit like coming home to her, more so than going to see her own father anyway. As she rang the doorbell, Lynnette peeked through the beveled glass of the exquisite front doors.

Meanwhile, Anna, Elliot's housekeeper, served the third course of dinner in the formal dining room. As Elliot sat back in his chair, he found it hard to believe what Jake was telling him. What an amazing coincidence! It was nearly impossible to fathom. He smiled at his niece, Melody, so enthusiastically full of questions for Jake as she continued interrupting her brother's story to ask the kind of specific details only a woman finds interesting. Elliot just couldn't believed the odds of Lynnette and Jake meeting on a flight to Cabo San Lucas, especially considering he was unknowingly the same man her father was forcing her to marry. It was truly amazing.

"Jake, I'm so excited for you," Melody jumped out of her chair, ran up behind Jake and threw her arms around his neck. "It's so romantic and you sound so in love. I honestly never thought it would happen to you, you're such a heartbreaker," she finished with a big smack on his cheek.

Elliot chuckled. Jake grunted. The doorbell rang.

Anna left the room to answer the door as they continued their conversation over dinner.

"So," Elliot inquired, "you plan to continue your relationship with Lynnette, but what about the arrangement we had? Are you going to tell her about it?"

"What arrangement was that again?" Melody asked not following the conversation completely.

Jake looked concerned, knowing he should have already let Lynnette know he was the one her father had arranged for her to marry.

"Yeah, well we need to talk about that because she still doesn't know it's me she was supposed to marry," Jake admitted. "I haven't told her yet."

Just then, Jake looked up to see Lynnette standing across the room. She looked shocked. Or was that the look of fury. He noticed they were both similar and all too familiar lately.

Elliot attempted to diffuse the situation.

"Lynnette, honey, please sit down to eat with us. Anna, please pull up another chair."

"What are you doing here?" she directed at Jake, not acknowledging Elliot or Melody. "How do you know my Uncle Elliot?"

"Lynnette," Jake stood to approach her. She raised her palms, stopping him.

"Wait a minute. What did you just say?" she asked, suddenly recalling the words he had said when she'd entered the room. "You're the one my dad arranged for me to marry?" she accused. "Is it true?" the anger in her voice growing.

Melody gasped.

Swallowing, Jake clenched his teeth and resolved himself to face the situation head-on.

"Yes, Lynnette, it's true. Your father and my Uncle Elliot asked me to marry you, but you have to listen to me," he insisted moving closer to her. "I didn't know at the..."

"What do you mean your Uncle? Elliot is your uncle?" she questioned in further disbelief.

Lynnette spun around to face Elliot. "You were in on this too?" she accused. "You, the only one I've ever been able to trust? You planned this horrible thing with my father?"

"Yes, dear, but only at your father's insistence," Elliot answered. "He was adamant on the point of you marrying immediately, Lynnette, and I thought the wisest course was to ensure the best choice for you rather than to leave the selection to your father. Dear, I'm truly sorry for my part in the deception, but once you've had time to think it through, I assure you that you'll agree you and Jake are a terrific match for one another. I've known that for a long while now."

Lynnette stood in the doorway, frozen in place. She felt like time had stopped. Melody sat on the edge of her chair feeling certain something was about to happen and didn't want to miss a thing. She remembered Lynnette from the airport, but was still rather confused about the facts. She also wondered how the woman had found them here at Uncle Elliot's house.

"Could someone please tell me what's going on?" Melody asked in frustration.

Jake knew from the look in her eyes that Lynnette was working herself up for a scene and wasn't looking forward to it at all. Elliot also saw the look in her eyes, so he took immediate charge of the situation.

Pouring her a glass of the wine, Elliot rose easily from his chair to move over to Lynnette's side. Putting his arm comfortingly around her shoulders, Elliot handed her the glass and carefully guided a shocked looking Lynnette from the room. Over his shoulder he said, "Jake, you and Melody continue your meal while Lynnette and I go have a talk in my study."

This wasn't going to be easy to resolve, Elliot knew, but he must try. Lynnette was terribly hurt at the moment, she felt deceived and it was his fault.

Jake sat back down at the dinner table, crossed his arms over his chest and just sat there staring, unseeing, out the window. Melody couldn't wait for answers and began pelting her brother with questions, each one going unanswered as Jake sat there, ignoring her. He sure had messed things up with Lynnette, hadn't he? How could he ever make it right again? How could he gain her trust?

"How could you do this to me, Uncle Elliot?" Lynnette demanded once Elliot had closed the door to his study. "Why would you be a part of this scheme with my father? It was wrong and you knew it," she stated in anger.

"Lynnette, you have to realize the relationship between your father and me in order to understand my reasons," Elliot explained. "You also have to know the depth of my love for you and the fact I've tried to cushion your father's actions toward you over the years," he replied gently. "Sit down here with me, my dear. I have some things I need to finally share with you."

"Is Jake really your nephew?" Lynnette asked, taking a seat on the couch.

"Yes, he is, just as Melody, his sister, is my niece. Their parents were killed years ago in an auto accident. Their mother was my sister, Ruth. They were little ones back then and their godmother and her husband raised them. I was single and traveling a lot on business, so it was the best choice at the time," Elliot explained.

Lynnette stared down at the carpet, trying to make sense of everything she'd heard.

Elliot continued.

"I will answer all of your questions, but the one thing you must remember at all times, my dear, is that I love you like a daughter and have always looked out for your happiness and best interests. That fact should never be a doubt in your mind, alright?"

Lynnette looked at Elliot a long while before slowly nodding her head in agreement.

It was taking forever, Jake thought, taking a deep breath and glancing across the table at Melody. Lost in thought, he had forgotten all about her. Sighing, he wondered if Lynnette would ever believe anything he had to say again once she knew the entire truth. Damn it, this isn't how he wanted her to hear about the marriage arrangement.

"Melody, I'm sorry the visit turned out like this," Jake offered.

"That's okay, but before I leave, someone needs to explain everything to me," she announced.

As soon as Jake heard Elliot and Lynnette come out of the study, he jumped from his chair to run after her as she went out the front door. His uncle put up a hand to stop him.

"Let her go for now, son. She has a lot of thinking to do and you'll see her again tomorrow at Mac's."

Dejected, Jake stopped, dropping his head in disgust. He was more seriously concerned that Lynnette seemed hurt instead of angry with him. He could handle her anger. That was easy, but he really couldn't stand the fact that he had hurt her. His headache was now coming back with a vengeance.

"Although Mac probably intends to still force this marriage to happen," Elliot continued, "we'll use the opportunity to change his mind and to get Lynnette to understand. We're both in the doghouse with her, but it'll be alright in the end, Jake. You'll see. Come on, now. Let's go relax over a brandy and cigar out on the deck."

In her usual bad timing, Melody cheerily commented that Lynnette seemed to be very lovely.

"I didn't get a chance to say goodbye to her," she said. "Will I get to see her again before I leave?"

At the bar, Elliot frowned as he poured two glasses of brandy. Jake selected two cigars from Elliot's humidor and slipped out on to the patio without a word. Elliot joined Jake on the deck after getting Anna to help Melody get settled into the guest room. The two men sat back comfortably in the patio chairs in silence, each one in deep thought as they enjoyed the brisk night air and their aromatic cigars. Elliot sipped his brandy, before speaking.

"The meeting I just attended in D.C. has resulted in a new assignment, Jake. I know your mind is on other things, but we'll need you down in Belize in two weeks time. We just uncovered an arms dealer using a new route through the Yucatan Peninsula, but we need more information. You'll be sent in on a covert mission to gather the specifics we need to effectively cut off their trafficking route."

"No problem," Jake replied, welcoming a diversion. "I'll report to C.I.A. headquarters next week to get my orders."

Lynnette felt numb driving back home down the coast. She vaguely recalled pulling into a drive-thru to order dinner then pulled away without ordering, unable to decide on anything to eat. Once home, she sat staring at the wall, thinking. She finally undressed for bed, fluffed the pillows and opened her paperback to pick-up where she had left off. She sat there staring unseeingly at the same page for what seemed like forever. Why can't life be simple and have a happy ending like these romance novels? After a long while, she fell asleep, but awoke later from a bad dream.

She dreamt she was back in Jake's stateroom during the storm, lying there scared in the darkness as the boat was tossed about, then suddenly was being attacked by a man. It was Eric at first, then Jake's face was above her attacking and then it remained Eric's face as the torment continued. She fought him off unsuccessfully and this time, Jake never showed up to rescue her. She awoke with a scream in her throat, sweating and scared. Glancing at the clock, she saw it was almost two o'clock in the morning.

Jake stood at the railing of his penthouse deck looking out at the view of the Queen Mary and the city lights of the marina, wishing things had gone down differently today. He had no idea what would happen tomorrow, but he was going to try to get Lynnette to understand. He was falling in love with her and that is all that mattered to him now. Sure, they had gotten off to a bad start and from her perspective it looked pretty bad for him. He just needed to be able to explain to her what happened and how he also got caught up in this mess. He had to speak with her alone before getting to Mac's though. There would be too many possible interruptions. There was also something nagging at him as he pushed away from the railing and decided he needed some sleep if he was going to make any sense when he spoke with her tomorrow.

The next morning began as any other November day, overcast and chilly. After Lynnette's morning run and coffee, she ate a bowl of cold cereal for breakfast and then took a long hot shower. She dressed and got ready, realizing she had some extra time and feeling drawn to the place she always went when life became overwhelming, she jumped in her car and drove up the coast to that special spot on the point overlooking the harbor. From this vantage point, she could look out over the rooftops of the houses of Balboa Peninsula and out across the Pacific Ocean. On a clear day you could see Catalina Island from here, but not today. There was a thick fog bank laying low on the water out about a quarter mile off the coastline.

Taking the red and black wool blanket she always kept in her trunk, she carried it over to her favorite spot and sat down on the bench snuggled up in the warmth of the plaid wrap. Looking out over the water, she allowed her mind to wander, trying to make sense of everything going on in her life. It was a form of subconscious therapy she had used successfully in the past. She would allow her thoughts to mull around in her head disorganized and then at some point, things seemed to arrange themselves in her mind without her knowing how, and she would feel better. Things would start to make sense again. This process had never let her down in the past, not even once. She just needed to relax and let her thoughts go wherever they went, staying out of the way and not forcing it. There was no hurry. Just relax and look out at the water, she willed herself.

Jake showered, dressed and drank a protein shake straight from the blender he had made it in to save washing more dishes. He'd slept in later than usual, but felt rested and ready to tackle the difficult day ahead. At some point in the night, he had awoken realizing what had been nagging in the back of his thoughts earlier. He recalled the time Lynnette had confided in him that one morning onboard Ariel, that there was a special place she always went whenever she had trouble in her life. She had said it was a cliff above Newport Harbor, overlooking the ocean. There was only one area he could think of that fit that description and he thought he might find her there, if he hurried. It seemed logical she would go there since everything was all messed up between them. He needed to speak with her before they all showed up at her father's house in a few hours time. It was imperative that he personally explain everything to her.

The fog was thick in places, but he chose to avoid the freeway and to take the coastal route anyway, not only to enjoy the feel of driving his Ferrari, but also to try to clear his own head. Heading south through town, he passed the popular shops of Corona Del Mar, strangely quiet on a cold winter day, and turned right when he came to The Five Crowns restaurant. Making the sharp curve in the narrow road when he reached the cliff, he headed north along the waterfront, looking for Lynnette at one of the park benches. Only the diehard workout fanatics were out running on a cold winter day like this one, he noticed. Finally, he spotted her at the last bench along the cliff, sitting alone there in the cold and wrapped up in a blanket. He stopped the car a moment and observed her hair blowing softly back, away from her face. From this angle, he thought she looked angelically peaceful sitting there, so innocent and amazingly beautiful.

Jake swung the car around and stopped at the curb. Getting out, he slipped on his jacket to brave the cold air and headed across the grass toward her. She hadn't moved a muscle and didn't seem to notice he was even there. He watched her for several more moments as she continued to just stare out at the ocean, as if in a trance. Finally, she turned her head toward him ever so slightly, as if finally sensing his presence.

"Hey," he said.

After a pause, she quietly asked, "How did you know where to find me?"

Resting his palms on the bench beside her, he leaned down before answering. "I remembered your description of the place you told me you always go when you have trouble in your life," he answered gently. "I figured it was along here somewhere, so I came looking for you."

"Oh?" she replied and then slowly sighed.

After a long while, he came around the bench and sat down next to her. She didn't speak so he just waited patiently for her lead.

"How long were you aware I was being forced to marry you?" she finally asked.

Looking over at her, he answered carefully and honestly.

"I found out about their plans when we were aboard the Ariel, right before the storm hit. My Uncle Elliot phoned and said he needed to finally call in a favor I owed him."

That got Lynnette's attention. She looked over at Jake, her irritation already apparent. As soon as Jake had said it, he realized how bad it sounded, as if marrying her was some kind of payment for a debt he owed. Damn if he wasn't already messing it up.

"Lynnette, I'm really sorry for how bad that just sounded. When I first made the promise to my uncle that day to marry you, I didn't know it was you he was speaking about at the time. I swear," he insisted. "He told me your name later in that same call, but he was totally unaware we had already met and I hadn't told him we had until last night."

"Why in the world would you ever agree to marry someone you didn't know anyway?" she asked in anger. "Especially after all the hell you gave me for doing the very same thing?"

"You're right. It's complicated though. Listen, the only thing I have is my word, Lynnette, and when I told my uncle I would do anything he asked of me, I meant it. If it weren't for him, I don't know where I'd be now, but it wouldn't be good. He changed the course of my life for the better and I would have done anything he asked me to do. Anything."

"What would you have done if it hadn't been me he asked you to marry?" she asked quietly.

After a bit, he simply said, "I don't know."

She sat in unemotional silence for the longest time until Jake could take it no more. He had to admit he would rather she be yelling at him or pissed off instead of this silent treatment. He had to do something to break her out of this lethargic, disconnected state she was in currently.

"You know what, Lynnette," he began in anger, "I'd really like to know what in the hell I've done to piss you off!"

She just looked over at him. Well, at least she was looking at him now, rather than through him. That was an improvement. He had her attention, so he continued pressing.

"Well, I'll tell you what I've done," he stated forcefully. "From my point of view, I helped you out in Mexico when you had no place to stay, I saved your ass from the bad guys, I kept your money from being taken by your dumb-ass ex-step brother and your sister, by the way, and then I saved you from drowning in the Pacific Ocean." He was now yelling. "I seriously cared about you, so what the hell did I do that was so damn wrong anyway?" he shouted at her.

He could see it was working. There was a fire in her eyes now and she no longer looked lethargic. She was still holding back though, but it wouldn't take much more to push her over the edge, which is right where he needed her to be in order to begin communicating again. He needed her angry. He continued on.

"You know what?" he pushed further. "You've been nothing but a big pain in my ass from the moment I first met you and you're still a pain in the ass now!" he hollered at her, standing up for an intimidating effect.

"Me?" she cried out, jumping up. "I was a pain in your ass?" she yelled back aggressively.

Jake held back his smile, but inwardly felt ecstatic that she was finally reacting to him and fighting back. He finally saw in her what he loved most about her. Her spunk. At last she was standing up to him again.

"You're the one who insisted I stay at your friend's house on the beach, weren't you?" Lynnette hollered. "You were the one who wouldn't turn the boat around until I told you about Todd so you could help me with Keira, right? I didn't ask for your help! You insisted on being involved in my business from the start, so don't you dare go blaming me for all your troubles, mister," she yelled up at him. "This was your fault, not mine," she finished.

"Oh yeah?" he pushed her further. "Just how do you figure that?" he shouted back.

"When you found out I was being forced to marry you, you should have told me. You should have been honest then," she shouted, her anger now raw and intense. "Damn you, Jake" she cried out, pounding her fists against his chest, "I fell in love with you and you had to lie to me and ruin everything." Her tears began to flow in earnest now as she continued punching his chest with her fists in fury. He didn't stop her, but rather let her punch him until her anger was spent. All he could think of was that she had just admitted she loved him.

"We could have been so good together and trusted each other and it would have been so wonderful," she choked out through her tears. "But, no. You had to go and mess it all up by lying and now it's ruined," she finally finished the assault on his chest, dropping her face into her hands as she wept.

"It's not ruined, sweetheart," he stated simply, pulling her hands away from her face, kissing them sweetly. He wrapped his arms around her and pulled her close as he looked out over the water. He noticed the fog along the coast was finally lifting and the sunshine was breaking through.

Sobbing into his chest, she said, "We can never have a loving, trusting relationship together without honesty. Don't you see? I found the man of my dreams and now you turned out to be a liar," she exclaimed, although her words were somewhat muffled into his chest, but he got the gist of it.

Grinning, he kissed the top of her head and spoke carefully.

"Sweetheart, what I'm hearing from you," he said gently stroking her hair, "is that you think I'm the man of your dreams and you're really upset because you think I lied to you, right?"

"Yes," she agreed, her voice still muffled as she spoke into his chest.

"Lynnette, when two people meet, they don't expose everything about themselves immediately. Don't you think I too needed to protect my feelings from being hurt? I've been hurt by women before and in the beginning of this, honey, well, I honestly didn't know if I could trust you not to hurt me either," Jake explained. "Sure, I didn't tell you everything about myself or that we were promised to be married, but that was because I really wanted you to decide you wanted to marry for love, not money. I also didn't want you to marry because you're being forced to marry by your father. I needed to know you wanted to be with me. That's all I was after, honey. I didn't lie to you. I was honestly waiting for the right time to tell you. I love you, Lynnette, and I would love to spend the rest of my life with you," he finished, raising her chin up with one finger. He gazed into her eyes. "I'm not a liar, Lynnette. I can't prove it to you now, but in time you'll see it's the truth. Just give us time, alright?" he asked simply.

She waited, hesitating, as she gazed up into his eyes. She felt her doubts drift away like the fog. She had never felt anything was as right before as being with Jake. She knew without a doubt she loved him. Slowly, she smiled up at him and he knew at that moment, he had her.

"So," she said, wiping her eyes, "you think you can prove you're not a liar, huh?" she taunted.

One of Jake's eyebrows rose suspiciously in question of her teasing tone. Gone was the upset girl and back was his sassy woman. She sure had spunk. What was she up to now, he wondered.

"So," she began slowly, "Keira tells me you actually own the Ariel. Is that true after you told me you only work on her?"

Looking rather sheepish, he had to agree. "Yep."

How about the house I stayed in at Santa Maria? I suppose you own that too?" she accused.

"Yep."

"Then you not only own Ariel, but you also have a fleet of charter yachts around the world?" she questioned further.

"That's true," he admitted.

"So, you lied to me, letting me believe you worked on that boat and didn't have any money of your own," she accused.

"Yacht," he corrected, yet again.

"What?" she asked.

"It's a yacht, sweetheart. Not a boat."

"Back to the point, Jake," she continued. "You lied to me."

"No, I didn't lie. I just didn't correct your mistaken assumption that I worked on that boat. As a matter of fact I never said either way. For your information, I worked my butt off to build up my business and opt never to share the status of my wealth with any new women I date. Too many women are only after money, so I choose not to reveal what I own until I know they…"

"Yacht," she said.

"What?" he asked.

"You said boat. Ariel is a yacht," she corrected him.

Spanking her on the bottom, she squealed and ran away. He caught up with her, laughing and pulled her close for a long and thorough kiss. By the time he was through, she was weak in the knees and sighing.

Jake thought of telling her more about the truth about Keira and her role with Todd in the attempted blackmail, but thought better of it, not wanting to ruin the wonderful moment they were sharing.

The sun was now shining brightly and the view all the way to Catalina Island was as clear as a bell. Gone was the grey, gloomy water and it now glistened a gorgeous bright blue. Taking her hand, he decided to take time for a walk.

"No," she hesitated. "I'm due at father's by one o'clock."

"We both are," he replied.

"What?"

"It seems I've been summoned," he moaned. "We're both going and we're meeting up with your father and my Uncle Elliot at one o'clock."

"Summoned?" she asked. "That's how this whole thing began! I was summoned to my father's office."

"Just great," Jake replied. "There's time. Come on. Let go for a quick walk. This view along here is too beautiful not to enjoy."

She allowed Jake to lead her by the hand down the winding path that ran along the top of the cliff overlooking the Pacific. Taking the stairs down to the beach, they walked hand in hand along the water as the waves lapped gently against the sand.

After several minutes, she shrugged and said, "Well, falling in love with you does have its upside, I suppose."

Grinning down at her, he took the bait. "And just exactly what would that be, my love?"

Smiling up at his handsome face, she explained. "Well, considering the fact that you're already rich, at least I won't have to support you if we ever get married."

As she laughed, Jake grinned and reached back and spanked her behind once again.

It would not be the last time either.

They would be late to Mac's that afternoon, losing complete track of time as they continued down to the beach, hand in hand, not caring about anything other than the love they felt for one another.

The End...?

L.L. Lunde

L.L. Lunde was born and raised in sunny Southern California and always loved the ocean. She was drawn to the Pacific at a young age, majoring in marine biology, enjoying sailing, snorkeling, body surfing and anything pertaining to the ocean.

To weave her entertaining stories of love and adventure, she draws upon her own life experiences, which include romance in foreign countries, skippering sailboats in exotic island ports and surviving many harrowing adventures in various places around the world. She and her loving husband currently reside near the coast in Orange County.

www.LLLunde.com

The Ocean's Series by L.L. Lunde

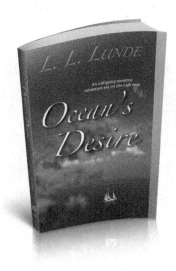

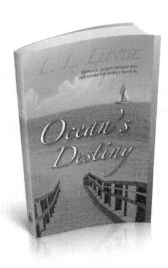